TOUGH GUYS

Other Books by Adrian Cole

**The DREAM LORDS saga
(Zebra, USA):**
A Plague of Nightmares
Lord of Nightmares
Bane of Nightmares

**The OMARAN saga
(Unwin Hyman, UK):**
A Place Among the Fallen
Throne of Fools
The King of Light and Shadows
The Gods in Anger

**The STAR REQUIEM
(Unwin Hyman, UK):**
Mother of Storms
Thief of Dreams
Warlord of Heaven
Labyrinth of Worlds

**The VOIDAL saga
(Wildside, USA):**
Oblivion Hand
The Long Reach of Night
Sword of Shadows

Individual novels:
Madness Emerging (Robert Hale, UK)
Paths in Darkness (Robert Hale, UK)
Wargods of Ludorbis (Hale, UK)
The Lucifer Experiment (Hale, UK)
Blood Red Angel (Avon, USA)
The Crimson Talisman (Wizards of WC,
USA)
Storm over Atlantis (Wildside, USA)
Night of the Heroes (Wildside, USA)
The Shadow Academy (Edge, USA)

Collection:
Nick Nightmare Investigates (Alchemy,
UK)

Young Adult:
Moorstones (Spindlewood, UK)
The Sleep of Giants (Spindlewood, UK)

Edited by:
Young Thongor (Wildside, USA)

For more information about the works of Adrian Cole
visit his website at:
adriancscole.com

TOUGH GUYS

Adrian Cole

PARALLEL UNIVERSE PUBLICATIONS

Contents

Contents

Adrian Cole - From Nightmares to Voidal to Nightmare

by David A. Sutton

"There's a storm coming. Old night is stirring"

It seems I've known Adrian (Ade, to his friends) for a thousand years. Too long, some might say, for this to be an earthly relationship! Early on in Adrian's involvement in the genre and The British Fantasy Society, he spoke on a panel at the very first British Fantasy convention; under discussion 'Sword & Sorcery: The Gutter Press of Fantasy?' That was 1975 and even by then Adrian had been writing fiction for around four years.

Back-track a couple of years and I remember when Adrian took over the editorship of the British Fantasy Society journal, *Dark Horizons*, in 1973. In those days fanzines were invariably reproduced using the mimeograph or ink duplicator. If you had an electric one, you had the equivalent of the latest all-singing, all-dancing photo quality laserjet printer of the day. I had a second-hand, *manual* Rex Rotary duplicator and it was such fun to see Adrian attempt the impossible — to get evenly printed sheets from that manually inked, manually cranked pile of scrap metal! And then there was the almost suicide-inducing task of collating and stapling hundreds of pages... His issue, however, number 6, marked a turning point for the BFS. Perhaps it was the optional monochrome or magenta covers? Or the spoof piece 'Wired Tales' in the line-up of its contents? Or perhaps that first step towards the hallowed dream of litho printing (for the cover and interior artwork only of that issue) marked the BFS' move away from the cheap and cheerful 'fanzine' of the sixties. After Adrian's mind-altering experience with the Rex Rotary, he felt his days editing *Dark Horizons* were over. It would be much easier for him to become a starving fantasy writer in a garret...

Influenced in his early writing by Tolkien and the sword and sorcery genre, he cites the work of H. Rider Haggard and Edgar Rice Burroughs as key favourites from his younger days. In later life he developed an all-encompassing interest in comics, amassing a wide collection that includes British comics such as *Dan Dare* and *Garth*, as well as sword and sorcery comics like *Conan, Slaine* and so on. Add to that an interest in ancient history, particularly Celtic, Norse, Roman and Dark Age, and one can see how all of these interests informed his writing.

Whether rock music had an influence on his output, other than passing references, I'm not sure, but I have to recount our trip to the Birmingham Odeon in 1973 to experience a Hawkwind concert. The band had released 'Space Ritual' that year, which had science fictional elements and the involvement of Michael Moorcock and his influences. Suitably attired in very smelly Afghan coats (all the rage) we staggered out of the darkened auditorium half way through the gig. Hawkwind's infamously mind-altering decibel level concerts were perhaps outdone that day, and we two fans, at least, remained deaf for several days afterwards. No doubt it may have addled our brains too. In fact, it was probably why we ended up demolishing several bottles of Retsina every time we went to a certain Greek restaurant in Birmingham that is, probably thankfully, no longer in existence.

Adrian began publishing novels around the same time as his short stories began to appear, with his short yarn 'The Horror Under Penmire' appearing in Mary Danby's *Frighteners* in 1974, just pipping at the post the first volume of his 'Dream Lords' trilogy, *A Plague of Nightmares* by a year.

His short fiction has been widely published. From fantasy to horror anthologies, including *The Berserkers* (edited by Roger Ellwood), *Cold Fear* (Hugh Lamb), *Worlds of Cthulhu* (Robert M. Price), *Kitchen Sink Gothic* (David A. Riley), *Fantasy Tales* (Stephen Jones and David Sutton) and *Fear* magazine (John Gilbert). He's appeared in *The Year's Best Fantasy* (Lin Carter) and *The Year's Best Fantasy & Horror* (Ellen Datlow).

Following on from the 'Dream Lords' trilogy of novels (*A Plague of Nightmares, Lord of Nightmares* and *Bane of Nightmares*), came the four-volume 'Omaran Saga' and 'Star Requiem' quartet of books. Ever prolific, a string of one-off novels interspersed these series, including *Madness Emerging, Paths in Darkness, Moorstones, The Sleep of Giants* and more recently, *Blood Red Angel* and *The Shadow Academy* amongst others.

Moorstones and *The Sleep of Giants*, both written as 'young adult' novels, are set in his native West Country. Adrian was born in Plymouth and returned west from Birmingham in adult life, after working for the Birmingham library service. He is married to Jude and together they raised two children, Sam and Katia. Ade became a business manager at Bideford College for twenty years before retirement. The couple live in a rambling old forge and Ade has always a ready story to tell about his (sometimes hair-raising) adventures in home maintenance and DIY! And if you happen to see a lone swimmer in the chilly seas off Westward Ho! that'll be Ade, taking the waters.

Adrian describes his Dream Lords trilogy as "a mixture of fantastic adventure, sword-and-planet-and-sorcery, very much inspired by Burroughs, Frank Herbert's *Dune* and Dennis Wheatley's black magic books". Although Adrian had not read any works by Robert E. Howard at the time he wrote the series (he became a big fan later), they were promoted as being "In the tradition of Robert E. Howard". The first volume, *A Plague of Nightmares* even splashed, "Fantasy and horror in the tradition of Tolkien and Lovecraft!" But the overstated influences aside, there was something maybe prescient in these overblown comments, for Adrian has become a craftsman in writing in the hybrid genres, or 'cross-genre', 'genre busting' work, initially in his creation of the Voidal and latterly in the Nick Nightmare stories.

The author says, "the Voidal, [is] a warrior doomed to wander the limitless worlds of a bizarre omniverse, in search of his past, his identity and his soul". He adds, "Inspired by a combination of fantasy works, including Clark Ashton Smith, H. P. Lovecraft and the extraordinary French artist, Philipe Druillet, it was the beginning of a strange and tortured odyssey". Adrian doesn't say if the tortured odyssey is his or the Voidal's! But the odyssey has continued for forty years; the first Voidal yarn, 'The Coming of the Voidal' was published as a chapbook in 1977. 'First Make Them Mad' and 'Universe of Islands' followed in 1979 and 1980. One of the stories, 'Astral Stray', introduced the character Elfloq, a companion of the Voidal. The story was reprinted in Lin Carter's *Year's Best Fantasy Stories*, volume 5, from DAW Books in

1980. In 2001 Wildside Press collected eight of the Voidal yarns in *Oblivion Hand*, most revised for this edition. This was followed in 2011 by both *The Long Reach of Night* and *Sword of Shadows*, both containing reprints and new Voidal stories.

Adrian's penchant for genre-busting writing continues to this day, with his latest incarnation, Nick Nightmare, "Private Eye – Public Fist". Hard-boiled tough guy, Nick is a pulp hero, taking on assorted horrors in his native New York, which include the Old Ones, Voodoo, femme fatales, the freakish mobster The Vogue Prince, Dagon and the Heavy Mob from the Deep, to name a few. Characters spawned from this fevered imagination include Sharkbait Bill, pulp writer Bart Kraggs, Dr. Moribund and Montifellini who drives the Magic Bus.

Adrian first hit upon his pulp hero after reading Peter Cheyney's *Sinister Errand* and the work of Carter Brown, the Mike Hammer titles by Mickey Spillane and Lovecraft's Mythos stories. The first story to be published was 'The Vogue Prince', in *The Alchemy Book of Pulp Heroes*, volume 1, edited by Mike Chinn. (2012), followed by 'You Don't Want to Know' in the Stephen Jones edited *Weirder Shadows Over Innsmouth* the following year. Also that year Jon Harvey's Spectre Press published 'Nightmare on Mad Gull Island' as a hardcover limited edition chapbook (*Cthulhu 4*). Nick Nightmare's most recent appearances have been in *Nick Nightmare Investigates*, a smashing, beautifully designed, limited edition hardcover from The Alchemy Press/Airgedlámh Publications (2014). This contains all the previously published Nightmare yarns, plus four new tales (including 'Fire All of the Guns at One Time', a crossover tale by Ade and Mike Chinn, bringing in Mike's two-fisted, gun-toting ghost-hunting pulp character Damian Paladin). *Nick Nightmare Investigates* won the British Fantasy Award in 2015 in the Best Collection category.

So, talking about tough guys, here you hold in your shivering hands Adrian's latest collection, *Tough Guys*. Previously unpublished here are three novellas and a short. Based on the title theme, these four works are completely different in subject matter and tone.

There is, of course, A Nick Nightmare story herein, 'Wait for the Ricochet', in which the gumshoe is entrusted to convey a message about "The Malleus Tenebrarum", a book that names the properties and powers of dark and light, to the Mechanic, one Oil-

Gun Eddy... His adversary is the sinister Lucien de Sangreville, plus assorted non-human denizens of the murky lower levels, and his sidekick the sword-wielding business-woman Ariadne Carnadine. In contrast, in 'If You Don't Eat Your Meat' the reader enters a post-apocalyptic world where the very unsavoury Ryan relates his story of rival families and cannibalism. It is gruesome and unflinching horror. In 'A Smell of Burning' a hospital patient finds he is having out-of-the-body experiences. On his astral journeys he visits a man recalling his abused childhood and this leads to a shocking revelation... Finally, 'Not If You Want to Live' explores the fate of Razorjack, who is a Redeemer, a dead man used by a shady organisation to bring back others from death. An intriguing and engrossing story of love between Razorjack (aka Jack Krane) and mobster's moll Rebecca Fellini, with science fictional and satanic elements. And all four stories are engrossing reads, so now without further ado, I'll hand you over to... The Tough Guys!

David A. Sutton
Birmingham, February 2016

WAIT FOR THE RICOCHET

They say every cloud has a silver lining. Darkness always comes before the dawn. Things get worse before they get better. They say all that stuff. What they don't say so loudly is that every sunny day has its clouds. You're a long time dead.

Who are they anyway? And what the hell do they know?

I was sitting on the sidewalk outside my local burger joint, enjoying a fat hot dog, a pot of black coffee and a scan through a couple of daily rags, mostly focused on the racing pages to see if I could find a nag or two worth backing with a few bucks, more for amusement than profit. I don't win much at the betting game, but it's a low-key habit, a mild stimulus.

I could see over the top of the newspaper that I had company. Slippery Al, a local errand boy for anyone that tipped him a handful of dollars, was hovering around me like a blow fly and twice as nervous. He was well named: he had long, lank hair, greasy as an axle and pale skin that looked like it had been oiled. If you wrapped your arms around him (though Hell knows why anyone other than his mother would want to do that) you got the feeling he'd squirt out of your grip like an elongated bar of soap.

I lowered the paper and met his uneasy gaze. With him it would always be cloudy. He had a way of jerking his head this way and that, as if anticipating rough words or a hostile move from anywhere around him.

"Sit down, Al. You want coffee?"

He eyed the pot like it was an alien artefact, shaking his head, and perched himself anxiously on the edge of one of the metal seats, ready to slide away at any moment. I was used to his eccentricities so I didn't take it personally. "What news from afar?"

He rummaged inside his jacket, like a wino digging about in a trashcan for a bottle. I watched as he tugged out an envelope and thrust it towards me, evidently glad to be rid of it. I studied the scrawled writing, my name, Nick Stone, followed by a single word, 'Urgent.'

"Who gave it to you?"

"A guy called McLennon. Said he was slipped it while he was

visiting a pal in Sing Sing prison. I do a bit of this and that for McLennon. He knows I got contacts." Whatever else anyone thought of Slippery Al, he did have contacts, some of them useful. I gave him a few greenbacks and he was up and away, quick as a flea.

I used my forefinger to open the envelope and slid out the single sheet within. I recognised the scrawl now. I hadn't seen it for a long time, not since my own less than Halcyon days in that delightful Correctional Facility. It had a new, institutional name now, but to me and those of us who had been its guests, it would always be Sing Sing. Cagney would have felt the same.

I need to see you, Nick. It's important. Big time. **Nam et ipsa scientia potestas est.** Zeff.

I sat back with mixed emotions. Mostly guilt – I hadn't visited old Zeff Radwawski since the day I got out. I used the excuse that he'd told me to swear never to set foot inside the prison again, even as a visitor, but the truth was, I couldn't face going there, even to see the man who had taught me so much. I'd done three years in that hole, three years for a murder I didn't commit, until my lawyer dug up enough fresh evidence to spring me. Someone had paid that guy a fistful of spondulicks and I'd always had a hunch it had been Zeff Radwawski. Anyhow it wasn't me – I didn't have enough then to buy a pack of gum.

Zeff had taken me under his wing and made me learn things – books, music, the Arts. Stuff he said would not only enrich my life, but get me through it better. Three years of hard labour it had been – I hadn't been an easy pupil – but now I was glad of it. I was a mine of information. And, hell, I even knew a bit of Latin. Enough, anyhow, to translate what Zeff had written.

Knowledge is power.

I put the letter away and sipped my coffee. I'd have to go, of course. Whatever Zeff wanted, I owed him a visit. And my guess was he was due for release soon, not back out into this world, though. He was due for the last sleep, the long one.

I took a final look at the racing pages. There was a nag running in the 3.30, its name sprang off the page like an omen – *Roman Holiday*. What those ancient guys called an augury. It was worth a ten buck stake, even at long odds. (I found out some days later that it had come in last, just about in time to beat the racecourse lock-up.)

*

To the Governor and his Merry Men in Sing Sing, I would always be an ex-Con, a former guest, no longer their responsibility, a minor irritation in the daily flow of prison life. Never mind that I'd been framed and put in the slammer to rot by a bunch of slick operators whose toes I'd trodden on once too often. I didn't expect to be welcomed back, even on a visit, with open arms and a bunch of roses.

So I was surprised when my reception committee, two uniformed heavies, politely and indifferently took me into a small library, sat me down at a long table and asked me if I wanted anything to eat or drink. They were both dead ringers for the Incredible Hulk, except that their skin wasn't green, but that was all. Slightly disarmed by their unexpected respect, I asked for coffee. This library was a big improvement on the one I'd spent so many hours in with my erstwhile tutor: it sure looked like money – public money, grants, I guessed – had been lavished on it. Part of the prison's drive to establish a new image. The days of frying its inmates in the Big Chair were long gone. Now it was all about rehabilitation. Although the place was empty. Not even a librarian to shuffle a few tickets.

I didn't have long to wait before my hosts brought Zeff in and set down a pot of coffee and a couple of mugs on the polished mahogany table. I knew at once Zeff was on borrowed time. He would be in his seventies now, and those long years of confinement – he'd been in here for twenty or more – had taken their toll, aided by the wasting disease that gnawed at his bones. He was deathly white, the last wisps of his hair like mist about his head. The lines on his face were deeply ingrained, lines of pain as much as age.

Even so, he grinned as he saw me and reached out a gnarled hand to grip mine. There was surprising strength in those fingers, a reminder of the fire that had once burned in him. He lowered himself into a chair and the uniforms left us, retreating out of sight.

"Don't say it," he grunted. "I know I look like hell. I've not got long left, Nick. But time enough to say what I need to say." He could read my guilt at not visiting him like it was chalked up all over me. "Listen, son, don't beat yourself up for not coming here sooner. This is no place for you. Never was. Are you doing okay?"

15

I nodded, my throat drier than a *wadi* at midday. "No little thanks to you, buddy. All that stuff you crammed into me. Three years of it – you were tougher than the guards."

"You had a brain, son. I didn't want to see you waste it. From what I hear – and you'd be amazed at what news filters in to this place – you've been busy." He coughed, his entire frame shuddering.

I wanted to hug the guy. "I've had a few good breaks."

"You've met up with some tough customers. And you know what's out there."

"Yeah. But like you said in your note, knowledge is power. You taught me that."

He grinned through his pain. "That's what it's all about, Nick. There's always someone – or something – that wants it all. There's a darkness out there that would snuff out the last candle if it could." He leaned forward. "You never were a religious man."

I smiled sardonically. "If there are gods, they're no better than us little guys. The only difference is, they've got more clout."

"Some of us are given certain – gifts – abilities that enable us to tilt the balance of power a millimetre or two. You've met some of those people, Nick. The dark recoils from them, at least for a time. We're going to need them and their like, Nick. There's a storm coming. Old Night is stirring. A vast power that reaches out and threads all the other black strands of evil that want to rise up and spread like plagues. A power that's older and darker than any of them. Men have given it many names since the tide of history began."

I thought about some of the bizarre cults and demi-gods I'd stumbled across – once I'd have dismissed it all as bunkum, but I had the scars to prove that you mocked it at your peril. "You're talking about beings with names that you need an extra tongue to pronounce."

"Light and Darkness have been at war since the whole shebang began, right across everything that exists. In the beginning, as far as we know, there was darkness. Science has been busting a gut to find out how light came into existence. You can take the simplistic view that God created it."

"I always thought that was a mite too pat, too convenient."

"Yeah, well, we could speculate until doomsday. Point is, Nick, there's an on-going conflict. Now and then it flares up and

16

centres it attention here and there. Right now, it's here, or will be."

"The stars are right, is that it?"

"Partly. Whatever is stirring up the darkness has more strands than a spider's web. And there are more unholy alliances than any of us could possibly imagine. Something's coming. We need to react early, before it gets too strong a hold and opens doors that we'd never be able to close."

"So this is the Apocalypse you're talking about?"

I hadn't meant to sound flippant, but Zeff glared his annoyance. "You have to take this seriously, Nick. Dammit, it's not a game. It's war. For real. Mostly it's subtle. What we're up against is nothing if not devious beyond belief." He coughed again, fighting back whatever was inside him, dragging him to a slow death.

"Okay," I said quietly. Part of my reaction was due to the fact that he'd never spoken about this stuff when I'd been with him in here. I knew there were a million horrors out in the world – Jeeze, most of them were based in the city as far as my own experiences went – but this kind of religious zeal that had gotten a hold of Zeff was disturbing. Was he losing it? All that time cooped up in here, with death closing in on him like some avenging angel – or demon?

"I said some of us have been given gifts," he went on. "Talents. Others are guardians, keepers of knowledge. There are powers – weapons – that can be used against the dark. You know about some of them."

He was right. I'd seen certain artefacts in action, even used some, though always with caution. There was a danger of contamination when you monkeyed about with such things.

"For example, there's a certain *mechanic*," he said very softly, letting the word hover between us like some kind of spell.

I just nodded. He was talking about the irrepressible Oil-Gun Eddy, who was a lot more than he looked and who knew a thing or two about dangerous artefacts, not least the terrifying weapon that housed the Dancers of Ruin. I'd seen them in action, and boy, they were not to be messed with.

"The weapons and all the powers they control have got to be co-ordinated, and soon, Nick. You have a part to play. It's what I helped to prepare you for. You think I've lost my marbles, eh? But you can't take that chance," he added before I could object.

17

I owed him more than I could ever repay him. "You want me to do something, just name it," I said. "But remember, I'm just a gumshoe. A small cog."

"The big wheels don't turn without the little ones," he said with a grin. It evaporated quickly and he leaned as close as the table would permit. "There are keys to power, dark and light. Where the war is confined to earthly realms, these keys can be very potent. They can define success or failure on a significant scale. There is a book that names them all, their properties, how they can be used. And where they can be found. *The Malleus Tenebrarum*. Nothing on this earth is more sought after than this book, and no other work is so jealously protected."

I had a choice: start giggling at this hocus-pocus, or get very nervous. Very nervous won out. I decided Zeff was as sane as I was. I glanced around me at the walls of books as if they had a life of their own. Maybe they did. So was this ultimate volume here? Was that why he'd brought me?

He shook his head, like he'd read my mind. "I know where it is, but when I die, no one else will, unless I pass the knowledge on to a new keeper first."

"You're not going to tell me that's me?" Jeeze, I had enough trouble dodging the million and one freaks I'd wound up over the last few years without stirring up the kind of monstrous powers Zeff was hinting at.

"No. The mechanic. He safeguards many of the artefacts. The knowledge is for him. You must pass it to him."

"So this is *Casting the Runes*, only for real?"

He gave me his don't-be-so-goddam-flippant look again. "If the book has to be used, he must be the one to open it, and he alone. The artefacts protect him."

"And me, old buddy? Who's looking after me?"

"You'll be shielded – to an extent. Enough for you to pass on the knowledge. You only need carry it for a short time. But you have to be discreet. The enemy must not know. Once you've passed the knowledge on, the mechanic will erase all memory of it from your mind. It'll be as if you never knew. Then you'll be safe enough."

I sat back. There was no question of my refusing to carry out Zeff's crazy wishes, but I didn't get a nice warm feeling about it.

"You called yourself a small cog, Nick. That's what's needed.

Someone who can slide through the cracks. Someone who won't be noticed."

"A mug."

He didn't smile, shaking his head. "That's the last thing we need."

*

On my way back to the city I was torn between mulling over what Zeff had told me about his all-powerful book and its whereabouts and trying to close down my mind on the matter altogether. Hell knew who – or what – was listening in. I thought I was imagining it, but I kind of got the feeling that I was a marked man, both on the boat that brought me back down the Hudson and in the streets of the city, heading via the subway for the dubious sanctuary of my office. There was something in the air and my psychic radar had picked it up. It was faceless, but that was okay – my guess was it would be the last word in ugliness.

I was about to board the train, when I sensed a more physical presence further down the platform. The train wasn't crowded, but there were enough people getting on and off the car to obscure my view. Even so, I picked out one face, briefly, further down the line. The muggy air was turning cold. I tried to convince myself it wasn't one of the guards who'd escorted me around Sing Sing. The eyes gleamed briefly. Inside my coat, my fingers closed around the solid silver cigarette lighter Zeff had given me, his parting gift. I don't smoke, but I took a morsel of comfort from touching the delicate filigree, telling myself it was silver for a reason.

I pushed deeper into the car and hung on to a strap, keeping myself as nondescript as I could. I was expecting the watcher to be easing his way along the cars to be nearer to me, but a few discreet glances showed me nothing. Maybe I had imagined it.

People got off, station by station. I began to notice that not so many were getting on. The cars started to empty, like they would have done nearer the termini. We were in the city centre. So where the heck were all the travellers? I stared down the cars and about three down could see the back of a tall, thick-set man who could have been that guard from Sing Sing. I asked myself, why should anyone be following me? Surely they'd know the location of my office, maybe even my apartment. Zeff had given me the answer, though. I was the known messenger. They wanted to see who I spoke to. When I passed on what I knew about a certain book, they wanted to be in on it.

I decided I'd slip out of the car and lose the goon. Then I noticed that the door beside me had stopped operating. So had those nearest to me. Locked tight. This was no accident. Those that did work were still disgorging passengers. Now, no one was getting on. A couple of the lights started flickering. And we weren't stopping at all the stations. A few zipped by. I took my hand off the silver lighter and curled my fingers around one of my two Berettas. That felt so much better, like a vital organ had been restored.

The train slowed, all its lights dimmed now. If there were any other passengers on board, they were well out of sight at either end of the cars. Somehow I got the feeling that there weren't any, just the guard, his back still to me, like he wasn't interested. Fat chance.

We were in between stations, but we must have been close to my stop right in the centre of the city. As we came to a complete halt, I watched the guard casually move along the car towards me. His face was in shadow, but I had been right all along. He was from Sing Sing all right. The shadows and the silence curled around us. Beside me the doors rumbled open to reveal a black hole that yawned as invitingly as a mausoleum. Its chilling air had a feel of malevolence.

The guard was very close to me now. "This is our stop, Mr Stone," he said, in the same polite tone he'd used in the prison. He had the build of a quarter back, a jaw like an anvil. If he was armed, his gun was out of sight. Somehow I didn't think if I got the drop on him he'd pay much attention to threats. He was just the hired help. Whoever was running this show was out there in the darkness.

The guard nodded towards the open doors. I could just about make out a sort of platform. I'd like to have assumed it was some kind of maintenance point, but I would have been kidding myself. I disembarked slowly. There was only one way to walk along the narrow platform and a greyish light was seeping down from a point ahead. I made for it, moving slowly, ready to act if I had to. Somehow I didn't think I'd been brought here to be mugged. There was more than a good chance they wanted to pry my head open, though. They would want to know where the goddam book was.

The platform widened and there was a flight of steps going upwards into a marginally better light. Cobwebs had wrapped a bulb so tightly that they barely allowed light through. I looked around for spiders. They were not my favourite creatures. Up ahead there was a door.

"Go ahead," said the guard. "Open it."

I did so and pushed the door inward. It revealed a long, low-ceilinged room, lit by a few more mouldering bulbs. There was graffiti on the walls, daubed in thick paint, clumsy work that some joker had slapped on in an effort to suggest pentagrams, inverted crucifixes and a beast that I assumed was a goat, seeing as how it had two curling horns. All it needed was a *Satan Rules – OK?* slogan. Half way down the room was a bare table and some chairs. A figure sat behind the table, wrapped in darkness like some kind of vampire just up from his bed of dirt, though the guy was sharply dressed. No dirt – or flies – on him. My fingers eased off the Beretta and back to the silver lighter. It felt suddenly warm, like I'd got hold of a small, living animal. That was fine by me.

Behind me, the guard leaned up against a wall, like someone had switched him off. I wasn't going to take that for granted. I reached the table. Count Dracula's cousin looked at me with hypnotic eyes. Oh, he had the gift all right. Those eyes were unique. Burning blue, if there is such a thing. I made damn certain I didn't lock into that gaze. Anyone who succumbed to it would be putty in his hands, sure as eggs was eggs.

"Do sit down, Mr Stone," he said very smoothly. It wasn't a Bela Lugosi voice, but it had a powerful timbre, the kind of voice used to being obeyed. He wasn't a Yank – a Brit maybe.

I took a chair and dropped into it, feigning calmness. "You'd better have a good explanation for this, buddy. I don't take kindly to being shoved around."

"Really, Mr Stone, I think you're exaggerating. Ronnie there hasn't laid a finger on you, has he? All I want is to have a little – chat." He leaned forward, interlinking his fingers and regarding me like a cat chewing over which part of a small bird it's going to – well, chew over.

"Chat away, but make it snappy," I grunted, but my tough guy act washed right over him.

"Of course. Let's, uh, cut to the chase. You've been to see an old friend. Zeffron Radwawski. He's an old acquaintance of mine, too. And he gave you something. Some information."

I went on avoiding his eyes, but I could feel their intensity. Like a snake was trying to mesmerise me. "Sure. He wanted to see me one last time. He was always a mite sentimental. So what's it to do with you?"

"It's very simple, Mr Stone. You just give me the information, about a certain book, and you'll be back up in the city and getting on with your life. I can't imagine the book would be of any use to you. In exchange, you get to live, with your health and sanity intact."

I was in a jam. I had my back to Ronnie the gorilla. He could shoot me easily enough – no doubt to maim as I'd be useless to them dead if I didn't squawk. My best bet was to pull my own gun on Dr Mesmer here. My right hand had slipped inside my coat. He knew what was in my mind, but it didn't seem to faze him.

"What's it to be?" I think he was using his nice voice.

Again I avoided his eyes, but I could sense that he was getting mildly irritated by my silence. "Perhaps I can help you make up your mind," he said, his tone changing to one of menace. Now we were getting down to it.

He stood up and backed slowly from the chair. The air around him shimmered, like heat haze on a desert road. It grew darker, the bulbs overhead dimming like someone had wrapped a paw around them. I watched, fascinated, as my host began to emanate an even darker cloud, like it was flowing out of him. It coalesced on either side of him, taking form. Two forms, in fact: ink-black shapes, half the height of a man, hunched and neck-less. Both had eyes like rubies and again I avoided their baleful glare. My guess was they were imps, conjurations that served their master. Whether I was imagining this or not, they meant business, that business being my deep pain. They both reached out long, black arms, dense as oil, intending to fasten into me.

Right then I felt the inside of my head *itching*. Like someone was groping about in there, trying to get a hold of something. My host was doing his damndest to read my mind and rip out the information I was carrying. I could feel the silver lighter glowing inside my jacket and I tried to focus on that, diverting any thoughts about the forbidden book.

I was pretty sure my gun wasn't going to be a lot of use against them – like shooting smoke. But Ronnie the Hulk behind me was still a threat. So I flung myself sideways, rolled, pulled out the Beretta and loosed off a couple of shots in his direction. I was close enough to him not to miss. I heard him yell and he crumpled, the sound of his rasping breath loud in the chamber. I'd taken my host by surprise, which gave me time to get to my knees, my gun aimed at his chest.

He glowered down at me from beyond the table. "You're wasting time with that toy, Mr Stone. I'm afraid I have to get very unpleasant." As he spoke, the two shadow-things converged on me again and I could feel something vile emanating from them, a kind of pure malice. It almost unnerved me and it was all I could do not to throw up. My free hand dug inside my coat and grabbed the silver lighter. I yanked it out and held it in front of me.

The reaction was instant and shocking. The two imp-fiends wavered and my host drew back, an expression of mingled horror and fear on his face. "*Put that away*," he hissed in a voice that sent shivers down my spine – nasty ones.

I got up slowly and held out the lighter. The temptation to flick it on was too great. I thumbed it and it flamed into life. It was no ordinary flame. Instead it was like I was holding a miniature flame-thrower and a long, fat tongue of fire shot upwards like I'd released a stream of napalm. The whole place was bathed in brilliant white light, dazzling and blazing hot. I heard shrieks, as if a bunch of animals had been roasted. I even let out a shriek or two of my own.

When I took my finger off the lighter, the flame was gone. So were the two imp shapes. My host was at the other end of the room, one arm covering his face, as if I'd tossed acid into it. I watched in amazement as he just – disappeared. Like he'd been no more than a projection. There was a thunderclap that left my ears ringing so loud I thought my eardrums had burst. When I recovered and peered through the smoke – thankfully not the thick black stuff of the imps – I was alone with the slumped form of Ronnie the guard.

Cautiously I went over to him, picking up his fallen gun and tucking it out of the way in my belt. I bent down to the guy. There was a spreading stain across his chest. I was lucky to have caught him with one of my slugs – he was lucky that it hadn't ripped into his heart.

"Listen up, Ronnie-boy," I said, tapping my Beretta lightly on his arm. "It's very simple. Either you show me out of this place and I lug you to the nearest hospital, or I leave you here to bathe in your own juices until all your lights go right out. My guess is you've got an hour, two at best, before you croak. What do you say, pal?"

"Get me outta here, Stone. Don't leave me to those bastards. You don't know what they're like. They're not human."

"Let's go." I heaved him up, which was no mean feat. It would have been easier lugging a dead ox out of there, but I got him to the door, kicked it open and managed to get us down the stairs without collapsing. His breath rasped in my ear, but it was all he could do to fight the agony in his chest and keep on his feet. He wasn't about to try and jump me.

We got to the narrow platform, which was just about lit. The train had gone, leaving only the tunnel curving away to left and right of us. He glanced briefly to the utter darkness to our left, which for all I knew lead down to the bowels of Hell. It kind of pulsed, emanating a palpable flow of evil, like some kind of invisible talon. Thankfully Ronnie-boy nodded to the right. "That'll take us back to the public line. We got to use the track. Mind your feet."

I had no intention of frying myself, so I didn't need the warning about the live rail. I got us down off the platform and he yelped with pain. His chest was soaked with blood. I hadn't been kidding when I'd told him he had an hour left if he didn't get help. We stood unsteadily between the rails. What light there was just about picked out their curling extent. We moved on, me keeping him up like we were two buddies struggling across the front line of a war zone.

"So who do you work for? Was that your boss?" I said between deep breaths. Jeeze, this guy weighed a ton.

"His name's Lucien de Sangreville. One of the big shots in the organization," he grunted.

"I guess you're not talking about Bloomingdale's."

He shook his head and blood was seeping from his mouth and down his chin. "It's a cabal."

"Keep talking, buddy. It'll inspire me to move you quicker. Clam up on me now and I might just run out of energy and dump you here."

"No!" he snapped, craning his neck to look back down the tunnel. His expression suggested he was expecting something big and disgusting to come out of the dark behind us and he wasn't thinking trains. It sure felt – and smelled – like he was thinking correctly. "I'm just a bit player. Guys like me don't get told much. Just do our job and get paid. If not, they get ugly, real ugly."

"Black magic, is that it?"

He nodded, shuddering. "I've seen some of it. Used to laugh at that stuff. Not anymore. I'd have taken off by now, but once they get hold of you, you don't argue. You saw those things back there."

"Looked like smoke and mirrors to me," I snorted, but I for one was not convinced.

"If they'd grabbed you –" He turned again, ignoring the pain. Now there really was something back there in the darkness, something big and very ugly and it was salivating. One of Satan's sidekicks was going to make an appearance if we didn't get the hell out of here. I put in an extra effort and was horrified to see that this tunnel was shut off ahead – a circular wall of steel blocked the way to freedom and there was nowhere else to go. We were about to be engulfed by the steadily oncoming tide of darkness behind us. I could hear something, like the murmuring of a host and it wasn't the kind of stuff you'd want your mother to hear.

"There!" said Ronnie, staggering forward, almost crumpling but recovering enough to jab a finger at something on the wall. It was a black gizmo, an electrical fitting. I unclipped its lid. Ronnie reached in with a last ounce or two of energy and prodded at what must have been a small keypad. To my intense relief the circular steel door groaned and then started to slide aside, letting in the wan light from beyond, revealing the public section of the subway.

Ronnie had sagged down, leaning his back on the curved wall, no more than a foot or two from the exit. His face was grey, his eyes glazing. The entire top half of his body was gleaming. Damn bullet must have torn an artery. I stared back the way we had come: the darkness boiled, churning out a dozen thick ropes of blackness. There was a roaring sound in my head, threatening to smash me to my knees. De Sangreville had dug deep into the realms of nightmare to dredge up whatever was coming for me. I struggled to break free, backing out into the main subway.

There was nothing I could do for Ronnie. I watched in revulsion as the tendrils of darkness reached him and coiled about him, lifting him to his feet as easily as I could have lifted a doll. His mouth opened wide, blood running from it and from his distended eyes, like he was looking into the hungry gaze of Satan himself. No sound came out of him as the darkness shook him. And he began to – collapse. Like all his bones had suddenly become water. All that was left was flesh and blood. Lots of blood. The darkness tossed him aside like an oversize, dripping sponge.

That did it for me. I ripped free of my trance and headed up the track. Any minute now, I thought, that bubbling horror would close on me. I heard a crash, the sound of thunder, and it took me a while to figure out what it was. The steel door to the branch line had slammed shut. I risked a look back and let out a huge sob of relief. The crawling dark had withdrawn behind it. There was just me and the subway track.

In a moment or two I heard voices up ahead and flashlights speared me. I was perfectly happy to be speared by flashlights. I raised my arms and waited. A large figure pushed forward from the group that was approaching. It was impossible not to recognise the vast bulk of Police Chief Rizzie Carter.

"Chief!" I called, grinning my most winsome grin. "Am I glad to see you."

He lowered the fat handgun and glowered at me. "Nick Nightmare. I might have known. I got a hijacked train that reappears as suddenly as it disappears. I got some kind of private tunnel branching off the main subway. I got a whole bunch of commuters scared half witless, gibbering about demons and I got what sounds like a goddam thunderstorm down here underground! And here, right in the thick of it –"

"I know, I know. I can explain. Can we go somewhere a little more salubrious?"

"Will the precinct do, or d'ya want I should book us into a hotel?"

"I'm heartened to hear you haven't lost your sense of humour, Chief. You're gonna need it."

*

"So how come they rubbed out their own goon?" the Chief asked

26

me in his office, after I'd given him a pretty full account of my escapades in the subway labyrinth. I'd edited the facts a little, not wanting to say anything about a certain valuable book.

"My guess is, they wanted to shut him up before he blabbed too much. They'd have known I was lugging him to daylight and medical attention."

"So you didn't get a lot out of him?"

"Just a name. Lucien de Sangreville. Mean anything to you, Chief?"

He leaned back in his chair and I thought it would buckle under the not insignificant pressure. He punctuated his words with sweeps of his right hand and a mug of coffee that he somehow, miraculously, never spilled, and equally wild sweeps of his left hand, in which was clutched a fat bacon roll that he was quickly destroying, bite by monstrous bite. "So, let me get this straight – you were on a subway train when this guy jumps you and another bunch of guys, who you didn't see, hijacked the train, using a branch line that appears to belong to a cabal of black magicians, and took you to some kind of voodoo chamber – "

"Not voodoo, Chief. If your men examine the place, look at the walls. It's devil worship, European style. They worship Satan – all that kind of stuff."

"European. That figures, if it's anything to do with de Sangreville. He's a Brit. A man with a proud ancestry that he claims goes back a long ways. And big, big money. I'm surprised you haven't heard of him, Nick. Especially as he's in cahoots with that rich lady friend of yours."

I tried to react like I hadn't been slapped in the face. "Ariadne Carnadine? She knows this guy? You sure about that?" I couldn't believe my occasional employer would have anything to do with Satanism. She was strictly on the side of the Good People. True, she made a pile of money from her business empire, but it was strictly legit.

"Money attracts money," said the Chief, shrugging. "This guy de Sangreville fronts a big industrial corporation – it's an international giant. Women's fashion mostly – he employs some of the biggest names around. And half the Hollywood ladies are customers. Also he does jewellery, perfume. You might say, he's the ultimate ladies' man. But I guess you need to travel around the top circles to meet him. He keeps a low profile. His empire is

27

worth billions. Like I told you, Miss Carnadine does business with him."

So, I mused, she wouldn't necessarily know he was mixed up in this black magic stuff. I was damn sure she wasn't. It would be too much to take.

"So why was he after you, Nick? Something you left out of your story?" He shoved the last of the bacon roll into his mouth and worked his jaw furiously. It never stood a chance.

I reached into my coat and took out the silver lighter. "I've picked up a few bits and pieces over the years, Chief. Things that have certain powers."

"If anyone else was trying this on with me, I'd slap them around until they thought better of it. But I know the kind of weird stuff you get mixed up in. You've earned your nickname. So what does that thing do? No – don't show me. Just tell me."

I did so and he nodded. "So de Sangreville wants as many of these objects of power as he can get his mitts on. All to fuel his own armoury."

"Yeah. He's planning something. Big and nasty. Can you have him watched?"

"What sort of thing? Not planning on raising the Devil? I thought all that stuff died out with *The Exorcist*."

"I wouldn't be too sure."

*

Most people would have found it impossible to get within a mile of Ariadne Carnadine, head of the illustrious Carnadine Industries, one of the biggest players in city financial circles, but it took me no more than a few minutes to get her on the end of my phone.

"Nick!" she exclaimed. "I thought you'd run out on me. What took you so long?" It was true; I hadn't been in touch with her for a month or so.

I was completely embarrassed by her honest enthusiasm – completely thrilled, of course – and for a moment my mouth dried up on me so that she had to prompt me to speak.

"Miss Carnadine –"

"This is a private line," she laughed. "No need for formality. Or can't you speak?"

"Sure, sure," I laughed nervously. If I hadn't been sitting down, I would have done so – my knees wouldn't have sustained me. "I've been a bit tied up."

"How intriguing. I'm jealous."

I think my mouth was probably gaping, but I managed to get a grip on myself. "I need to see you. For lots of reasons, not all of them good. It's pretty urgent."

She laughed softly. "You better come over."

"Is there a back way in? I don't want to be seen."

"How deliciously mysterious. I do love a mystery. But seriously, are you okay, Nick?" Her voice had changed and there was no mistaking the underlying toughness. I remembered what she had been like in action and she was one feisty lady when the chips were down.

"I'm fine. I just want to stay that way."

Later, in one of her numerous offices, where she assured me we had absolute privacy, we sat as easily as we could. I wasn't a great one for cloak and dagger, but this was one time when I appreciated it. I couldn't afford to let anyone know who I was associating with right now, given the poised threat of the satanic crew I'd stirred up. So Ariadne had arranged for me to go into one of her vast fashion house stores close to her office block and for one of the sweet young things to slip me surreptitiously down to the basement, along some echoing corridors and upstairs to a private elevator. With any luck my meeting with Ariadne would remain secret.

She sat slightly stiffly in one of the plush chairs, wearing her usual sleek business suit. In her early thirties, she had pale skin and hair that today she had dyed ash-blond. Her brilliant gaze fixed me and she interlocked her small, delicate fingers on the desk. She had sensed my mood at once and dispensed with the playful banter. Hopefully we could return to that later.

"You know a guy name of Lucien de Sangreville?" I said, diving straight in.

She arched her brows, her patrician features sculpted into a slight scowl. She'd drawn her hair back in a neat bun, exposing delicate ears and the two teardrop earrings that hung from them. They were cut from the sort of rocks that minor wars would once have been fought over. "Lucien. Yes, of course. We've done battle in a few boardrooms. I think he'd like to buy me out if I'd let him.

He could afford it, too. But I'm not for sale." She sipped at the tea she'd had served to us.

I joined her. It was a little ceremony that I'd come to love. I couldn't disguise my unease, though. "So he's not a big buddy."

She laughed, a gentle sound that played havoc with my nerve endings. It reminded me of FiFi Cherie the nightclub singer, one of Ariadne's *alter egos*. When she transformed herself into that persona, the rest of the world just dissolved. "He'd like to be. He rather thinks that all women would succumb to his charms. He's tried his seduction techniques on me more than once. Oh, he's about as charming as a man can get, but it doesn't work on me. I prefer an altogether different type of guy." She smiled wickedly at me and again I felt a flush. What the hell was I, a teenager?

"He's not a man to cross, I guess?"

She shook her head. "No, absolutely not. I've deflected him diplomatically. So why is he bothering you?"

I gave her the gist of it, leaving out details about the *Malleus Tenebrarum*. "He's on a power cull. Gathering as many of the artefacts of control as he can. I'm told it's in preparation for some kind of coup, involving the dark arts and everything hellish that implies."

She sat back, real concern shadowing her perfect features. "Yes, it tallies with my instincts when I've met him. From your experiences in the cellar, I'd say he was a mage, and of a very high order. If he can project himself in that real a form, he will possess very great powers. Most people dismiss black magic as so much mumbo-jumbo, something that went out of fashion and favour years ago. But it still thrives. I'm not speaking from first-hand experience, you understand." Again that wicked smile. One way or the other, she did have the Devil in her.

"And de Sangreville is a front runner?"

"I wouldn't be surprised. He's from a long established blood line that he proudly traces back to the Templars and beyond. His family mixed English and French blood. Their original money – mountains of it – came from the Crusades and Heaven alone knows what other diabolic dealings they would have had. The de Sangreville roots run long and deep, especially in Europe."

"A sort of Unholy Roman Empire," I quipped.

"That probably sums it up, Nick. So treading on Lucien's toes is a very bad idea."

I nodded. "Right now, I'm a target. I need to pass some information on to a contact of mine. Once I've done that, I'll just be a plain old gumshoe again, low profile and of no consequence to the big shots. But I have two problems with all this stuff. One – I need to meet up with my buddy without de Sangreville knowing, or muscling in. Gotta be an exclusively private affair."

She nodded thoughtfully. "Maybe I can help with that. Secondly?"

"It bugs me that by passing the information on to my buddy, I'll be landing him in a pile of trouble. The Bad Guys will be after him. He's tougher than a ten ton rhino, but I wouldn't want to jeopardise his health."

"Hadn't you better let him decide that?"

I gaped at her. "What? Oh – yeah. Sure. Never thought of that." Now that I did, it still bugged me. There was no way that Oil-Gun Eddie would refuse to take on the burden of responsibility. Whatever, my guess was, I had to speak to him.

"So when do you want to meet him? Soon, I should think, before you find yourself engulfed by demons and whatever other unpleasant forces Lucien will invoke."

"You're not doing my heart rate a lot of good." So what was new?

*

We found ways to get very discreet messages to my favourite haunts as well as some of the insalubrious ones, and Ariadne's brows rose in wry amusement at the latter, but she duly dispersed her staff to make sure the cooked-up information got through fast, namely that I would be out of the country for a few days. Whether or not de Sangreville's network of spies would buy this was debatable, but the man himself might expect me to be winding my way to whoever I was to pass the information on to. It would buy us time to set up a private meeting with Oil-Gun Eddie. Yes, I said us – Ariadne had decided that she would accompany me and when Ariadne makes up her mind, a poor sap like me has no chance of changing it. I confess, I was glad, though. If I was going to be bagged by a bunch of Satanists and turned inside out over a roasting spit, there was no one else I'd rather have holding my hand.

"The best way I can think of to get hold of Eddie is through

31

Montifellini," I told Ariadne.

"The driver of that extraordinary bus you told me about?" she said. "Now him I'd like to meet." She said it without sarcasm – I'd told her about Montifellini, whose vehicle was not the clapped-out wreck that it seemed. It visited places that no vehicle should be able to reach, under normal circumstances.

"We may need to get him to drive us to our rendezvous. That bus can slide through the cracks in time. Believe me, I've done it. If anyone can give de Sangreville's satanic crew the slip, it will be Montifellini."

"I'll get my best outfit together."

By the time we were ready to leave, about to descend via another of Ariadne's private elevators, one of her aides was on the phone to her. There was an outside caller. To my surprise, it was Chief Rizzie Carter.

"You gave us the slip," he grunted. I'd forgotten I'd asked him to keep me under watch. "But it shows you're sharp. Me, I can be smart, too – I figured out where you might be. Listen, I got bad news."

I felt the knots beginning to squeeze tighter in my gut. "Shoot."

"I had your office watched, like you asked. You had a visitor. Only – he was being followed. A bunch of real weirdoes. Made the Goths look like a gang of Sunday afternoon picnickers in Central Park. All they needed were horns and cloven feet and they'd have fitted the bill as your black magic hooligans. Or so my men told me, once they'd stopped shivering and untangled their tongues. These freaks scared the living crap outta them just by being there. Hell knows what they'd have done if they'd seen my men. And that's not all. I had another crew keeping an eye on your friend Mr de Sangreville. They lost him pretty quickly and they're now complaining about things following *them*. Horrible things, Nick. You've kicked over a hornet's nest the size of the Empire State." It was a long speech for Rizzie. Showed how very, very nervous he was.

"Who was the visitor?"

"He was wearing a heavy oil-skin coat and leather boots buckled up to his thighs. Couldn't see his face – his head was wrapped up against the wind like he was a mummy, they said, and he wore thick goggles that musta come from the Forties. And he rode the grandmother of motor bikes. Had an engine like something from a jet plane. From their description, I know I've seen him before. At that big dust up we had at the Swinging Citadel nightclub, when we did for that crime syndicate."

He didn't need to elaborate. Oil-Gun Eddy. He had been paying me a visit. Now there was a coincidence. "So what happened to him?"

"They got him trapped in the alley below your office. My men said it was like a black smog, thick oily clouds, like someone was burning a ton of old tyres. Something poured into their heads, too. By the time they came to their senses, the place was deserted. Your visitor and his bike, the clouds, the Devil's brigade – all gone like they'd never been there. Like a gate to Hell had opened up and swallowed them."

I shuddered at the perceptiveness of his image.

"Whaddya want me to do now, Nick? I got no clues as to where the biker is, or de Sangreville. You could be on your own in this."

"Thanks, Chief. I'll be in touch."

Ariadne could see from my face that I'd been kicked in a soft part of my anatomy, figuratively speaking. She put a hand on my arm. "What is it?"

I told her the bad news. "It may be a coincidence," I said. "My place was being watched and Oil-Gun turned up out of the blue." I was trying to think straight, which wasn't easy given the pace of events. "The Chief said his men weren't seen by de Sangreville's goons. So he's not to know the police are keeping an eye on me. And he wouldn't necessarily know that Oil-Gun was the one I was going to pass the information to. My dough is on de Sangreville having picked up my red herring about me being out of the country."

"So why did he have Oil-Gun abducted?"

"My guess would be he's going to try to use him to get to me. He knows I wouldn't leave Oil-Gun in a jam. Where do you think de Sangreville would have taken him?"

She exhaled deeply, pouting her lips in an exasperated way. "Now you've asked me, Nick. He has that many places, most of them private fortresses. Even if we knew where to go, we'd have a hard time of it getting in – and out."

"I have a theory," I said, pulling out a strip of gum and chewing on it hard. It aids my concentration, if it doesn't add to my personal allure. "If de Sangreville has snatched Oil-Gun as some kind of hostage – bait maybe to draw me in – then he's going to try and contact me. Maybe not directly since he thinks I'm away. But he'd find a way to get a message to me."

The internal phone rang and we both leapt up as if we'd been stung by hornets. Ariadne stared at the machine in momentary horror, and then flicked the voice box. Her P.A.'s voice came crisp and clear.

"Sorry to interrupt you, Miss Carnadine, but you have an outside caller. A Mr de Sangreville."

Ariadne and I stared at each other and no doubt she felt the cold shudders just as I did. Jeeze, was the guy psychic? It was like he'd been listening in to our conversation.

"Put him through, Marilyn."

The voice that broke the stillness of the room now was just as I remembered it down in the cellar off the subway. Its almost mellow tones would have melted stone, but not this one. "Ariadne, dear lady. I'm so glad to have caught you in. If I didn't know how busy you are, I would have sworn you've been avoiding me."

"Lucien, what on earth makes you think that?" She pulled a face that suggested someone had just dropped something putrescent under her nose.

The soft laughter from the phone was eerily unsettling. "Have you thought any more about my offer?"

"There have been so many. Business and pleasure."

"I meant about tomorrow night. My little *soiree*. Music, some very interesting patrons of the arts, some excellent business contacts and I'm keeping a number of bottles of superlative wine on one side so that I can toast any mutual contracts we might consider. I cannot believe you'd want to miss such an occasion."

To her credit, Ariadne laughed with just the right amount of coquettishness. It made her sound very convincing. "Lucien, you're so persistent." She made a perfect show of resisting and refusing, but then seeming to relent. "Tomorrow night, you say? Well, as it happens I do have a window. All right, I'll come, but don't get any funny ideas."

"*Parfait*! What possible excuse can you have for not joining me on Snake Island? It will be a masque to end all masques. Shall I have you picked up?"

34

"No, no. I do my own driving. So what time is this bash starting?"

"Be here at seven for aperitifs." De Sangreville chuckled like he was anticipating something not quite legal. I had the coldest feeling that he was standing in front of us, flesh and bone, and that his eyes were trying to bore into mine, trying his mind rape tricks again. I looked away, but he had signed off.

"You okay?" Ariadne said. "You look a bit pale."

"That guy's a freak show on his own. And how did he know to call you up right now?"

"I'd forgotten he tried to invite me to this *soiree* of his. But as it happens, it'll be convenient, won't it?"

I grunted. To me it sounded too much of a goddam coincidence. But I knew she would already be deciding on which outfit to wear.

*

I spent the next day preparing for the night's revels, though with little enthusiasm. I mugged up on Snake Island, which was one of many beyond the estuary of the city's rivers, down the coast a score of miles or more in an area of long mud flats and marshes that the developers hadn't got round to draining and converting into money, one way or another. I studied a few photos of the place: all of them were bleak and cheerless. Snake Island offered not-so-splendid isolation, but no doubt that suited de Sangreville perfectly.

I was slowly going up the wall trying to figure out what he was up to. Of course, it was me he wanted, or at least, the contents of my head. Oil-Gun must be the bait, but I got no messages, veiled threats or otherwise. I didn't think de Sangreville was trying to get at me through Ariadne. There was no reason to suppose he knew about our association, nor that he knew about her other persona, FiFi Cherie or the nameless female ninja who had accompanied me on the wild outing to the remote promontory of Black Wake, where we'd dug her brother out of a hole. Inviting her to the masque on Snake Island had to be coincidence, even if my mind was uneasy about it.

For two bits I would have called in the Marines – or the brotherhood known as Vengeance Unlimited, to which Oil-Gun belonged. Hell, maybe that's what de Sangreville wanted – to get them cornered. Between them they had remarkable powers – and the artefacts to go with them – exactly what the Satanist was trying to amass. And yet the combined powers of the group would turn Snake Island upside down and sink it if it had to. No, de Sangreville wouldn't risk it. He'd simply go to ground at the first sniff of a full-blooded assault on his fortress. Picking off the team one by one, now that made more sense. Maybe Oil-Gun wasn't bait after all. Whatever, it was driving me nuts turning it over and over.

So the plain fact was, Ariadne and I had to be subtle, though it had my nerves strung out, taut as piano wire. I was mighty relieved when the evening wore on to the time when I slipped away to our rendezvous. She was in a limousine with several of her toughs. They were dressed as monks, wearing thick black habits with deep hoods and they gave me one to put on. I was happy to do it – it would shield my identity pretty well. Ariadne hadn't been able to resist wearing her black ninja outfit, complete with twin samurai swords. I told her it would draw attention to her, not disguise her, but her eyes – all that could be seen of her face – gleamed. Jeeze, she was enjoying this.

"If I can deflect attention from you, dear heart, that'll be fine."

An hour later we drove up the long, flat promontory to Snake Island. It was humped up ahead of us, rising out of the marshlands like the back of a giant alligator. It was partly covered in trees and rose to a nest of crags, from some of which could be seen the walls and buttresses of a building that could have been an old church. Probably built by de Sangreville for effect, I reckoned. The limo pulled up before a pair of thick gates, beyond which was a quayside from which a stone bridge spanned an arm of the sea that wrapped itself possessively round the base of the island.

Two thick-set guards in militia-type uniforms met us, both carrying state of the art machine guns. Ariadne spoke to one of the big lugs as charmingly as she could, but even her most seductive voice cut no ice with these zombies.

"Yous need passes for all of yous," growled one of the men. He had a hatchet face, the kind that could chop up a dozen logs before breakfast.

Ariadne's voice changed, hardening. "Why don't you get on that cell phone of yours and speak to Mr de Sangreville? I think you'll find if you turn me away, he'll have your thick hide for a smoking jacket."

The thug glowered at her like he was deciding whether to do as she'd said or cut loose with his big toy. I'd have turned his head to sushi first – the folds of my monk's habit concealed my Berettas. Thankfully there was no need for drama. The guy did use his cell phone and having grunted into it a few times, handed it to Ariadne.

"I'm at the gates, Lucien. Your commando unit are anxious to boot me off the premises as you neglected to send me a formal written invite." She laughed softly at whatever he said. "I do have a few of my own men with me. Like you, I never go anywhere without bodyguards. Well, that's all very well, Lucien, but I won't be joining the party without them." It sounded like he didn't much care for men with guns that he didn't control, but he must have relented and a few minutes later the limo was cruising over the bridge.

There were houses the other side and a few small boats moored up to a quay. More guards waved us on up the gradual incline of a road that took us past lawns and terraced gardens that looked a shade out of place in such a remote place. De Sangreville's money mountain took care of all of this – the island reeked of it. So did the enormous fleet of cars that were parked up around the sprawling car park in front of a big house. It looked like it had been shipped in, stone by stone, from Versailles, a real palace. It could have housed an entire township and still had room for a baseball stadium.

The cars – at least a hundred of them – were very flash, every one of them worth a king's ransom. We could have been in Hollywood. What guests I could see leaving their vehicles were dressed up in their party finery, their costumes varying across all ages and aspects of history, film and literature. Scattered around I could see more of de Sangreville's guards, about as discreet as piranhas in a punch bowl.

We got to the wide steps at the front of the house and climbed up to meet our host and his immediate cronies at the top of them, where de Sangreville was nodding enthusiastically and shaking hands with the incoming guests, like the President distributing largesse. Ariadne curtseyed to him and he smiled wolfishly, towering at least a foot over her in an immaculate black suit. He was the only person there not in costume, but I guessed he'd slip into his Christopher Lee outfit later.

"Delighted that you came, my dear," I heard him say to Ariadne. So he knew it was her, even though, like I said, the only part of her that was exposed was her eyes. "Do go in. Nearly everyone is here."

He nodded curtly to us bodyguards and we kept our cowled heads down. Even so I swear I felt his eyes boring through the cloth, as if he could pick through my thoughts. I kept thinking, food and wine, food and wine. Yeah, like that would throw him.

Inside, the central hall was big enough to have swallowed Westminster Abbey more than once: it had a forest of candles, some as thick as oak trees, many of them black. Nice effect. There were hundreds of garishly dressed up guests, a regular Masque of the Red Death and an orchestra, a warehouse full of food and chandeliers overhead that scintillated in a way that suggested they were the real, expensive deal.

Ariadne turned to me and said softly, "Why don't you let me do the mingling and you go off and see what you can sniff out."

That was fine by me. I was starting to wilt inside my Mysterious Monk costume and also I was getting the distinct impression that some of de Sangreville's muscle-men were very edgy about us unwanted bodyguards. Much more of this crowding and there was going to be a dogfight and I didn't want to be a soft target. I slipped away easily enough. The place was so stuffed with revellers and so labyrinthine that I was able to give any watchers the slip. I found a narrow hallway and a small door that led back out into the gardens, glad to get into the fresh night air. The grounds were lit up, but the base of the huge house was shadowed, which suited me. I melted into the dark and eased my way along the wall until I found what I was after – a set of steps that led down to another door.

It was locked, but I had some special keys that would have opened hell gates had the need arisen. I slipped inside and re-locked the door. There was just enough light to see by, so I didn't need to use the silver lighter Ziff had given me, which I still carried. It was a cellar, vast and cold, huge columns supporting the low ceiling that put me in mind of some medieval abbey. Perfect for any forthcoming Black Masses, as the mob above me would have appreciated. I rooted around for a while, finding a whole bunch of tombs and stuff, which on another day might have been intriguing. My real interest, though, fixed on something much more revealing.

Propped up against one of the massive stone columns was a two-wheeled colossus of a motor-bike. Bingo. Only Oil-Gun Eddy could own this beast. I'd ridden on back of it a couple of times, an unforgettably terrifying experience. I kept myself in darkness, in case the bike was guarded, and that was a good move: leaning against another column was one of de Sangreville's ruffians, lazily drawing on a cigarette and watching the clouds of smoke he was exhaling. Time to relieve his bore-dom.

It was a piece of cake to slip up behind him, jam one of the Berettas under his ear and warn him not to move on pain of having his brains swiftly removed and redistributed. I'd mastered the art of tying anyone up with one hand a long time back and soon had the sap turkey-trussed to the pillar. He gave me the usual spiel about how de Sangreville would roast me over a spit and personally feed my heart, liver and other vital organs to the Devil, until I gave him a tap across the bridge of his nose. The flow of blood shut him up.

"Okay, let's keep this simple. A straight trade-off. You give me some information and I leave you here without two very shattered kneecaps. Deal?"

He spat blood but nodded. Once he started blabbing, I got what I needed. Oil-Gun Eddy was indeed a prisoner, being held in the old chapel up on top of the hill behind the de Sangreville royal residence. Later tonight, after the main party was over, there was to be a second, livelier do, some kind of ceremony. It was obvious this guy didn't want to be part of it. He didn't exactly say that the Devil and all his horned horrors were top of the guest list, but I got the message.

Satisfied that I'd squeezed about as much as I could out of the guy, I gagged him and left him to sweat. My guess was someone would relieve him in the morning. He would be pretty shook up, but he'd live. I must be getting soft.

Back upstairs, I blended with the cavorting, capering hordes and even helped myself to a mouthful or two of grub, which I admit was damn tasty. I drank some iced mineral water, which was safe enough. I didn't want to risk even a slug or two of booze, which could have been spiked. One or two of the broads, dressed in nothing but sequins – as many as half a dozen of them – made passes at me. It must have been the monk's habit. I politely declined and found my way as close to Ariadne's side as I could without crowding her, like any good bodyguard would.

We all passed a couple of hours shuffling about, the guests dancing, eating, drinking – all the usual party stuff. Some paired off and slipped away to play the games that the grown-ups like to play, but slowly the great mass of bodies thinned out. Sometime before midnight, de Sangreville started manoeuvring key people into a side chamber, including Ariadne, so I made sure I was still close by. So as not to allay her host's suspicions, she discreetly dismissed her other monks, leaving me the lone hooded soul in the diminished company. She'd removed her own face mask, but kept her hair neatly tied back.

This hall was even more lavish and as its doors closed on the selected party, I studied the tapestries, paintings and sculptures. They were all superb works of art, no denying that, but this was Kinky Central. I won't describe the stuff in detail, but it consisted mainly of people without clothes, amusing each other in ways which would have made even the Marquis de Sade blush. I could tell by the expressions on the faces of the present company that they were all waiting for de Sangreville to give the word and life would be imitating art very quickly. I can tell you, I was sweating rivers under my cowl. And I would only have to shed the hood to cause a stir, never mind anything else.

Fortunately de Sangreville hadn't brought us here to indulge in anything more outrageous than listening to him outlining his plans for the impending overwhelming of the world's economy and his presiding over a kind of new, Mephisthophelean order.

"Those who ally themselves to me, those who are willing to go as far as to merge their souls with mine in the name of the Great Beast, will have access to immeasurable power. Power over world politics, religion, finances, everything. You are all key players in world affairs. You cannot imagine how much further we can all go."

There were about a hundred people in the hall and I didn't see or hear any dissenters. They were like a crowd of dope addicts, about to shoot up on their favourite fix, big time. No power like power.

"Since the dawn of time, there have been many ways to tap

this power and numerous artefacts which enabled pre-human races to control the world. I am in the process of gathering the most puissant of them and you will share in this wielding of authority. I will demonstrate this tonight, in the ceremony we will soon hold. I have brought to the sacred place, a person who controls certain artefacts himself, though he uses them for trivial reasons, not appreciating the immensity of what they could achieve. He possesses a weapon that I cannot take from him and use, as it would turn upon us all – unless we make a sacrifice of this man to the Great One and thus wrest control in his name."

I kept still with difficulty. Bad enough that this lunatic was planning to carve Oil-Gun Eddy into dog meat, but if he intended to take control of the Dancers of Ruin, all hell really was going to break loose. Pandora's Box would have nothing on this.

De Sangreville finished his address and began to usher his selected guests out of the hall and into the night, where a path wound upwards to the promised chapel. Its ruined outline could be clearly seen up on the hill, its interior lit by braziers of hot coals, no doubt to set the mood. It had a certain style, I'll give it that, but my bowels were clenched like a big, cold fist. Ariadne gave the outward appearance of being cool, but she must have been as spooked as I was. We were going into this without a clear plan. Hell, I could blaze away happily with the Berettas and she could wreak havoc with her twin blades, but at the end of all that, we'd finish up as so much mincemeat, whatever havoc we unleashed. De Sangreville must have been confident, and why not? He held all the aces, not to mention the pretty picture cards.

He dropped in beside Ariadne as the company filed excitedly up the hill towards the gates of the chapel, leaning over to speak to her quietly, though I could just make out the words. "I've obtained some wonderful things. I'm sure you'll appreciate what they can do for us all. But there's one item I really must have. It's a book."

I didn't get her reply, but she was playing along convincingly.

"The *Malleus Tenebrarum*," he went on. "It lists all the artefacts and their locations. And it enables its owner to wield and control them."

"Do you know its whereabouts?" She leaned towards him so that I would hear this time.

I couldn't see his face, but his tone was angry. "No, only one man has that knowledge. It's an on-going chain, linked back through time. Right now the single custodian is a grubby little private detective. A man called Nick Stone. He's out of the country at the moment."

"Oh, but I know him, Lucien! He works down in the underbelly of the city. Quite a useful contact when you need someone like that. I've used him myself. Surely you must be mistaken. He's a nobody!"

"I'm sure that's precisely why he was chosen. Discreet and secure."

"Well, you're right about his being out of the country. One of my aides tried to get hold of him the other day, but he's away. Do you need to see him?"

De Sangreville released an unpleasant sound that I took to be a laugh. "Oh, yes. Very much so. I will be waiting for him."

"I'll have my aides meet him and I'll bring him to you myself, if you like."

"Really? That would be excellent. I must say, my dear, you do seem to have changed your tune. And there was I thinking I could never persuade you to join in my crusade."

She laughed, the perfect actress. "I always have a price, Lucien. What you are offering does rather meet it."

We'd reached the gates, which were much older than I'd realised. Matter of fact the whole ruin was unusually old. I'd thought it must be some kind of replica of a medieval chapel, but I got that wrong on two counts: it was much, much older, as if the guys who'd thrown up Stonehenge had had a sudden brainstorm and made an architectural leap, and also it wasn't any recognisable style, not medieval, not anything you'd find in a history book. The building had a weirdness to it that reeked of the alien, like it was something created by those pre-humans de Sangreville had talked about. My guess is that people had added chunks over the years, refining it so that something of the medieval style dressed its bones. It felt freaky, though, devilish. Good place for an Inquisition, or a Black Mass, which figured.

The centre of the ruin opened out into a huge pit, like a miniature, dried-up volcanic vent. It just needed a few sulphurous fumes to complete the image. No doubt we'd get that later. Slowly the company shuffled around its edges, fanning out on two sides. There were more black candles, set in extravagant holders that looked as though they'd been filched from a major cathedral or two, like Milan or Rome, except that the figures sculpted in their metal were engaged in the wrong kind of congress for a Catholic church. And not all the figures represented were human. Whoever had done the carvings or cast the bronzes, they sure had a twisted imagination. There were big, golden crosses here too, many of them with representations of inverted crucified victims welded into them, and as with the other sculptures, not too many of these were human.

Across from where Ariadne and I emerged, we saw a large altar, behind which the overlord of this perversion of religion was enshrined in a huge stone figure – revoltingly life-like – rearing up. It had the face of a goat, eyes like heated coals and curling horns as wide as tree trunks. And the goat had teeth like I'd never seen on a goat before – not made for chewing the cud, brother, no. These were elongated and very sharp, like something out of an *Alien* movie, only much bigger. What made them even more ghoulish was the fact that they *moved*. Either there was some very smart mechanical gizmo behind this, or the thing was alive. My head went for the gizmo, but my guts definitely opted for the live thing.

Coupled with this eye-boggling scenario were the twin sense-assaulting smells and sounds. Incense, sweet and sickly, was rich in the air, drifting over and around the pit in thick clouds that boiled from a score of fat braziers, behind which some truly muscled guys – a very mixed race bunch – stood with folded arms, like oiled djinns, waiting to do their master's bidding, like maybe bite someone's head off. They all looked like they would have kicked Charles Atlas' butt sideways *after* he'd done the body-building course. The air throbbed and thundered to the sound of drums. You can't have a good Black Mass without drums, I guess, and here we had drums enough to service a dozen at once. It was like being in the belly of a thunderstorm. Overhead was a deep darkness, cloudless, moonless and starless, like it was a hole into some other dimension.

I gritted my teeth and re-clenched my bowels against all this unnatural, quasi-human discord but what really got to me was what was on the altar. Stretched across it, spread-eagled in a chained "X" shape was a single figure. No prizes for guessing who it was – the motor-cycle garb, even the goggles, gave it away. It was Oil-Gun Eddy, snared and ready for the oven, or whatever nastiness de Sangreville had in store for him.

Ariadne sensed my horror and must have thought I was about to blow my top and run amok – she gripped my arm through the thick fabric of the habit as if to say, "Keep calm." I couldn't think of a snappy response – my eyes had picked out another, smaller altar, to one side of the main one. It was a block of stone, some six feet square and three feet high, and on it a long object rested. It looked like some kind of elongated baseball bat, made from dark wood. I couldn't see from here, but I knew that it was carved around with capering naked figures. The Dancers of Ruin. Oil-Gun Eddy was its personal custodian. He'd let me use it one time when we'd tangled with a particularly nasty bunch of characters and I was in no hurry to touch the damn thing again.

De Sangreville was very cagey about the artefact – he had had a dozen bizarre lamp-like objects placed all around it on the altar, like they were holding it in check. Very sensible arrangement. He'd left our side, though not without another of those sideways glances that gave me the impression I may as well not have been wearing my habit and cowl, like he saw through its disguise. Certainly his amused expression suggested as much. Was I being played for a sucker here?

"He's going to sacrifice Eddy," I said to Ariadne. "He reckons by doing it he'll get control of the Dancers. I'm going to blow his brains out before I let that happen."

She nodded, but not convincingly. Miss Cool was losing it, the sweat standing out on her brow. Her face said it all – brother are we in the crap, neck deep. Yet at the same time I could still feel the resolve in her.

De Sangreville had reached the far side of the pit and stood beside the large altar. Behind him, the huge goat-figure shuddered, its thick hide rippling, then opening to reveal not the body of a goat at all, but an impossibly immense human torso, gleaming muscle, deeply bronzed, almost black, but not in any human sense. This was a very different kind of darkness and it personified every demonic image the mind could dredge up. Power radiated from that naked superhuman torso, not least from its intimidating phallus, wide as an arm.

Seemed like there were to be some preliminaries to the sacrifice – de Sangreville lifted a long, silver blade and used it like

44

a conductor's baton to direct the acolytes, Ariadne and me included, to walk one by one past the altar and the horrendously endowed living incubus behind it. I didn't want to think too much about what we were expected to do as we filed by, but I had one hand on one of my Berettas, both eyes on the supine form of Oil-Gun Eddy. My guess was they had drugged him.

The drums rumbled on at an insane pace, even more insistent and de Sangreville was shouting out the words of an incantation, which was taken up by the moving acolytes. I thought maybe it was a variation on Latin, but the drums rose towards a crescendo, drowning it out. The mists overhead coagulated like a swamp, and from it I could see swirls and eddies of life – demonic life. No tricks here, this was the real deal. I could hear shrieks from the pit, ripping through the deeper sounds of the drums and aerial thunder. We were being joined in this little party by whatever the underworld could disgorge.

Across the pit, where Ariadne and I had entered the chapel, a new figure emerged into the nightmare ceremony and I felt yet another kick in the guts. It was the guard I had tied up in the cellar. Someone had found the bozo and freed him. And here he was, spilling all he knew to de Sangreville's muscle-bound bravos. I was no more than a few minutes or two from discovery and I had to act fast.

I barged my way along the queue towards the smaller of the altars. Time to take a risk or two. I'd handled the Dancers of Ruin before, so maybe they'd work for me again. Eddy had warned me that over-use of the artefact was very dangerous and would probably mean the wielder would be sucked into the weapon's awful power – hell, I'd seen our enemies suffer exactly that fate. I knew, though, that if I took out a Beretta and tried to shove my weight around with just a couple of clips of bullets, I'd be toasted fast. Nothing for it – I had to take a risk with the Dancers.

So I pushed forward and made a grab for the weapon. The lamp-things around it had no effect on me and I was able to grip the long artefact by its handle. It felt lighter than I remembered it, and the carvings didn't seem quite so intricate. Ariadne had realised something was wrong as soon as I grabbed the Dancers, but she was with me and whipped out her twin blades, kicking the nearest acolytes to her backwards, so that the two of us formed a space between the altars. De Sangreville stopped his bawling and glared at us, deep waves of hate streaming off him like radioactive fallout. Yeah, he was real mad. The huge goat-thing towering over him turned its head our way and the teeth opened to reveal a vivid pink mouth and a tongue the size of an overblown python.

What really bothered me, though, was the artefact I was holding. The Dancers of Ruin. Or rather, not the Dancers of Ruin. It was an elaborate fake. Oil-Gun Eddy had not been carrying the real McCoy when they'd snatched him. A precaution, maybe. This thing I was holding, like Babe Ruth about to hit out a record home run, was a bat, an ordinary bat. Wood, dead and useless against the seething mob of acolytes, demons and whatever else was gathering in the smoky gloom.

It had sure fooled de Sangreville, but not anymore. He could see it wasn't the precious artefact he lusted after. He was bemused, I was bemused, so what the crap? – I threw it at him. He wasn't that bemused that he didn't react fast – he lifted his right arm and the bat blew apart in a blue blaze of fire. In the excitement, my hood had fallen back to reveal my less than composed features. De Sangreville knew at once who I was and a satanic smile curled his lips – kind of appropriate for the occasion.

"Stone! The bad penny returns. Well, there's no one else I'd rather join our little celebration!" He waved his nearest thugs forward, but I'd already got the guns out and let the first one have it. He tumbled backwards into the pit as the bullet smacked him in the chest and Ariadne de-activated two more of them with dazzling sweeps of her swords. All this had de Sangreville bubbling with volcanic fury and he hurled some kind of blue bolt my way. I felt it thud up against me like I'd been hit by a big wave, and I was knocked sideways. Dazed, I realised that the silver lighter had baled me out again, at least, it had done enough to weaken the effect of the blow.

I fell across the edge of the pit and could just about see Ariadne straddling me, hacking away at de Sangreville's private army like she was carving a way through a jungle. I knew, however, that the odds of us getting out of this mess were very poor. Inevitably I gaped down into the pit and my eyes almost popped out of their sockets at what I saw coming up from below. The hill on which the chapel squatted was about to give up the contents of its stomach, a disgusting, bilious tide. It was as if a massed crowd of people had been fused together and were clawing their way upwards to us, but those faces – twisted, distorted, leering and snarling, like maniacs on a really bad day. And they all had tongues like ropes. Worse, they were all trying to lasso me.

The prospect of being snarled up in a demonic flesh-fest did wonders for my energy level and I got to my feet, emptying a few rounds down into the closest of the rising faces. Zero effect. Ariadne shoved one of her swords at me and I tucked my Berettas away, accepting it uneasily. We stood back to back and I was thinking, this would make one hell of a movie.

"Let's take as many of the bastards with us as we can, Caruthers!" I shouted to her and, dammit, she laughed, a blood-covered Valkyrie. My kind of woman. Yeah, if only.

Overhead, the storm had broken, big time. Lightning flashed, multiple tongues of it, the glare giving an even more horrific taint to the pit and the revolting things spewing upwards, now just a few feet away. Complete chaos had taken over the human element of the conflict. The Goat-Thing behind the altar must have decided it would rather watch the kids play than interfere – it had become no more than a statue again, frozen into immobility, for which Ariadne and I gave thanks.

There was a lull in the action. The acolytes had no appetite for a fight – well, to be fair to them, they didn't have any weapons. They'd come here looking for an orgy of sexual frivolity and a few more bottles of expensive wine, not to be decapitated by two over-excited supplicants looking to get into the *Guinness Book of Records* with some new body count record. So they had fled the scene, back to the chapel gates and away down the hill to somewhere saner.

So Ariadne and I were faced with two fronts – de Sangreville's heavy brigade, now armed to the teeth, though not with guns, and the gibbering escapees from the pit. I'd heard de Sangreville screaming above the general hullabaloo that he wanted us both alive, so that bought us a little time. We were surrounded and knew that there was no way we were going to cut our way free. Besides which, how the blazes were we going to rescue Oil-Gun Eddy? He hadn't as much as twitched, lying supine on the big altar. Then there was the small matter of the chains.

De Sangreville knew he still had the trumps. He watched us closely as he moved with contemptuous arrogance toward his victim and rose up over the sacrifice. The storm lashed around him, seemingly encouraging him as he once again lifted that long, wickedly sharp blade. There was nothing Ariadne or I could do to prevent his next act.

To my utter horror, he plunged it down into the breast – and heart – of the prone Oil-Gun Eddy, down into the unresisting flesh and organ until only the hilt protruded. I wanted to scream, to roar with anguish and fury, but my body was locked, seized up with revulsion. Instead, I could do nothing but watch as the blade rose and fell twice more. Blood ran out over the leather jacket of the mechanic, darkening the altar as de Sangreville's face gleamed with unholy joy at the murderous act in the name of his repulsive master.

As Oil-Gun's blood dripped down the altar and into the pit, the creatures within it shrieked in lunatic glee, the first of them lapping at the scarlet flow, drawing some frightful energy from it. I ripped myself free of my stupor and would have leapt for de Sangreville, but Ariadne held me back. She was no less horrified than I, that much was clear from the look on her face, but she kept her cool, where I would have lost it altogether. Instead of hurling myself at the Satanist and doubtless being overwhelmed by his power and that of the ascending demonic horde, I fell back with Ariadne. The wild delight of the creatures, milling around the blood of the sacrifice, momentarily distracted them from us.

I fought the last of de Sangreville's human defendants as we forced our way back around the edge of the pit, but others had formed a cordon near the gates, trapping us. We would be dragged down by sheer weight of numbers. Only my intense fury at Oil-Gun's murder kept me going in those moments. Ariadne and I fought back to back, our bodies pressed close to one another. I was about to make a final, hopeless charge for the gates, when a new sound erupted above everything else. Deafening, continuous, it was the awesome noise of a machine gun – and some beast of a gun at that. Miraculously the swarm of thugs ahead of us broke ranks, bodies flung this way and that as if smashed aside by a huge scythe.

Someone else had joined the affray, a uniformed figure, its jet-black outfit seemingly pasted to its skinny form, its head concealed in a tight-fitting black mask. It carried a weapon that spat round after round, like a Gatling gun in overdrive. De Sangreville's servants became wheat falling to the scythe, chopped

48

down and trashed in a thick drizzle of blood. Small compensation for the loss of Oil-Gun. Ariadne shoved me forward and in a daze I followed the gunman, out through the gates and down the slope. Behind us we could hear a rising cacophony of frustration as the demonic swarm bent its attention to us.

We had just enough of a head start to reach the big building and our rescuer didn't bother about niceties when it came to getting inside – he just blew the nearest cellar door to pulp and splinters and motioned us inside. We wove through the ill-lit columns until we reached Oil-Gun's motor bike, which had been left unguarded. The black-clad guy tossed his weapon to me and leapt on to the bike, kicking it into life and gunning the engine. It roared like a dozen banshees, filling the cellar with black smoke. Ariadne and I didn't need telling what to do. She jumped up behind the biker and I was behind her a moment later, trying to keep my balance and swing the machine gun up with me. Its weight almost dragged me off the bike.

Next thing, we were flying through the cellar. I had a vague impression of clawed hands trying to rip me off the bike, shrieking faces, those curling tongues, but somehow we evaded them. Our driver headed directly for the wall to the outside. He may have been confident, but I wasn't – I just gaped at the oncoming stone – it would have been several feet thick. We were going to be pasted across it for a distance of many yards unless – unless we went through it like it was made of silk.

Which we did. Oil-Gun Eddy's legacy had saved us. His amazing bike possessed similar qualities to Montifellini's Magic Bus. Sound and light were shut out and we were in a vacuum: we could have been flying. I had one arm wrapped around Ariadne, and one arm hanging on to the gun, which threatened to tear my arm off at the socket. However, we had thrown off the demonic pursuit. Wherever we were, it had not followed. I was just starting to feel the first stirrings of smug relief, when something did shift in the darkness.

Somewhere beside us, flying along like an express, a shadow form was writhing into a semblance of being. A leering face glared at us, keeping pace with the speed of our progress. De Sangreville, or at least, his sending.

"You can run, Stone," its mouth bawled at me. "There's nowhere that can shelter you for long. Your precious mechanic is dead and you can't pass your knowledge on to him now. You are stuck with it, my friend! Stuck with it until I come for you. And I'll drain your mind, believe me. Run! Run and hide. It's a game you cannot hope to win." And naturally, we had to have the burst of lunatic laughter to accompany the threat. Only it wasn't laughable. De Sangreville meant business and I didn't see the funny side of it at all.

Finally we popped out of whatever interstice between worlds or dimensions the bike had taken us to and came roaring in to a flat, tarmacked area. In front of us some tumbledown buildings rose up from an all-pervasive fog. I recognised the place and a sign bore me out. *Eddie's Auto Emporium*, it said. Oil-Gun's private garage, somewhere in limbo. About as safe a haven as I was likely to find for the time being. But my relief at seeing the place was buried under my returning sense of horror at what had happened to its owner.

I dismounted, staggering, dropping the gun, and gaped at Ariadne, about as close to letting my grief out as I had been for many a long year. She just took me in her arms and held me, speaking softly to me while all I could do was shake. At any other time I would have been as excited as a college boy on his first date, but I was wrecked. After a while we broke apart and turned to our rescuer. He finished checking the bike and the formidable gun and came to us, pulling off his mask.

It was like someone had rammed a piston into my gut.

It was Oil-Gun. Alive, flesh and blood.

He shook his head, his grimy face deeply sad. "I'm sorry, Nick. We had to kid you along. It was the only way we could bamboozle de Sangreville. We had to make him think he'd killed me. Only consolation is that de Sangreville's victim was dead already when the knife cut into him. An old trick – arsenic in a false tooth."

"So you're the real Oil-Gun Eddy?" said Ariadne. I'd forgotten she'd not met him before.

"That I am, ma'am."

"So who died back there at the chapel?" she asked him. I was too speechless to comment.

Oil-Gun turned that unhappiest of expressions on me. "I'm sorry, Nick. It was Zeff Radwawski. Things changed damned fast after you went to visit him. When he gave you the information about *The Malleus Tenebrarum*, he expected to die in Sing Sing, soon

50

after. All you had to do was pass the knowledge to me and that woulda been that. Then outta the blue the Governor took pity on Zeff and released him. So we decided to pull one last stunt and throw de Sangreville right off the scent, by faking my death so he'd think the information would be lost with me. It woulda paid off if he hadn't figured you'd not passed the information on. I'm getting too old for this game. Too many mistakes."

I went to him and hugged him to me, the smell of oil and grease overpowering but so very welcome. I was still finding it impossible to talk, my tongue had swollen up and my throat was constricted.

"Let's get some coffee on the boil," said Eddy. "Later you can pass over to me the information de Sangreville was so all-fired anxious to get. Once it's lodged with me," he added, tapping his head, "it won't go nowhere. He can throw as many demons and supernatural creeps as he likes at me, but I'll just burn 'em up, worse'n Hell itself."

We went inside, skirting the piles of machinery and broken bikes and autos. Ariadne studied them, intrigued, but let Oil-Gun prepare the coffee, which was as good as it always was. We sat in a huddle, reflecting on the horrors we had seen.

"I'm a mite concerned about one thing," I said. "Not that I'm complaining, but if the knowledge about the book is hidden with you, Eddy, de Sangreville won't know it. Right now he thinks you're dead, so he'll be after my head. I don't give a lot for my chances."

Eddy grinned. "He'll just have to get in the queue, Nick. How many other crooks and nasties would like to get hold of you? It's an occupational hazard. Maybe we can see if we can strengthen your defences. You're safe enough here until we do."

"That's supposed to reassure me?"

Eddy was on the point of outlining some plan or other that I just knew would be as crazy as anything else his mad brigade of crusaders could dream up, when Ariadne hushed us. She pointed silently to the doors, crouching down in her most unnerving ninja mode. Someone, or more likely some*thing* was prowling about out in the darkness. Eddy swore under his breath. He wasn't expecting anything, satanic or otherwise, to breach the walls of this place.

Ariadne and I followed him quietly to the door and as he slid

51

the bolts, we hung back in the shadows, studying the swirling vapours outside, where the night heaved like a dark ocean swell. Eddy had snatched up some kind of long, metal spar. My guess was it housed latent power, puissant as a magician's staff. Ahead of him the mist pulled gently aside like thick curtains and we could see a shape forming within it. One of de Sangreville's agents? I was holding on to my silver lighter, but all that was left of it was a solidified misshapen blob.

The shape outside became a figure, hunched over almost double, as if in great pain: it raised its gaunt face which even in this poor light radiated lines of age and stress. Ethereal as the mist that surrounded it, it was a spectral thing, a ghostly facsimile of Zeff Radwawski. I gasped, wanting to rush forward, but Ariadne gently pulled me back. Eddy lowered the rod.

"Nearly brought it off," came the faint voice of the spirit, barely above a death-rattle. "But it's not over. De Sangreville will stop at nothing to find the book."

"He won't pry it out of me," Eddy growled.

"No, but he's insane enough to call up the worst of Hell's servants. Right now he's preparing a ritual that will awaken the Chthonic Serpents. He'll feed them my re-animated corpse and they'll burrow deep into my dead psyche, pour their toxins into me and maybe, just maybe, suck out its secrets. What I passed on to Nick may yet have a faint residue in me. If they find it, they'll uncover the whereabouts of *The Malleus Tenebrarum*."

Eddy swore again. Before he could say anything else, the shifting form of Zeff Radwawski began to melt away into darkness, the last visible aspect of it those sad, pain-filled eyes.

Ariadne broke into my frozen outrage. "What exactly are these Chthonic Serpents?"

Eddy looked deeply disturbed. "The worst kind of demonic conjuration. Very powerful, both in physical form and in mental strength. Like Zeff's spirit said, they get inside your head and they can do some very nasty stuff. No psychedelic drug made by man can compare to what they can unload. We can't let Zeff suffer that. He should have gone in peace to whatever's beyond this life. If the Serpents use him, he'll be in some kind of Hell forever after. That can't happen."

"So," I muttered, still badly shaken up by the whole farrago of events. "We go back for a second helping?"

Ariadne had started wiping down her twin blades with some old rags. "That's what I call a plan," she said, with a grin that made me shudder. These modern girls did like to party.

Eddy took me to one side. "I need to think this one through, Nick. Firstly, give me the details of the book. That's one weight you can relieve yourself of."

That was the easy bit. It was a relief to unload that particular burden. Then, over coffee and a plate full of fried food that even Ariadne dug into like she hadn't eaten for a week, we went over the plan. There was no point my telling Ariadne that she shouldn't be putting her neck on the line any longer. Our cause was her cause and that was that. And if I'd tried to tell her I was worried about her, she would probably have said, not as much as I'm worried about you and this crazy biker pal of yours.

*

So we went back. Silent as ghosts, black as the night that surrounded us, and tooled up so that when it came down to it we were ready to re-run the siege of Mafeking. The three of us. I'll admit I was less than confident. You'd think anyone who got himself into as many scrapes as I did would get used to it. No. What I'd seen in the pit on Snake Island and the goat-thing in all its tumescent glory had stirred up new levels of dread in me. If Ariadne was as shaken as I was, she hid it well and since she was game for this showdown at the gates of Hell, I was just going to have to get into line. I had to draw on my fury at Zeff's death to fuel me and drive me on. That wasn't so hard.

I'd wondered if maybe we should have taken a few buddies along with us, like a couple of hundred marines, but Eddy said Montifellini was tied up somewhere else and besides, Eddy's plan relied on stealth and the unexpected. So being hugely outnumbered was a minor detail. I admit, though, it made it easier to get on to the island. We used a low rowing boat to glide across the murky waters, well concealed by the darkness and the undulation of the Atlantic tide. We came ashore like so much driftwood and hauled the boat up a mud flat and into some tangled flotsam and jetsam dumped there by countless older tides.

From there the going was easy enough at first – slipping through the scrub and low trees, ducking and weaving. There were lights at the boundary of the big house's grounds, but thankfully not searchlights. De Sangreville didn't believe in total overkill regarding security, probably because he didn't expect an invading army. Besides, we assumed there would be guardians of a very different nature lurking in the darkness, products of his diabolism. Eddy had given Ariadne and me a thin vest each, made from some sort of metal alloy that he said would deflect more than bullets. I didn't doubt his skills as a smith, and my guess was there were more than a few hexes woven into the material.

Whatever, we got to the wall and found a stretch that seemed obscure enough to allow us to shin up and over it like a trio of monkeys. There were things in the night skies overhead, and we got through a few nervy moments when something cold but invisible seemed to sniff the air around us. Eddy's protective stuff was effective. He reckoned it would be too smart for any CCTV system that was in use, so the chances were good that we'd make the house without being detected. From the bottom of the long grass lawn where we emerged from more bushes we could see the house, glowing with light as if there was yet another party in full swing up there. Scores of windows radiated hot red light like so many baleful eyes. Maybe it was a trap. Maybe we were just being naïve in thinking we could stroll in unannounced.

Eddy had also given Ariadne and me a sword each. She would have demurred, preferring her own twin blades, which God knows, were about as effective as such things get, but when she hefted Eddy's blade, a smile crossed her face that had something of the Devil in it. "Come to mummy," she had purred. Me, I just hefted my blade, which seemed surprisingly light, and muttered appropriate sounds. I still had my two Berettas tucked into my belt.

"You can cut dust in half with that blade," Eddy told us. Yeah, that would be the easy part. He carried a familiar weapon – the Dancers of Ruin, zipped up in a long, concealing pouch, and this time it was no forgery. Rather him than me, I thought.

We had come up right under the walls of the big house, still unmolested, still part of the darkness. The night itself was very calm, a direct contrast to the mayhem of the earlier storm. I could feel rather than see elements of the night curling and twisting just on the edge of things and I tried not to think of feline monsters poised to pounce and rend. Then Eddy chose his moment and waved us forward. He dispensed with the standard cry of "let's do this," or "show time" and just hopped up on to the sill of an open window that gaped invitingly.

We were inside, dropping on to a plush carpet in a large, unoccupied room, although its many lights overhead were blazing away extravagantly. Still no one appeared. Eddy led the way to a tall door and gently opened it a fraction. There was a hallway outside and we flowed along it like shadows, totally enclosed in that peculiar silence. I didn't trust it one iota.

It was broken eventually by a low murmuring which I recognised as a crowd of people praying or chanting softly, the rise and fall coming from beyond two tall doors. Eddy glanced over his shoulder at Ariadne and me, as if to say, *this is it, guys. We're going over the top.* He pushed one of the doors and it swung quietly inwards to reveal a large, baronial hall, lit by another small forest of thick candles, the air pungent with incense. Several large braziers, heaped with red hot coals, diffused long, straight plumes of smoke upwards to the high beams. The whole place looked like a church, with de Sangreville and his immediate followers out front on a higher area, another massive inverted crucifix behind them.

Below the Satanist, stretched out on a raised slab, was the corpse of Zeff Radwawski, now stripped of all its clothing, a pale, naked form, from which the blood of the knife wounds inflicted earlier had been cleaned. He looked little bigger than a child and again I felt the blazing fury rising in me like bile. It was as much as I could do not to use both my guns on de Sangreville. Eddie had warned me, both about the consequences of letting my anger loose and that it would bounce off the Satanist like water off a duck's back. It was going to be hard to stay calm, though, when de Sangreville began that goddam ritual that would drag Zeff back into some semblance of life and probe his mind.

As we entered, the acolytes on either side of us, all of them robed in freshly laundered purple silks, kept their heads bowed as if we didn't exist, their low voices continuing their chanting like a subdued Sunday congregation in a village church. It was mildly disconcerting. Eddy went down the aisle like a wraith, stopping short of the slab, masked head raised, arms folded in an impressively scornful pose. Just behind him, Ariadne and I stood on either side, arms at our sides. We had been primed by Eddy and he'd warned us that timing was going to be everything.

I could see now that the floor in front of Eddy was open, a dark rectangle that must be a window down into whatever chamber lay below, unless, as I suspected, it was another branch of the pit we had seen in the chapel. Wisps of greenish smoke curled upwards from it and something shifted down there among the sibilant stirring of its haze.

De Sangreville studied the three of us calmly. He seemed like he'd grown a foot or two, but maybe he had put on his biggest platform soles for the occasion. His robes hid them – robes that looked like something you'd expect to see in the Vatican. "Well," he said in a sort of amused voice. "I recognise you two runaways. Nice to have you back, Mr – Nightmare. And Ariadne, still dressed for battle. You should have made the most of your escape. Whatever possessed you to return? In this realm you are like rats in a trap. And who is your champion?" He glared dismissively at Eddy. "I'm afraid his conceit and bald confidence is totally without grounding here. It will be a particular pleasure to demonstrate that fact."

Eddy slowly unzipped his mask. "My friends call me Eddy," he growled in a laudable impression of Lee Marvin in a bad mood. "You can call me Trollhammer." He slid the leather-bound Dancers of Ruin from where it was clipped to his belt and took off its casing. "I believe you were looking for this."

He held the long club up in front of him and I could see the naked forms writhing around it as though eager to be unleashed. I winced at the thought.

De Sangreville had undoubtedly been taken unawares. However, his face quickly shaped another grim smile. "Indeed. The Dancers of Ruin. Good of you to bring it to me. Pity your dead friend can't employ it against me. After all, there's no substitute for the appointed wielder. You must be deluded if you thought you could play the role of Trollhammer. That esteemed member of Vengeance Unlimited lies before you, lifeless as clay. You must be the idiot brother."

I had a job keeping a smirk off my mug. The jerk had fallen for our ruse.

Eddy was the personification of cool. As he faced de Sangreville down, I realised that the fumes rising from the opening in the floor had intensified, thickening and coalescing into two high columns that rose up right and left of us. Their shapes took positive form. Snakes – huge serpents. These would be the promised Chthonic Serpents, right on cue.

"Let's see who's the idiot," Eddy said calmly. Right now I was thinking, that's me you're talking about, my rationale being prompted by the now very corporeal monsters that weaved their heads several feet above ours. Thick strands of venom dripped from their sabre-long teeth, enough toxins per drip to mind-warp an entire city. These serpents were as thick across as Eddy's motorbike, their eyes scintillating in the bizarre light of the hall. Needless to say, I avoided looking at them.

De Sangreville was holding out his hands as if expecting to be given something – not the Dancers of Ruin – but other powers, as if he were clawing an unseen darkness, pulling from it the kind of demonic stuff we'd seen earlier. Eddy knew what he was about and directed the top of the weapon at de Sangreville's chest. The air crackled and popped, sounding like a transformer was discharging megawatts of electricity – I could feel myself trembling like I was about to burst into flame. The two serpents swung their flat heads around to study the two opposed figures. A cloud of darkness surged out from the Satanist to be met with an equally vivid emission of light from the Dancers. I expected them to flow from it, those naked, capering horrors that would inflict incalculable destruction on those who came within their reach, but it was as though they remained trapped within the artefact. De Sangreville's demons, attempting to pour from the darkness he had conjured, seemed likewise contained.

Stalemate. Just as Eddy had predicted. And he'd given Ariadne and me instructions. While he and de Sangreville went through this cosmic arm-wrestling, neither of them gaining any advantage over the other, the air around us trembled on the edge of an explosion that would have sent the entire island and every living thing on it into eternity. The twin serpents drew back for a joint strike at Eddie that would have swung the outcome against him. Ariadne shouted to me and we drew our blades simultaneously. It was our big moment.

It was all in the timing. We drew back the blades – sharp enough to splice a cobweb strand – and as one, we swung at the Chthonic Serpents. In perfect synchronicity the two huge heads were sliced from their trunks, releasing a bubbling spume of oily blood. The headless shapes writhed and thrashed about for several desperate moments, almost toppling both Ariadne and me into the opening, but we managed to avoid them. The heads crashed into the still praying acolytes, where complete chaos and confusion took a hold. None of the robed figures, most of whom were splattered with serpent gunk, had the stomach for a fight, and they began exiting the hall like a bomb was about to go off. Devoid of life, the serpent heads became two lumps of granite.

The collapse of the serpents put a huge dent in de Sangreville's concentration and his hands fell to his side. Eddy stood on the very lip of the floor opening and held the artefact out over it so that its top almost reached the deathly pale shape of Zeff. The corpse stirred as if in sleep and I swear I heard a great sigh heaved out of it, Zeff's wrinkled face smiling briefly. I knew that for him, it was truly over. Wherever he'd gone, it wasn't into some infernal darkness.

Da Sangreville was enveloped in his own clouds of darkness – they wrapped him like a shroud, preparing to whisk him away out of here. Eddy seemed content to step back from any kind of follow-up. I'm sure he could have released the Dancers then, but he chose not to, turning instead to Ariadne and me. Maybe he didn't want de Sangreville sucked into the unique dimensions of the artefact along with its other monsters, where he could stir up a revolution.

"Nice timing, guys," he grinned. "One split second out and all hell would have broken loose."

"Now he tells us," I growled to Ariadne, but behind her mask, her eyes had never been more alive.

*

Back at *Eddie's Auto Emporium* we showered, cleaned up and helped ourselves to more of his unique coffee. He leaned back in one of his ancient, creaking chairs, wiping a smudge of oil from his cheek. "Gettin' too damn old for this kind of caper," he snorted. "Same as the others. MacFury and Montifellini say the same. We make too many mistakes. Besides, we're getting' past it physically."

"Maybe it's time to wind up Vengeance Unlimited," I said. "You guys have done your bit, fighting crime most of your lives.

You've earned your retirement a dozen times over."

Eddy glared at me as if I'd spoken some kind of heresy. "Zeff told you what was happenin', didn't he? He wasn't just talkin' about de Sangreville. This was just the thin end of the wedge. There's one hell of a storm brewin'."

Ariadne leaned forward. She'd somehow changed into lighter clothes, but she still managed to look like the proverbial million dollars. "Sounds like you need a new Vengeance Unlimited," she said.

Eddy grinned, exhibiting as many gaps in his teeth as he had teeth. He was right; he was definitely an old guy. "Now, there's a woman with brains as well as brawn. A new Vengeance Unlimited. Phoenix rising from the ashes, huh?"

Why did I not like the sound of this?

"Don't tell me," Eddy went on, stabbing a greasy finger at me, "you didn't know that Zeff had been groomin' you all that time for something special. Don't ya get it? You and Miss Carnadine here – you're two new core members."

My jaw had started to sag open again. I let Ariadne do the talking.

"Who are the other three?" she said calmly, like she'd already signed the contract.

"Five," said Eddy. "There were five core members, and two more who worked closely with us. Zeff was one of them. As for the rest of the new crew – you'll find 'em. And you'll know 'em." He got up and yawned, studying the first hints of dawn outside. Then he left us to it, disappearing into the jumbled maze of metal and motor wreckage.

Ariadne and I stood in the doorway, watching the daylight spreading pinkly. I heard music start up, filtering through speakers buried somewhere in the heart of the workshop. Eddie was already selecting spanners for some work and I recognised the harmonies of Vanilla Fudge. Eddie accompanied them – less melodiously – on *Some Velvet Morning*.

Ariadne slipped an arm around my waist. "Rising from the ashes. Surely a tough hombre like you would be up for that?"

I think I grunted.

"And what's a girl got to do round here to get kissed?"

That was easy. I knew the answer to that one. Some Velvet Morning. Yes, indeedy.

IF YOU DON'T EAT YOUR MEAT

They'll catch up with me one of these days. Sooner rather than later. And they'll nail me up, just like that bloke the Jesus people are always on about. A lesson for all. They think. Anyway it'll be too late. There's too many of us now. Not as many as them, not yet, but there will be. Then we'll see. Fuck me, yeah.

Eating each other is supposed to be one of the worst things people can do. There's always been laws against it. Strong laws, more bollocks from the Jesus people, to make everyone back off doing it. Laws are supposed to protect people, but they don't always – sometimes they get in the way and make life harder.

On the farm where I grew up, we had our own laws. My old man always said, you got to survive. That's the first law.

We had a hard time of it, me and my family. Apart from mother and father, there was eight of us kids, five boys and three girls. Our farm, Blackstones, was on the edge of the moors, but most of the time we grew enough food and milked the herd to live well enough off it and trade in the local market towns for clothes and stuff. The family had been at the farm for donkey's years. Same as other farms in the area. Long before the Virus came.

Our lands were remote, so not much changed. It was tough, but no one interfered with us. No one was bothered. Too busy sorting out their own messes in the cities. I suppose we were happy, doing what we always did. Us kids all had to go to school, but most of the time it was a fucking pain in the arse, getting in the way of our chores on the farm. We all had chores, starting at sunrise. We did half a day's work before we went to school, trudging four miles in all weathers to get there. Then home again to get the day's work finished. Same as the kids from the other farms.

Winters were always the hardest. More fuel to gather for the fire, more work to do keeping the animals alive, more repairs to the farmhouse and barns. Being high up, we always got snow, sometimes so bad we were almost buried. We always managed.

61

Had to. Father gave us the belt if we didn't pull our weight. Got used to it. In the winter, it was worse, so you made sure you got your chores done. I liked the winters. Meant that we kids could all snuggle up together under the blankets. We used to do things with our sisters. They showed us what to do and we learned things. Amazing. Never knew nothing like it.

One of my sisters had a baby, Jerome, and me and my brothers all took turns being his dad. He was a laugh, all pink and useless to start with, but like the pigs and sheep, he got bigger all the time, until he could crawl about and eat proper food. I liked Jerome. I liked his mum, too, Aggie, but mother told me she didn't want her having any more babies, not yet, so we were all warned not to play those games under the blankets with her. Father said if we did, he'd cut our dickies off with the really sharp knife he used for skinning animals. When you saw that knife, it made your dicky shrivel up to nothing.

One winter was the worst ever. We knew it was going to be bad because it started early, at the end of September. There was already snow up on the higher moor. Me and my brothers used to go up there and have snow fights, before the winds got too strong. They came over from the east, which was always bad. Father said they were *Siberian*. I think that was like Hell, only cold instead of hot. I didn't know much about Bible stuff and church, only what I heard at school. Our family didn't go to church. Father said church people had a funny idea about God and his son, Jesus, who a lot of people worshipped. We had different gods, much older ones. They'd been in our lands forever. They were the proper gods.

That winter, that really bad one, father said it was our gods showing everyone – especially the Jesus people – that they still ruled and if they wanted to blow cold and angry, they'd do it, and fuck everyone. I asked father if the gods were angry and he said, maybe. If we survived, it meant the gods had allowed it. If anyone died, the gods had taken them. Seemed fair enough to me and the family.

Kids at school from most of the other farms said the same. Only twats like our neighbours, the Tregathicks, liked the Jesus stuff. It meant we had arguments with some of the Jesus kids at school, but we liked to fight, so that was okay. We always beat the shit out of the Jesus kids so the teachers always sided with them. We never told the teachers about our gods, not unless we were tortured. Like when they twisted our arms up our backs or made us stay in the showers when they were freezing cold. Most of us farm kids closed up even more if we were caned, or tortured, but a couple of the younger ones blabbed about our gods. The teachers, the nasty ones, hated all that stuff. One of them said that, years and years ago, they used to *burn* people who liked the old gods. Yeah, well, if they'd tried that on me and my family, I'd have burned their fucking church down. And all those fucking Jesus people with it. You have to protect yourselves. No other bugger will.

Anyway, that winter, we missed a lot of time at school, being holed up on the farm. By February, we were still snowed right in. We couldn't even get the tractors up the lane. We cleared it of snow, but then another blizzard came along and a whole day's shovelling was wasted. Father said there was no point going against the gods. They wanted us holed up. So we got on with it. Kept fed, kept warm, kept the animals alive as best we could. The gods took some, but that was okay. Same on the other farms.

The problem was, people started to run out of food. We'd done a lot of trading around the harvest time, a few months back, filling our stocks up from our crops and making sure we gave something to the gods. Blackstones would have been okay. Father knew what to do in hard times, so even in that winter, he'd prepared us. We heard tales of the villages, where supplies were low and they had to have stuff dropped in by helicopters. We heard them in the sky. We didn't have TV at Blackstones. I only saw TV at school. They reckon that before the Virus, *everyone* had TV, but I reckon that's bollocks.

Other people's problems were nothing to do with us, father said. It was up to them to provide for themselves. We'd done it, so why shouldn't they? Law of survival. That was okay, but then we got a problem. It was me that found it out.

It was my turn to go and check on the cattle. The herd was split into three barns, where they were spending most of the winter, under cover. If we'd left them out in that snow, none of them would have lived. There was enough room in the barns to shelter them and we'd got another small barn stuffed with straw bales for the winter feed. When I went into the barns that morning to check on the cows, they were fine. Warmer than us, crowded together, but cows don't mind that. They don't get irritable like the dogs, or the cats. The cats were always spitting at each other, too cramped for comfort.

The cows were in good shape, except that there was a problem. I counted them. They're not like dogs, they don't have names, and you don't remember their faces like you do dogs. So you just count them. There was one missing. I did the count three times and each time I got it to one missing. I told father, so he went and did the check for himself, saying if I was wrong he'd give me the belt. I knew I was right.

When father came back, he looked like hell. I was right. One missing.

"That cow didn't break out on its own. If it had, the others would've gone with it. The dogs would've gone mad. They weren't disturbed."

"What you thinking?" said mother. We could all see father was puzzled.

"Some bastard's been here last night and taken it. It snowed, so the trail will be gone."

I'd never seen him look so mad. He turned to me and my brothers. "You boys – get your thick clothes on. We need to find that animal."

Mother was looking worried, like she could smell trouble. A fight. "Can't we manage with one less cow?" she said.

Father growled something. "It's not the fucking cow, woman. It's the principal. Some bastard stole it, which means it won't be the last time. We got to make the bugger pay. Make him know that no one steals from Blackstones without reprisals. You all understand that?"

All of us, mother included, said yes. So we went out, father, me and my four brothers. The snow was deep and the sky was heavy with more, all dark and fucked up, like the gods were still pissed off by something. Maybe they were angry that someone had nicked one of our cows. We tried to find some kind of trail, or clues to which way the cow had gone, but the night's snowfall was a perfect cover for the bastards that done it.

"It won't be the villagers," father said. "Too far away. Anyhow, they wouldn't risk it. The PPU would be on 'em." Father didn't have much time for the People Police Units: I think he had a lot of trouble with them when he was a kid, but he never said much about it. My older brothers reckoned as how father had even been in prison for something he'd done – maybe smashing some bloke up, even killing him. Father wouldn't say and none of us was stupid enough to ask him. "When you need to know something, I'll tell you," he always said. Just told us to keep out of trouble with the PPU. "You can't fight those fuckers," he'd say. They were set up in the years after the Virus, and were supposed to make sure everyone was okay, even remote ones like us, but father reckoned they were Government lackeys and did what they wanted.

Mother wouldn't let on much either. She did say once how father'd had a hard time of it before he met her, and he'd been beat up a few times, so bad it had messed up his head so that he got headaches and lost his temper. We saw that sometimes, but always kept out of it.

"Who d'ya reckon it is, father?" said Derrick, my oldest brother. He was seventeen and a big kid now, more like a man. He was fucking hard and could punch anybody right out. No one fucked about with him.

"Either someone's come from around the moor, someone desperate, or it's the Tregathicks." Father's face looked angry. "I saw old man Tregathick a while back and he said he was wondering if he had enough to get his whelps through the winter."

We reached a gap in one of the high hedges, which was almost buried, just a foot or so poking up from all that white. Father looked all around. There was still no sign of anything and worse, more snow was coming. You could see the clouds rolling up over the crest of the moor. Good job we all had thick coats with hoods.

"Derrick, you and Harold and Mick come with me. We'll skirt the low moor. Ryan, you and Wayne go and look over the Tregathicks' place. Watch out for anything funny. But keep out of sight, you hear me? Watch out for their dogs. You see anything, any sign of that cow, you come looking for me and your brothers. Got me? I don't want a fucking riot unless I'm in the thick of it. You clear on that?"

We all said okay and then we split up, me taking Wayne, the youngest, with me. I was fifteen, he was only twelve. I always kept an eye on him. He's the runt of the litter, although Amy is a year younger. She could beat him in a fight, so I felt a bit sorry for him. I was trying to toughen him up a bit. If I didn't, the little bugger would have a hard life. He was a good kid. The others cussed and swore at him, but I only ever wanted to give him a hug. Well, sometimes I cussed him when he was being a twat, but that wasn't often. The girls always protected him. Father said he should have been a girl.

Pretty soon we'd lost sight of father and the others. I knew the quickest way to the Tregathick farm, but it was really hard moving through the snow without getting buried in a drift. We kept away from the hedge lines where they'd be worst.

We were about half a mile from the farm, when Wayne started to shiver. The cold was really getting to him. Poor little sod, he'd tried hard enough to keep up with me, but he was pretty fucked. I made sure he kept his gloves on and I tightened up the draw string on his hood.

"Listen, Wayne, I got to take a look at that farm. Father will be like hell if I don't. You're going to have to wait for me."

"No! Don't leave me, Ryan. I'm scared." He was shivering even more.

"Be worse if you try to come." I forced a path through the snow to the nearest hedge. Like all the others, it was only showing the top scrub of blackthorn, like a few scrawny fingers. The snow had drifted tons of feet deep up to it. I knew this field and I knew there were some of our sheep in it. And I knew where they'd be. Father would have had us digging them out today if we hadn't been looking for the cow thieves.

I was right. A whole bunch of sheep had got up to the hedge before the snow had piled up. They were buried, but sheep are tough buggers. They can live okay under the snow. They make some kind of sheep house and shove up together. You wouldn't want to leave them there for too long, but a night or two is okay. Sometimes they live for a week like that. I found some now. They bleated at me like they were glad to see me and I gave them a hug. Then I got Wayne in there and shoved him up to the sheep.

"I ain't going to be long," I told him. "You just wait here. Cuddle the sheep. Keep wrapped up, Wayne. Keep your fucking gloves on, or you'll lose your fingers. I'll be back soon enough."

I left him. He'd soon be warm. Too fucking warm. Maybe he'd doze off, but that was okay. I made my way across the snow and started climbing the last fields before the moor's edge, except that you couldn't see that now. My legs were knackered, really aching, but I wasn't going to let father down. He was depending on me. I started to feel angry about whoever had stolen the cow. If we found them, we'd beat the living shit out of them for doing it. Being angry helped me get up that slope.

Took me a long time, but I got to a place above the Tregathick farm and was able to look down on it from the cover of some scrubby trees. The sky was very dark now and the farm had a few lights on. Like ours, it was proper froze in, the snow banked up around it so there was no way you'd get the tractors out, or the cars, even with chains. I noticed a few flakes of snow in the air. What was coming from over the moor was another fucking snowstorm. Maybe not so bad as the last one, not so much wind, but could be heavy snow.

I didn't have a lot of time. From up in the trees, I couldn't see much, so I wound my way down towards the outbuildings. They'd had paths cut around them, just so you could walk to and fro, like we'd done at home. I picked my moments carefully. It was a bit scary, but it was sort of fun, too. Like a game, only more serious. Me and my brothers were always playing war games, shooting each other and blowing each other up, but not for real. Just games. This was like that, only dangerous. I knew if the Tregathicks found me they'd break my arms.

One of the bigger barns had cows in it. Their set up was like ours – well, like most farms. We all lived pretty much the same kind of lives. And this barn had a smaller shed stuck to its side. There was a light in it, flickering, so I guessed it was an oil lamp. I could hear voices as I crept up closer. The snow was starting to fall more heavily, the beginning of a real storm, but I wasn't going to pull out now. I got to a place in the wooden wall where I could see through the planks into the shed. There were three figures in there, old man Tregathick and two of his sons. Ugly fuckers, the lot of them. Donkey shaggers, father called them. They had dogs with them, snuffling about in the straw.

Didn't bother me, but what did make me swear under my breath was what was hanging up in the shed, off a beam. It was the cow they'd stolen from us. Hung upside down on a steel hook, throat cut to drain out the blood into a rusty old bath, gutted and partly skinned. Jed Tregathick, the older boy, was holding a meat cleaver – he'd been doing the dirty work. His hands were bloody and he was standing in a heap of cow hide.

I wanted to bust open the planks, rush in and scream at the bastards, but I wasn't that fucking daft, or mad. I knew they'd just smack me down and toss me out into the snow. I must have made a noise, though, because one of the dogs started yapping and old man Tregathick swung round and looked right at the place where I was hiding.

"Who the fuck's out there?" he snarled. He waved his two sons to the door and grabbed a pitchfork. One stab of that and he could split me in two. He drew back his arm and flung the fork as hard as he could. It stuck in the planks, cracking one of them in half, the light spilling out.

There was nothing I could do here. I'd seen enough. I had to get back to father and tell him. He'd know what to do and we'd all have our instructions. Now all I could do was get the fuck out of there. I turned back to the edge of the path and could just about see my tracks where I'd sneaked into the yard. Already the snow was falling so heavy it was going to obscure them very soon. I had a hell of a job scrambling back up the slope, my legs aching so bad it was almost impossible.

Behind me I heard a shout and a whole lot of foul language as the two Tregathick boys threatened to rip me open and spread my guts over the whole field. Maybe they would, too. This winter had got to everyone. If they were that short of food they'd resorted to stealing cattle, their brains were screwed up. They weren't going to eat their own cows, any more than we would have back at Blackstones. We'd have stolen their cows first.

It was snowing so hard now that I could hardly see ahead. My earlier tracks were gone, but I just about saw the trees. I made for them, moving so slowly I thought the boys would be on me, but they were just as fucked as I was. Maybe not dressed for a chase, either. I thought the dogs would get me for sure, but the snow must have fucked them up as well.

Jed was a stubborn git. I knew him from school. He never gave up on anything, so he'd be chasing me, whatever happened. His other brother, Dale, was more likely to go back and get a thicker coat. Their old man was too buggered with arthritis to stand a chance of catching me up.

So I reckoned I only had Jed to deal with. He was a couple of years older than me and had more muscle, like a fucking bull. I wouldn't want to tangle with the bastard. I had to keep ahead of him. I got to the trees, my breath rasping, my throat burning. I looked back, but the snowfall was so thick I couldn't see. He'd be coming, though, sure as hell. He was funny in the head. Riled up like he was now, he'd be coming.

Half way across the snow field, I knew he was gaining. I'd burned up so much energy getting out to the Tregathick place, it was all I could do to put one foot in front of the other. Jed had the advantage of being a bit fresher. I was going to have to outsmart him. I only had one chance and that was bury myself in the snow. Hope he'd miss me.

The only place to do that was near a hedge, like I'd buried Wayne. I reached one just before Jed caught up with me – I could hear his breathing and his curses not far behind, just out of sight. I could feel my whole body starting to get colder and colder, and I knew I'd be frozen stiff if I didn't get out of this soon. I dived into a drift and just drove forward, like a swimmer in a pond - it was more like mud than water. I only got so far. I was stuck, but with any luck I'd be out of sight.

I waited, my face frozen. Ages went by. Nothing. It got so I couldn't stay under any longer. I pushed forward and the air hit me, like a slap. Jed was only a few feet away. He'd been waiting, like a fucking cat by a mouse hole, patient as hell. He snarled and grabbed at my coat, dragging me out of the snow and flinging me sideways before I could resist. He stood over me and pulled that meat cleaver from his belt. His ugly mug told me he was going to use it on me. He was that mad and that fucking screwed up, he was going to hack at me with it.

I was too exhausted to move. I watched the cleaver rise up, snowflakes whirling around it – the storm was still blowing hard. Jed was about to make his first chopping cut, when something in the snow around him made him stumble and then fall backwards. I got up as quick as I could. I saw what had happened. Jed had been standing on top of a sheep. More of them were buried here and when they'd felt Jed stomping about, they'd moved and opened up a gap in the drift.

Jed had sunk out of sight for a moment, but his cleaver hadn't. I got to it and snatched it up. I waited. Sure enough he started hauling himself out of the snow pit, swearing like hell. His face was blotchy with effort. His hands were like big hams, but he had no gloves on and his skin was blue with the cold. I held back, waiting until he reached for the lip of the pit. It was easy. I whacked the cleaver down and caught him smack bang on the wrist. That cleaver was sharp as a fucking razor. It went clean through skin and bone, taking the hand off.

Jed fell back into the snow pit, screaming. Blood was dripping from the cut, loads of it, but it was congealing in the cold. I waited, listening. I looked around me, but it was a whiteout, and I could see just a few feet in all directions. I grabbed the severed hand. Didn't want no evidence to show what I'd done. I shoved it into one of my deep coat pockets. More fucking blood. Then I realised I was being dumb. Jed was evidence enough, what with having no right hand. I had to deal with him. I made my mind up right there. No time to fuck about.

I lowered myself into the pit. Jed was laying against a bank of snow, groaning and blubbering, clutching his cut arm to his chest, blood over everything. He wasn't going anywhere. He couldn't even crawl. So much for the hard man. I went over to him and he looked up at me, his eyes filled with tears.

"You better get away from here," he said, although he could hardly speak for shivering. "When my old man finds you, he'll cut your fucking heart out, and your liver, and we'll eat you, boy. And your pissing family. We'll eat the lot of you!"

"You're not eating anyone, shit-face," I said and I let him have it with the cleaver. I knew how to use one. I'd done enough slaughtering when it was time to get the pig meat ready for market. The first cut opened his head from crown to chin. The second and third were so fast, he was dead before he could spit out another word. There was tons more blood, a lot of it spattering me, but I didn't care about that. I just got on with the job. I never killed anyone before, so a part of me felt like this was all wrong. I had to shove that aside. He'd have killed me, no question. I had to kill him and do the other, terrible things. Father's lessons about survival pushed me on.

I prepared Jed good and proper. It kept me warm. The secret of good butchery is having a really sharp cleaver and Jed's was perfect. I stripped him bollock naked, hacked off his limbs and stacked them with his head. Then I opened him up and quartered him. I'd never done a human before, but it was no different to preparing any other meat. The snow and the cold made it easier to contain the mess of blood and bits, although I did a pretty neat job. After I'd finished, I used his clothes to wrap up the sections tightly. The problem was going to be getting him back to Blackstones. It was going to take more than one trip.

I thought about that. Wayne would have to help me. I got up out of the drift. The snow had eased, so I could see where I was. I knew these fields, so was able to get a fix. I'd used Jed's belt to strap his arms and legs together, making a sort of bundle, like we did with wood. That's all Jed was now, fuel. I headed off for the hedge where I knew Wayne was huddled up to the sheep.

He was okay, warm as toast. The sheep didn't mind another body, even if it was human. Wayne gaped at the chopped up arms and legs, but I hadn't got time to fuck about. "Take these back to the farm. Don't fucking argue, Wayne. It was me or him. The bastard was going to kill me."

He was trying not to cry, frightened as shit. "What about the cow?"

"Yeah, it was the Tregathicks. They'd gutted it and strung it up. So now we're even, okay?"

"Sure, Ryan." He swung the bundle over his shoulder and soon after I watched him heading for home. Father would be evil, but he'd know what to do. I made my way back to where I'd left the rest of Jed. I used his trousers, which I'd cut into strips earlier and tied them around what was left of him. Four pieces, and the head, which was a pretty disgusting mess, cut to ribbons near enough, tied on to one piece by his long, greasy hair. Probably the only time it had come in useful.

As I dragged the stuff across the snow, I was knee deep in it, more in some places, and the weight of the bits of body got heavier. I was determined, though, and I also knew that at any moment the fucking Tregathicks might turn up. If they caught me out in the open, I was completely buggered. They'd cut me up right here and do the same for me as I'd done for Jed. So I kept on going, trusting Wayne to get home and divert father and my brothers my way.

I didn't have no remorse for killing Jed. Shit, it may have been a few years since anyone hereabouts killed off a rival farmer, but there'd been a time when it probably happened every fucking day, especially after the Virus mowed down half the country. There were always fights. How the fuck else was anyone supposed to survive? If you didn't get the fuckers first, they'd get you. The bloody animals do it, and let's face it, we're all fucking animals anyway, aren't we? That's what I told myself, anyway.

I was just about done in, when I heard voices, a shout. It was Derrick and behind him, father. Both had faces like thunder and I thought maybe I was in for a whipping after all. They got up to me and saw what I was hauling.

"Which one is it?" said father. You couldn't tell from the head that it was Jed Tregathick. I told him what had happened, and showed him the cleaver, and the severed hand.

"He was going to cut me up, father. If it weren't for the sheep, it'd be Jed dragging me back to his farm."

Father nodded and directed Derrick to grab two of the body pieces, while he took the other two. "Get your breath back," he said to me. "And cover our backs. The Tregathicks'll be out searching soon enough."

The snow came in handy, because I knew it would mop up the trail of blood and stuff. It would be weeks, maybe another couple of months even, before it was all melted away. By then it would be hard for anyone – like say, the PP - to find the trail. It wasn't going to lead to Blackstones, we'd made sure of that. As for the meat cleaver, father said he'd take it away and chuck it down the deepest mine shaft he could find – there were loads of them around the edge of the moors. No one would have a hope in hell of finding the cleaver down one of them. Nor Jed's hand.

It was mid-afternoon by the time we got back to the farm and the storm had risen up and unloaded another ton of snow. The Tregathicks would have given up their search. They wouldn't have been so stupid as to come to Blackstones. Oh, they knew it was us that had done for Jed, but they had no proof and they knew that if they came for us, it would be war. There were more of us and we were stronger, especially with Jed being dead, so they knew they'd get a fucking pasting. Father said they'd go home and wait.

"Reckon they'll get the PPU on to us?" said Derrick. No one wanted to mention the People Police, not with father's attitude towards them, but it was a question we all wanted to ask.

"They can't prove anything. No, the Tregathicks will try for revenge in their own way, in their own time. We'll be ready for them. Let me think about it. With Jed gone, they'll be easy meat in a fight." There was a look in his eye that made me wonder if he was of a mind to have a fight, a real fight. Burn the Tregathick place down, with all them fuckers in it, maybe. Make it look like an accident. Hell, we could toss Jed's body in there so's it would burn up so bad, no one would know he'd been cut to pieces.

Father had other ideas about Jed, though.

He called us boys together and I knew something was up, because mother took the girls away out of earshot.

"Listen, you boys. This winter will get harder before it breaks off. We're going to lose stock. Not all the sheep will survive. In the old days, before the Virus, things were done different. Long before my time, long before grandfather's time. Before history. Men had to fight to survive, tooth and claw, like the animals. That was the main thing. Survive. They made sacrifices to the gods. I told you about that before. They used to kill their enemies and give them to the gods, burn them and scatter the ashes on the land."

We were all nodding. Seemed natural to us.

"When things got real bad, when food was short, well, they did what they had to. They ate what they had. If they'd sacrificed someone to the gods, the gods had no problem with them taking part of the sacrifice and eating it. The heart, the liver, that's how it started. Men believed it made them strong if they did that. Then they went further. They ate some of the flesh. Shared it with the gods." He stared at us, one by one. Still we didn't say anything.

"You know, when I was a kid, before all you kids were born, I had some problems with the PPU. I was in a fight and I killed a man. Some scum who came creeping over the moor looking for food and shelter, thinking he could take advantage of my family. Grandfather knew him and took pity on him. Said he could be fed before moving on. The man was a fool. He thought he could take more than food. He got one of my sisters alone and put his stinking hands on her, thinking he could have his way with her. Force her. I caught him at it and beat the shit out of him. Killed him.

"It was a bad winter, like this one. Grandfather and I hid the body, froze it. The PPU must have got wind of the man disappearing. They were doing a search and they came to Blackstones. They had dogs and they searched the whole place. They didn't find the body, but they found things that belonged to the man, small things we'd missed when we were tidying up. Enough to know that he'd been here. They checked me out and there were bruises, so they knew I'd been in a fight. One of the PPU, an enforcer, told me he knew I'd killed the man. Told me to admit I'd had a fight and that the other man had run off, probably died out in the snow somewhere. Said if I did admit it, I'd do time in prison, but not for murder.

"I could have held out, but I guessed they'd have found the body and then I'd have been put inside for a long, long time. With grandfather being ill, the family would have suffered. Maybe even have broken up. I couldn't risk that. I went along with the enforcer's suggestion. He would do okay out of it. He'd have solved the crime, he said, and his bosses would be satisfied, even if the body hadn't been found. They'd soon stop looking."

We'd never heard father speak as much or for so long. He looked like he was letting out a whole lot of pain by telling us all this stuff, his face dark, his eyes flinty.

"Like I told you," he went on, "it was a bitter winter. Food was getting scarce. Grandfather knew what to do, once I'd been taken away. That body was brought out of the snow and ice. It was taken into one of the barns. Sacrificed to the old gods, in the hope that they'd look favourably on the family."

I knew in my guts what was coming next. The heart, the liver. They ate them. And the flesh. Like in the oldest days, they ate the flesh. To live through the worst times. Father said it now, told us outright.

"Without me to lead the family, they had no choice. They couldn't afford to kill off any of the stock. It would just have been putting off starvation until later. It kept them alive long enough to see the winter out. Grandfather told me about it when I was released. I did three years in the prison. When I came out, I knew they'd done the right thing. I got things back on a steady track and built up the herds. Met your mother and started my own herd." He smiled thinly. "Tough lot of bastards you all are, too."

"We'd have done the same, father," I said. "We'd have had no choice. We'd have eaten the flesh."

He put a hand on my arm, the closest he'd ever shown to affection. "I know you would have, Ryan. You boys all know what it takes. Now – I've never said anything about this. Your mother knows. She's a practical woman. She's soft with you boys sometimes – not often, mind. But when it comes down to it, she's as hard as I ever was. She does what she needs to do. I've spoken to her about Jed Tregathick."

"We don't want him found, father," I said. "Not by the Tregathicks or by the PPU."

"We have to dispose of him," said Derrick. The other boys nodded. We were all of one mind. We knew what we had to do.

"We won't starve this winter," said father.

*

The whole family fed for a month on Jed Tregathick. All of him, except for the bones and that mess that was his head. Father and a couple of us boys took them up on to the moor, deep into a valley where no one would see us and we made the offerings to the gods. We buried the last of Jed where they would never be found, not even by dogs on the hunt. The gods must have been pleased because there was another snowstorm after and we knew that the sacred place would be deep, deep under the snow. Father reckoned it would be the last of the winter's blasts and he was right. The thaw started soon after.

We'd heard nothing from the Tregathicks and they hadn't tried to get at us. Father said they wouldn't go to the local People Police Unit because old man Tregathick had been in trouble with them many a time. The PPU would have been glad of a chance to nail the fucker.

The snow retreated back up on to the moors, then even there it faded. The fields were like a mire, especially where we let the cows out. Most of the sheep had survived. There were a few casualties, but we had our hands full with lambing. We had a good crop. Maybe the sheep liked being buried in the drifts. Spent more time shagging, Derrick said. I asked him if we ought to go out and chase the Tregathicks girls – I'd met some of them at school – but Derrick said he'd rather shag a sheep than them. Mind you, another kid at school, Brad Tucker, reckoned Derrick was seeing one of the Tregathick girls in secret. I kept out of it.

One day we had visitors. It was a clear, sunny day, and you could see up over the moor and away into the distance down the valley, where the villages were, a dozen miles away. Some of them were almost deserted now, falling into ruin. What was left of their people had gone down to the city. Other villages had combined, not very big, but they had markets, which suited us when it came to trading.

Our visitors were the Tregathicks, or some of them. The old man was there, coughing like he was about to puke up his guts. He had his two eldest boys with him. They all had shotguns, but they'd broken them over their arms. Just as well. If they'd come in, threatening us, we'd have used our own guns on them.

Father squared up to old man Tregathick the other side of the gate into our big yard. It was like a couple of stags at a rut. One false move and they'd be at each other.

"What brings you across my land, Tregathick?" said father. I liked the way he got a challenge into his voice. Like a knife, or a cleaver. Most people would have buggered off at the sound of it.

Old man Tregathick was a tough bastard, though. He glared at all of us. "I've lost a son this winter. Jed. He caught some pig-fucker snooping about my farm back in the snow season. Chased him out into the storm. Never see'd him since." His eyes scanned all of us and settled on me.

I just kept still and ignored him, like I'd been told. I wanted to tell him I'd fed off his son and kept fat through the last of the winter, but I clammed up. Maybe there was something in me that said it was wrong, but this weren't the time to say it.

"Nasty winter," said father. "Reckon a lot of families lost kin. Too bad."

"Maybe it weren't the winter that took my boy. Maybe something else got him. Some whore's brat. Some dog turd that needs scraping up and flushing away." Each word was aimed at me – the Tregathicks knew it'd been me up there at their farm the night that time they stole our cow.

I wanted to tell old man Tregathick to fuck himself, but I just kept on looking out at the moors. I wanted to grin, thinking about Jed's head and bones, buried in that shrine we'd made. The gods would have rotted him down and took him by now.

Father was waiting. He knew what was coming. He'd already told us that some things were done the old way, the way they'd been done since men first tramped about up in these lands.

"I'll have my revenge," said old man Tregathick. "You watch your family. Don't let any of them out of your sight. We'll be watching. An eye for an eye."

I didn't know what the fuck that meant, but father did. "You can quote your Bible at me all day long, Tregathick. It don't mean fuck all to me and mine. You think you're a Christian now, eh? You think all that shit will help you? Well, you can tell your Jesus to kiss my arse. And I'll give his a good hard kick."

Old man Tregathick looked at all of us. You could tell he thought father had said something really bad. He was trying to look like some kind of demon, I guess. Didn't scare any of us, but we could feel his hate, hot as fire. "We'll see," he said.

"Next time you wander on to my land, guns or no, we'll shoot," said father. "I've got two of my boys with guns on you right now. They could take you all out where you stand."

Old man Tregathick spat. He was screwed and he knew it. But he'd only come here to lay down his threat. He turned on his heel and his sons went with him, back over the fields. Father watched him for a while. He was very still even after the men were out of sight.

Derrick, who'd been up in one of the barn lofts, his gun trained on the visitors, joined us now. "I heard it all, father," he said. "Them bastards are going to try and take one of us. If they do, will they do the same as we did to Jed?"

Father shrugged. "It's the way of things. They may be so-called Christians, but they're still scum. They took a cow. We took one of them. They try for one of us. We retaliate. Sooner or later one family's had enough and backs off. It won't be us."

"We have to stop them," I said. "Don't we, father?"

"There's a way, but it's risky."

Me and all the brothers were clustered about him. The sky seemed big that day, like it was open to the old gods, like they were listening in.

"These days," father went on, "we're more remote than we used to be, but there's far less of us. The Virus changed everything. We're isolated, but we can't get complacent. We don't want to draw attention to ourselves. If we start trouble with the Tregathicks, we have to handle things very carefully."

"Same if they start on us," said Derrick. "If they try snatching one of us, you could bring in the PPU, father. You could tell them now that we'd been threatened. Set them on the Tregathicks."

"The PPU wouldn't listen to me. I've got a record. I couldn't prove the Tregathicks said anything. No, we'll keep the PPU out of this. Trouble is, we can't be on watch all the time, every day. We've all got work to do. So's Tregathick, but he's sick with anger.

77

He wants his revenge. He won't cool off until he's taken one of us."

"So what do we do?" I asked.

"We hit them first."

I thought he meant for us to take another one of the Tregathicks. My brothers must have thought the same. They were all grinning. They were all eager to do this. Like starting a war. Part of me was all for it. My blood was up, especially after old man Tregathick had insulted mother and me. We'd see who was a dog turd, and who'd be scraped up and flushed away. Another part of me said this is dangerous. The PPU would find out. School would know, once kids didn't show up. They were hot on that. We'd had trouble with the schools if any of us stayed off for long. They always came looking for us.

"We have to do this in one hit," said father. "Sniping at each other, picking each other off one by one won't do. This isn't the fucking jungle."

"You mean a raid?" said Derrick.

"I mean a raid," said father, nodding. "You boys with me in this, or not? If we don't do this, they're going to take one of us, maybe one of the girls. If they take one of your sisters, you know what they'll do to her before they kill her. You think hard on that, boys. And what if they take your mother? Who says they won't try? Or Aggie's kid."

We were horrified, none of us wanting to look at each other. I couldn't stand the thought of anything happening to little Jerome. I'd *kill* anyone that touched him.

It was Wayne who spoke up. "I say we do a raid. Hit them first. We have to protect the family. I can use a gun. I can take a rabbit out at fifty yards."

Father tousled his hair in a rare show of affection. "That you can, Wayne. Maybe we won't need guns. Maybe we can use something that will take out the whole nest in one hit."

Father left us to think about it. He knew he couldn't organise it unless we were all with him. Maybe if we had had time to talk to each other we'd have thought better of it, and seen it as a kind of madness. In the end the decision was made for us. Old man Tregathick tried it on, quicker than we thought he would. He must have abandoned some of his own farm work, determined to catch us out. Two of his boys sneaked up on one of our fields where

Harold, our second oldest, was feeding the cows early one morning. He had a gun with him – we always took our guns now.

The two Tregathicks got the drop on Harold, but he was quick enough to get a shot off. Not at them, but enough to warn the rest of us. We lit up to that field like whippets and before the Tregathick boys could get hold of Harold, we had their exit covered. It was a stand-off: if they shot Harold, we'd blow the fuckers apart. If we shot at them first, they'd do for him. In the end it was a close run thing, but they pulled out and we got Harold back in one piece.

"I only turned my back for a couple of minutes," he said, embarrassed and furious with himself. "S'not possible to work and keep a lookout all the fucking time. Those Tregathick bastards don't work."

"Not your fault, son. Seems like they're prepared to run their shit-hole farm down before they give up on us," said father.

Derrick was in a right mood. "Fuck 'em! Let's do it, father. That raid. Let's do it."

We were all mad enough to agree, even the girls. Mother, too. I was a bit surprised, as she'd always been the one who tried to be reasonable, or a bit calmer anyway. The thought of her girls being abducted was too much. "Just get on with it," she said. "You boys. You do everything exactly like father says. Otherwise the next time the Tregathicks come calling, they won't slip up."

So we planned the raid. Father was a crafty bugger and he knew all the tricks. Derrick reckoned he'd always been a hard man, but that he'd got even harder when he did those three years in prison. Derrick reckoned prison was like Hell, where you got really fucked over. That's why you got sent there, to be given a really hard time for whatever you'd done.

"Listen, you boys," said father, the night of the raid. "I didn't tell you this before, but the man I fought and killed, the man I went to prison for. He was old man Tregathick's brother. That's when this started. He knew then that I'd done for his brother. He swore he'd have revenge. The PPU warned him off, telling him they'd be watching him. So he let things cool. It was a long time ago. The PPU won't be bothered about the Tregathicks anymore. Different enforcer in control hereabouts. Don't suppose they keep records that long."

"All the more reason to finish this," said Derrick. "Old man

Tregathick is hell bent on getting us."

Now I understood why mother had thrown in with us. That winter when father had killed Tregathick's brother had been like the one we'd just had. She and the family had fed off the body to get them through it. I wondered if old man Tregathick knew that.

"We're going to burn their farm down to the ground," said father. "With them in it. Take your guns, but I don't want anyone shot. No evidence of killing. The fire will do our work for us. They'll be incinerated. When the PPU turn up, all they'll find is ashes. Not much use to them if they want to prove arson."

He knew more about that than us, so we said yeah.

*

We got them hours before dawn. Derrick drove one of our old tractors. It was near enough clapped out. Derrick was good at fixing mechanical stuff and he got the tractor working, even though it had been pretty much abandoned for a year or more. He fixed it enough for it to get up on the edge of the moor and come at the back of the Tregathick farm from above. He'd been watching the farm for a few days, finding out what they did when they started the day. Luke Tregathick, now the oldest boy since we'd done for Jed, used to go up into the high fields and see to their sheep, checking out if anyone had nicked any. He'd be on his own in the half-light for about an hour before the rest of his family got going. Long enough for us.

Derrick put the old tractor in the field above Luke's. We hid ourselves along the hedge. We all had our boots on and had wrapped them in makeshift polythene, so that we didn't leave proper footprints. We'd smeared ourselves in muck of one sort or another, to put the Tregathick dogs off the trail. If all they got a smell of was animals, they wouldn't raise the alarm. We stank, but we had to do it.

We didn't have long to wait. Luke saw the tractor and couldn't resist a closer look. Once he was through the field gate and half way to the tractor, we had him. Derrick got a grip on him from behind so he couldn't move and we gagged him, trussed him up and took him to the tractor. We sat him on its rusty seat and tied him in good and proper. Fucker couldn't move. He'd be the driver until we cut him free. Except that we weren't going to do that.

The tractor was more rust than paint. Father soaked most of it in petrol. Luke's eyes were wide. We could see he wanted to scream. He was trying to pull his hands free, but no dice. Him and the tractor were one. Its tank was full of petrol, too.

There were maybe a few minutes when I wondered if what we were up to was right. Luke had never been friendly to me at school, even when there were fights between the farm boys and the Jesus kids. Would he have done this to me? His old man would have, and if I stood up against my old man, he'd likely throw me out, or worse. Best to get it done.

We rolled the tractor forward, through the gate on to Tregathick land. It was still quiet down below. Soon be time for the rest of them to get out to work. Father sent me and Wayne to open two more gates that gave the tractor a clear run to the main farmhouse. Once we'd done that, father got the tractor moving, locking it onto its course and then he set fire to it. Flames leapt up fast. They roared. Luke must have been trying to scream but we didn't hear him.

I watched as the tractor and the blazing figure rolled past me and Wayne. We were both amazed at how much flame came off it. And black smoke, billowing up high. Father's only worry was that it would be seen for miles, but he said if we did this quick, it would be okay.

The tractor rolled faster down through the open gates, once, twice, then across the flatter concrete yard. It smashed straight into the side of the farmhouse with a sound like a fucking bomb going off and bits of metal and wheel flew up into the air as the tank exploded. It must have thrown petrol all over the shop. Minutes later the whole of the house was on fire. The back door had caved in with part of the wall when the tractor hit it. Round the front, father had driven one of the Tregathick cars, a rackety old Vauxhall estate, right up to the front door – the only other door – and rammed it in place. At the side of the house there was a big steel tank and father said it was full of oil. Derrick had got to it and flipped off its seal. Then he tossed a lighted brand in and hared off quick. That tank blew apart like another bomb. Them Tregathicks were trapped like rats in a cage. A burning cage.

We knew they'd be so shit-scared of the fire they'd be trying to leap from the windows, but we moved too quick for them. We'd brought a low wagon, full of faggots, ready for this, and we made sure all of the windows had a fire blazing under them. It was like a scene from the Jesus peoples' Hell. I don't think even father realised how fantastic the blaze would be, or how quick it would eat up that farmhouse. The fire roared its way through wood and stone alike. All the big roof beams were alight, and I thought I could see someone among them, but only for a moment. It was so hot we all had to pull well back. Every single one of the Tregathick clan were in that house. We'd got the lot of them.

Something did burst out of the flames. One of the dogs, a big bugger, all snarls and teeth. Derrick saw it first and before anyone else could react, he shoved a pitchfork right into its gob. Its own weight forced the long tines deep into the dog's mouth. Derrick lifted the fucker clean off the ground and swung it back into the flames like he was pitching a bale onto a truck. We heard it shriek, then the flames roared and spat. The rest of the dog pack must've been burned up in there.

I stood by father, whose face was lit up in the glow like he was some kind of demon. "What about the fire brigade, father?" I asked him. "Someone would've have seen the blaze. Must be like one of them volcanoes."

"They'll come. And the PPU. That's as good a blaze as we could have hoped for. Another fifteen minutes and the place will be burnt to cinders. Okay, you boys, get off home – fast mind – and strip off. Burn all your clothes. Scrub down and wash your hair. I don't want no trace of smoke or anything on you. Later on, once the police get here, they'll call on us. Derrick, get that wagon home and hide it. Make sure everyone's ready. Ryan, you stay with me. We'll say we came up here to try to help."

I was afraid, but I did what he said. We walked around the blazing farm, though we couldn't get near. There were explosions and great blasts of heat, so we had to keep back. I could just about see our old tractor. There were just a few bits of it left, still burning up, the rest melted down by the heat. Nothing to say it wasn't a Tregathick tractor. First Jed was gone, like he'd never been. Now I guess it was the same for all the Tregathicks. From what I could see, there was nothing to show that we'd used the tractor and the old car to block off the doors, and all the faggots under the windows had gone, along with the window frames and walls where they'd been set. I'd never seen a fire like it. Didn't realise how much of the cob and stone it would burn.

"You keep your mouth tight shut," father told me. "Speak if they make you, but you're in shock, okay? So shocked by this that you can hardly speak. I'll do the talking." His eyes reflected the fire behind us. He looked mad. Maybe he was. Maybe we all were for this.

It wasn't long before the first of the fire engines came clanging up the lane. Six came in all and four PPU cars. Father met the firemen and I couldn't hear what he said to them at first. He just pointed. The firemen spread out, unfolding rolls of hose. Pretty soon they were training long jets of water on the farmhouse, but I knew they were much too late. Already the buildings were down to about a third of their size, just black and sooty. The water killed off the fire, sending out more clouds of smoke.

I stood to one side with father, trying not to look at him.

In a minute, a couple of men in PPU uniforms came up. I don't know if they knew him, but they looked angry. "Who are you, sir?" one of them asked.

Father said he was a neighbour and that he'd come over with me when he'd seen the flames. Said we couldn't do anything.

"You don't know how this got started?" said the other policeman.

"No," said father. "They had a big tank of oil next to the house. Always dangerous. They were smokers, the Tregathicks. Maybe they got careless. Once one of those tanks goes, that's it. Me and my boy here, we couldn't even get close to the place."

"Didn't anyone get out?"

"Didn't see anyone. We've circled the place but there's no sign. Looks like the whole family was in there."

"Okay. You better get yourselves home. We'll need to see you later, and take some statements, if you don't mind, sir."

"No, I don't mind." Father nodded at the men and we left them. I wanted to whoop, because it looked like we'd got clean away with it! Just like father had said we would.

"That was the easy bit," he told me, once we were well out of earshot. "They'll be crawling all over before the day's out. You all need to have your stories straight."

*

Father was right. That afternoon we had visitors. A few PPU cars, only this time two enforcers were with them, men in long coats, both of them with thin faces, stick men. I could feel the hate coming off them. They had a lot of questions. Some were for us kids, but we were all pretty good and pretending to be shocked by what had happened. Anyway, we were all scared, but we made it look like it was because of the fire.

The enforcers and the police and their dogs, all looked around the house and out in our barns. Father had warned us they would, so it was no good getting angry, or if we did, not to show it. Just play dumb, he'd said. He reckoned the PPU had their hands full in the cities and didn't much care for being dragged out into the wilds. They'd be in a hurry to get away.

They were there for longer than he expected, although it looked like they hadn't found anything to make them suspicious. It was like they wanted to catch us out, like they'd already made their minds up that we were mixed up in the fire. We had to keep our dogs out of the way, put in one of the cages, because the PPU had their own. They sniffed every room, then all the yards and barns. In the end it was one of the dogs that found us out.

An enforcer came into the dining room where father and mother and most of us kids were sitting around the big table. He was holding something, about the size of a small hand tool. He put it down on the table where we could all look at it. It was yellowish and had been carved.

"Does anyone know what that is?" said the enforcer. He was looking straight at father. Father knew exactly what it was, but he didn't give anything away. He just stared at it. I knew what it was, though I hadn't seen it before. It was a piece of bone. I recognised the carving – the sort of thing that Derrick did.

"Bit of whittling," said father at last. "The kids often do it. Old sheep bone. Must be more out in the fields. What of it?"

The enforcer nodded slowly and picked the bone up. "Whittling. Okay. Mind if I keep it?"

No one was going to argue. The enforcer looked all of us in the eye – he was a cold, hard-faced bastard. I suppose that's why he had his job. "If you country scum think the PPU will turn a blind eye to mayhem out here in the wilderness, you better think again. The country still has laws and by God you'd better respect them." It seemed like he'd said enough. He called his mate and the PPU and they left us, getting into their cars and driving off. Father waited until they were out of sight, well down the lane, then he swore. It was like a storm breaking. I never seen him so mad. He swung round to us boys.

"Which one of you?" he snarled. "Which one of you shit-heads carved that bone?"

Mother was scowling. "What's wrong? Why fuss about a bit of sheep bone?"

"Sheep bone? Fucking *sheep* bone!" father shouted. "It was a human bone. Fairly fresh." He swung round to Derrick. "What do you know about this? Tell me straight or I'll cut your balls off and make you wear them as a necklace."

None of us were laughing. We all knew this was bad. That bone must've come from Jed Tregathick. Derrick had kept it for a talisman and carved it.

He admitted it and it looked for a moment as if father would punch hell out of him. "They'll know," said father. "They'll know it's human and they'll likely trace it to Jed Tregathick. Then they'll be back here and we'll be done for. This has all been for nothing, you sodding idiot!"

"I can say I found it," said Derrick, but I could see he was shitting himself.

"They'll split us up," said father. "Then they'll trip us up. They'll go digging up all the old records about me and what happened with old man Tregathick's brother, they'll know this is the same thing. They won't give up until they've dragged it out of us."

"You said they wouldn't have records that old," said Derrick, desperate for something to cling on to.

"You want to take that fucking chance! *Do you?* You heard what that enforcer said. We may be scum to them, but they can't afford to have us become a law to ourselves. They can't let this go."

We all went very quiet for a while. Father must have been thinking hard. "Okay," he said, getting up. "Donna, take your sisters upstairs. Wayne, you go up with them. Do it now, go on." He waited while they did what he said.

The rest of us watched him as he paced about the room. "We can't stay here," he said.

Mother looked shocked. "What do you mean? Where would we go? We can't outrun them."

"No. Mother, you and the girls will be taken by the law. There's no way to avoid it. I don't want to risk anyone getting hurt. So when they come, you and the girls – and Harold, Mick, Wayne and Ryan – will go with them. They won't lock you up, but they'll have a lot of questions. You'll just have to ride it out. Me and Derrick –" He looked hard at Derrick, who was as miserable as I'd ever seen him – "will go up on to the moor. There's places we can hide for a while. It's our only chance."

"That's ridiculous," said mother. "You can't go on the run. If you do, they'll know it's you who's responsible. They'll find you."

"On the moor they won't. Once we get clear of it, give them the slip, we'll see."

I reckon we all wanted to argue. What father was suggesting was desperate. This was all happening too quickly. Him and Derrick wouldn't stand a chance once the PPU closed in. They had helicopters and all that. He was right about mother, though. Her best bet was to take the girls and chance it with the PPU. Say she didn't know anything about Jed Tregathick. They couldn't prove she did. I didn't want to go with mother, though. Not because I didn't care. If father was going to run, I wanted to go with him and Derrick.

"It's a mess," said father. "If we all stay put, they'll just round us up and they'll put me, and probably Derrick, in prison. Longer than three years this time. I'm not going back inside, if I can help it."

"Maybe you should have thought of that before you started all this," said mother and I could see she was a lot more angry than she had let on up to now.

"I do what's best for this family!" he shouted. "Always."

Mother lowered her eyes. "I know," she said, more softly.

"Okay, then. We can't waste any time. Derrick, get yourself ready. You'll need weapons. We'll head out as soon as it's dark."

I went upstairs with mother. The girls were crying, scared stiff. I tried to comfort them, but truth is I was confused. What the hell was going to happen to us? Father meant well, but I'd never seen him look so beaten before.

"They won't hurt us," mother said. "Father wants to take all the blame on to himself and Derrick. Give us the only chance we've got."

"I want to go with him," I said.

The girls, especially Aggie, looked at me, eyes full of terror. She was holding Jerome, and he was the only one who didn't know what was happening. I really wanted to hug him.

"Your sisters need protecting," mother said.

"The four boys will be with you. They'll see you're okay."

"Don't go, Ryan," said Aggie. I could see tears in her eyes and it almost made me start bleating, too.

"I killed Jed," I said. "It's his bone that's led to this. His curse is on me. I should be with father. If they take him, I should be there. Maybe if I hadn't killed Jed, this wouldn't have happened."

"Your place is with your sisters," said mother. "That's your job."

I didn't argue.

Soon after that, father and Derrick, dressed in thick clothes, said goodbye. There were more tears, but he didn't shed none. Nor mother. They knew what they had to do, I guess. Father and Derrick went out the back and up on through the fields, heading for the moor. They took three of the dogs with them. Derrick looked like a dead man, like all the fight in him had gone.

The rest of us just waited. Mother reckoned the PPU would come in the morning. She and the girls got ready and us boys did the same, all silent, mixed up. They wanted to fight, I knew that, but we'd have had no chance. Everyone tried to sleep, but I don't think anyone did.

I got up in the middle of the night and went downstairs, looking out through the tiny kitchen window at the moor. I was wondering where father and Derrick would be. There were old mines up there that they knew. They'd hide deep underground, but most were dangerous. They could easily get blocked in. I should have gone with them.

Mother had followed me down, quiet as a ghost. She made me jump. "Ryan," she said softly. "You know that your father and Derrick will be taken, don't you? They may get away for a while, but they won't make it far. Everything will come back on us now. The PPU will guess that fire wasn't an accident. They'll do everything to catch your father. He asked me to give you a message." She looked back to see if any of the others had followed her down, but no one had.

"Father wants you to make a break. If you go west of the moor and then south, you'll get to the city, down on the coast. He's going east. At best he thinks he'll last a few days before they find him and Derrick."

"What's he going to do?" I didn't want to think about it. "We should all be with him, us boys anyway. Give him more of a chance."

"Then none of you would escape. Father wants you to have a chance. If you get to the city, you can hide. You've a better chance there. Or if you can make your way to London. There you could go underground."

I'd never been to the city, never mind London. I'd sooner go to the moon.

Mother gave me an envelope. "Here's money. Father left it for you. Get dressed and take what you can carry. Me and the girls will be all right."

"When will I see you again?"

Her face hardened. Maybe to stop her crying. "Don't know, Ryan. No time to think about that now. We'll be okay. They won't hurt us." She kept saying that. "Look, even if you came with us, they won't keep us together. We'll be split up. It's how they work. Better if you try and get away. The PPU will be trying to find your father. They'll think he's got you and Derrick with him."

I was really screwed up inside. I couldn't stay, but I wanted to go after father and Derrick. But if I found them, father would be angry if he thought I'd gone against his plan to get me away safe. Maybe I should do what he said. Mother left me to think about it.

I got dressed and slipped a few knives into my belt. I decided not to take a shotgun. If I did get away, people would see it and I'd be picked up. I would have taken the last of the dogs, but I knew it would be the same as the gun. I thought that the PPU would hunt us with tracker dogs. All our trails would be easy to follow – that's what dogs do. The only way I'd get away would be if I went in a truck or a car. I could drive, but I hadn't taken a test – I was too young to be allowed to drive outside the farm lands. So if I was seen driving, I'd be caught. Then I thought maybe if I took a change of clothes, I could fool the tracker dogs. I bundled some up in a black plastic bag and slung it over my shoulder.

It was dark outside, just a bit of moonlight to show the tracks away from the farm. To start with, I headed along the route that I guessed father and Derrick would have taken – the shortest one to the moors. As I climbed, I could see smoke drifting up from where the Tregathick farm was. They'd have the last fucking laugh on us after all.

I reached the moors and stopped. I could see far away to the east to where the first light of dawn was on the horizon. The sun would be up soon. I would have a few hours before the PPU got back to our farm. Maybe it would be enough.

There were shafts in the side of the moor and places where granite had been mined. I headed for one of these abandoned quarries. A path led in between two high blocks of granite to a small lake. Me and my brothers had swum in that lake lots of times and it made me sad to think of that now. I knew the water was cold, even on a summer's day. I also knew what I had to do. I found the place at the back of the lake where there was a big cut in the rock, a tall cave that led in a good way. I went in, right to the back, where there was no light.

I took off all my clothes, everything. I stuffed them into cracks in the rocks. The tracker dogs would find them, no doubt of that. I still had the black bag over my shoulder and I stepped into the stream. Shit, it was icy! I splashed along it, back out of the cave to where the stream ran into the lake. I went in, holding the bag over my head, and swam as fast as I could across the lake. It was hard with the bag, and so cold I thought I would just sink down and drown. But I kept going until I got to the other side. The stream spilled out from the lake and back down the moor side.

I stood up, shivering like hell and got the fresh clothes out of the bag, dressing as fast as I could. I had a thick jacket and boots that tied up tight, so it wasn't too bad. When I'd done I put some small chunks of granite in the bag and slung it out into the lake. It sank quickly. I adjusted the three knives I'd brought, all long, skinning knives that you could shave with, checked that my money was okay, and headed off along the stream bed. If I'd done this right, the tracker dogs would go to the cave but then they'd lose my scent. There wouldn't be anything to help them find me. Even if they did, I'd be long gone.

I got down off the moor before I left the stream bed. The sun was starting to brighten up the fields, so I would be seen if I didn't keep well hidden. I moved quickly. There was enough gorse and bracken to cover me. I could see a narrow road a distance below me, but I didn't want to go near it yet. If I was going to get transport, I wanted to be much further away from Blackstones.

I kept wondering what time would the PPU go to our farm? As soon as they got there, they'd know three of us were gone and they'd be after us like a shot. Also I had to worry about helicopters. For sure they'd bring one or two. It'd save them a lot of time and I knew they didn't want to be up here longer than they possibly could.

It was still early morning when I saw a small farm below me. There were a few barns and a concrete area with cars and vans parked. I watched as a lorry drove up from a lane and stopped. It had a flat back and the driver got out and was met by a woman from the farmhouse. They talked for a bit and I heard the woman laugh. It reminded me of mother and I felt my throat drying up. The man went to the back of the truck and flipped the tail end down. He started unloading stuff – boxes, maybe food.

I crept down closer, watching out for dogs. The man finished and went into the farmhouse. I got to the edge of the concrete, hidden by the barn end. I waited. I heard a dog bark, but it was inside the house. Voices, more laughter. Two or three men. Maybe they were all eating. I took a chance.

I ducked down and ran across the concrete. I felt like a fucking rabbit, expecting to hear a shout, but I was up and in the truck really quickly. I rolled over among the other boxes and crates. There was a tarpaulin over some of them and I jerked it over where I was hiding.

It was a long time before the man came out. I heard him talking to the woman and another man, just outside the driving cab.

"You going up to the Tregathick's place?" said the man I hadn't seen. I guessed he was the farmer. "That fire sounds like a bad one. Road will likely be closed."

"I'll keep away until word comes through," said the other man. "Heard several were killed in the blaze. Radio's full of it. I'll be going back. See you next week." I heard him push back the tail of the truck and slip its bolts into place. I'd been lucky so far.

Soon after we were on our way. I was bucked about as the truck wound down the lanes, most of them full of potholes after the bad winter snow and ice. That was okay – I was getting further and further from Blackstones. By midday I was well beyond anywhere that the tracker dogs would have picked up my scent. The PPU must be at our farm by now.

I got out of the truck when it stopped in a small town, and I hid myself in some thick bushes along a river bank, beside a park. I'd been here a couple of times with mother as a kid. Kicked a ball about with my brothers in that park. Seemed a long time ago. I knew the city was maybe twenty miles away. I had plenty of money, so I could have got a bus. I knew a few still ran most days, but I reckoned that was too risky. I needed another lorry. Plenty went from here to the city.

Over the other side of the river, there was a big supermarket, the local point for distribution of food. Before the Virus there'd been lots of smaller shops, I'd been told. Now everything had merged into this one huge building and it had a massive car park and loads of cars. Behind it there was an area where the big trucks from up country unloaded all the supplies for the supermarket and took away the local produce. That was my best bet. I watched for half an hour as lorry after lorry pulled out of the car park and turned down the main road that led away to the city. So I knew that my chances of getting the right lorry were good.

It was easy sneaking into the back of a truck. I picked one that had a partly open back, so that I could jump out when it suited me. I just waited. It was very quiet. I heard voices now and then, and the sound of lorries coming and going. I was beginning to think I'd picked the wrong one – maybe it would stay put for a few days – but in the end it did start up. I felt a bit of panic when it left the car park, thinking it might go the wrong way, but it was okay. We were headed for the city.

I was getting hungry by now. There were tins of food in with me – beans and peas and stuff – but they were no good. I checked everything else, but it was all the same. I could've used one of the knives to bust open a tin and pig-out on beans – I don't mind them cold – but I thought about that. If whoever drove the lorry found out someone had nicked stuff from a crate, they'd be suspicious. It was the sort of thing the PPU would be on to. A clue.

We did reach the city, after a stop or two. It was late in the afternoon. The driver parked up and everything went quiet. Maybe he wasn't going to unload. Maybe he was going to leave things overnight. I shifted to the back of the truck and looked out. We were in an enclosed area. There were gates, shut but not locked as far as I could see.

I waited. It stayed quiet. Slowly I got down from the truck. I dropped to the ground and pulled my hood tight over my head. I got to the gates, expecting someone to shout. I tried to open them, but the fucking things wouldn't move. I could feel my whole body wet with sweat. There was no way I could climb over the gates, they were too tall. Then I realised something. I'd been trying to pull them open, but they needed pushing. I slipped the catch and pushed, enough to get them to let me through. I tried not to panic and instead of just running off, I shut the gates, so no one would know anyone had got through and out.

I was in a narrow street. I could hear people in some of the buildings – they all looked like stores or the back of abandoned shops. I kept walking, still with my hood up. When I came across people, I kept my head down, but no one took any notice of me. I kept expecting someone to grab me, or point me out, or shout, but it was like I was invisible. This must be why father had wanted me to get to the city. People kept to themselves. Pretty soon I was in much busier streets, people passing by on all sides, loads of them. Hundreds. I'd never seen so many. The Virus was supposed to have wiped out millions, so what must this place have been like before? Father told me once that the cities used to be packed, the streets shoulder to shoulder on busy days. Weird.

There were other young blokes like me, some of them with hoods. Slowly I started to get used to it. I was still sweating, my shirt soaking, but I felt a bit safer. So I had time to think about food. There was enough of it about now – a few cafes and food shops. I found one that sold pasties and pies and went in.

I was served by a kid not much older than me. He never even looked at me, just took my money and gave me a pasty in a bag. There were some chairs and tables by the big window at the front of the shop, so I sat down and ate the pasty. It was hot and that was okay. Nothing like the pasties mother made, but I was hungry enough to eat anything. Other people sat next to me, eating and talking, but no one looked at me, or spoke to me. I'd come to the right place. But I didn't want to get too fucking clever. Just when you thought you were okay, that's when they could get you.

There was a TV mounted on the wall. Father had said, in the cities, there were more TVs, in public places. I swung round a bit, so I could see it and hear it. There was a man on the screen, holding something. Most people were watching him, and as he spoke, more and more people turned to listen. I felt my guts crawling at his words.

"...following the tragic fire at the farm last night, the district People Police Unit has not yet been able to identify the source of the conflagration. Experts examining the remains of the buildings, which included a number of barns, have recovered eight bodies, all thought to be members of the Tregathick family. The PPU has not ruled out the possibility of arson. Members of another nearby farm, Blackstones, are helping the PPU with its enquiries. Three of the family, a man and his two teenage sons, are wanted for questioning, but so far the PPU has not been able to establish their whereabouts. It is not yet known if there is a connection between the fire and the missing men, but a widespread search is under way, centred on and around the edge of the moors..."

I felt myself getting all hot again and expected to see all the people in the food shop stare at me, but they didn't. Some of them were talking about the fire, but most of them were just watching, or eating, not really interested. I got up slowly and made for the door, pushing past the queue. I got away quickly. It was dark now and the city was lighting up. I kept to the middle of the street, where cars weren't allowed, so I was in shadow. Most of the people were either looking in the bright shop windows or getting on buses. To me there seemed to be a lot of them.

I didn't have any kind of plan. Mother had told me to get to London. That would mean a car, or another lorry, or maybe a train. I didn't want to risk a train. They were rare, so there'd be more chance of being seen. I thought I better stop here for the night. Better to make a run for it when there were a lot of people around. Use them as a screen. They could have seen the TV news, but it said the missing men were on the moor, not here. So I could be anyone.

I wandered around the streets for about an hour, still ignored; looking for somewhere I could hole up for the night. I found some back alleys and some bigger buildings that weren't shops or stores. Like huge barns, warehouses maybe. Couldn't see any windows in one and it was very dark around the side alley. I tried it. There were bins and piles of sacks. It smelled bad, but half way down the alley there was a door to the warehouse. I tried it, but it was locked. I took a knife out and tried the lock, working at it. There were screws holding the fitting in place, so I undid them.

A man's voice sounded back up the alley. "Hoy, what you playing at? Get away from that door. Come on, piss off out of it before I get the PPU About time you fucking scum were wiped out." He was wearing a uniform. As soon as he said he'd get the PPU, I got scared. He might have been bluffing, but I wasn't to know that. I just backed up against the door. Part of the fitting was hanging off. He saw it and swore.

He came at me and made a grab for me, but I was too quick for him. I slashed at him with my knife and ripped part of his sleeve. He swore again. He was a big bloke, bigger than me, about the same age as my father and I could see he was angry and spoiling for a fight. He pulled out a weapon, like a thick stick and I could see he was going to use it on me. I couldn't risk him giving me up to the PPU, if that was his plan. I reckoned he'd rather fix me himself, maybe even kill me. He could always say I'd attacked him and he had to do it. So I had to deal with him. My escape was blocked off – the alley was too narrow to make a break past him. I was going to have to kill the bastard.

He swung at me and I took a blow on my left arm. It hurt like fuck, pain shooting up into my shoulder. But it gave me some time to drive my knife up under his rib cage. It tore through his uniform and shirt and went through the flesh like butter, the point digging into his heart, like I was killing a pig. His mouth opened and I thought a big scream would come out, but there was no sound, just a gasp. He doubled up and I pulled the knife out quick. As he dropped to his knees, I used my left hand to yank his head up by the hair and the right hand to open his throat to the gullet. Blood oozed out fast as I let him sprawl among the bins before any of his muck got on me.

I hadn't made a lot of noise. I didn't think anyone else was about, so I was going to leave the alley when I saw shapes at the end of it. Five boys, one about my age, the rest a few years younger. They were coming down the alley, moving slowly and checking behind them, like they was on the run. It was dark but by the street lamp behind them I could see they were dressed in old clothes, scruffy, dirty. I couldn't avoid them. Maybe I could scare them off with the knife. I held it out. It still had blood on it.

"Who's there?" said one of the kids.

"This is our patch, mate. Fuck off out of it," said the leader, but I could see he was scared.

I went slowly forward. They'd blocked the alley, coming down it, three at the front, two behind. I was about to rush them, take them by surprise, but I couldn't risk getting caught. Five was a lot to take on in one go, even if they were kids.

"What's going on?" said the biggest one. I could see now he was thin, like he hadn't been eating much for ages. The others all looked like streaks of piss – a strong wind would blow them over. "Is that the security guard behind you? What you done to him. Fuck! You hit him?"

For all I knew they were mates of the man I'd gutted. I gripped the knife tighter. The older boy would have to go first. The others would likely make a run for it if I did for him. I didn't have to kill him, just make sure he was disabled.

"Is he hurt?" said one of the kids. "That's Worden. He's a bastard. Shit, have you knocked him out?"

The others started to laugh, but they were nervous of me.

"Serves the fucker right," said the older boy. "He's always giving us shit. Trying to get us moved on. Treats us like fucking rats. About time someone kicked his arse."

"Don't give me no trouble," I warned them.

"No, we won't, mate. We're just heading to our place for the night." He was edging closer, trying to get a better look at the guard. "When he gets up, he'll be like hell. We won't be able to stay here. You've fucked things up for us."

"He won't be getting up," I said. I stood aside and let them look.

The older boy gasped when he saw the pool of blood and the man's open throat. "Fuck! He's dead! You've killed the fucker!"

The others drew back from me like I'd got a plague. I waited to see what they'd do. I didn't want none of them splitting on me. I remembered the Tregathick farm. Father had said we had to burn out the whole nest. Maybe I needed to drop all of these if I was going to get away safely.

"What are we going to do?" said the older boy. "Shit, if the PPU find him, they'll blame us. You've dropped us right in it, mate." I could see he didn't know what the fuck to do about it, like he was going to piss his pants.

I shook my head. "So make sure they don't find the body."

They were all very quiet for a few minutes. One of them spoke up. "He's right, Dyl. Hide the body. Drop it in the harbour."

I shook my head again. "That won't do you any good. It'll sink for a day, maybe two. But it'll rise. They'll find it."

"You did this," said the older boy. "So you think of a way of hiding it."

"Okay," I said. "What's it worth?"

They were all looking at me with blank faces. I knew they were all shit scared, though.

"What do you want?" said the older boy, Dyl.

"Somewhere to hide out for the night. Tomorrow I want to find transport away from here, to London. A truck, or something." I didn't want to tell them I had money. I was going to need all of it for when I did get to London. "You hide me and I'll show you what to do with the body."

"Who are you?"

"Never mind that," I said. "You going to help me, or what?" I still held the knife where they could see it. They knew what I meant. They were more afraid of me than anything else.

"Sure," said Dyl. "Tell us what to do."

"Where's your hideout?"

"In the warehouse. Part of it's disused. Worden knew we holed up there, but he didn't follow us in. Just tried to scare us off."

"Get the body in there," I said. "Then leave it to me."

"What about the blood?" said one of the younger ones. "They'll find the blood."

"Is there a garage around here?" I said. I was doing their thinking for them. They weren't used to this kind of thing. "Garages have oil. Get as much as you can. Wash the alley down with it. It'll hide the blood. Long enough for you to find somewhere else to hole up. You can't stay here after tonight."

"He's right," said Dyl. "Fuck it! Connor – you and Mickey go and nick some oil. As much as you can. Do what he says."

I ripped open some of the plastic bin bags and used them to wrap part of the security guard's body, enough to stop anyone moving him from getting covered in blood. I got the kids to haul the body to the end of the alley. There was another door that looked locked, but they had a key and pushed it open. It was pitch dark inside, but Dyl had a torch. We all went in, dragging the corpse. They took me down some stairs to a basement area, through a load of old pipes, thick with spider webs and choked with dust. There were some rooms at the end of it and a wide area where it looked like old machinery had been removed. Boilers, maybe. My brother Derrick would have loved this place.

We sat on some low boxes, faces just about visible in the torchlight. Dyl gave the torch to one of the others and got a lot of paper and broken bits of box together and in a while had a small fire going, so they could save the torch battery. I was worried about the smoke, but Dyl said it went up through vents in the roof somewhere and no one would notice at night.

The body was slumped up against another box, like it was sleeping, or a scarecrow. "So where do we hide it?" said Dyl. "There's store rooms here, but it'll be found. This is Worden's patch. It's the first place anyone would search."

"You got any food?" I said. I was hungry again. I should have bought a few more pasties.

"No," said Dyl. "The controllers are getting wise to us in the market. We used to be able to nick stuff, but it's getting harder. More and more of us are going hungry and fighting over the waste, what there is of it. We'll just have to forage at first light, though people are getting wise to early starts. Sometimes we can get something when the deliveries come in."

"When did you guys last eat?"

"All we ever get is scraps," one of the youngsters said. Looking at them all, scrawny and white, I could believe it. My dogs were better fed, but I didn't want to think about them now.

We waited for the other boys. I realised these kids had accepted me as the person in charge, which was weird. Like they didn't have much of an idea about anything. How did they survive? Maybe they were that hungry they'd lost some of their energy. Needed to be pushed.

In a while the other boys came back. They'd found a garage and stolen some oil. It was easier than they'd thought. Easier to get than food. They'd spread the oil about the alley like I'd told them. One of them was holding something up. "See what I got!" He was laughing. "They left it in the garage."

It was a radio, old and chipped, but he got it working and we had it on low volume. They fiddled about with its knobs, getting different channels. A local news channel came up and I made them hold it. The tinny voice made me jump. The words made me go cold.

"...have been taken into custody. Social Control will be arranging care for the younger girls and the baby. In the meantime, the PPU have now confirmed that two of the men who they have been searching for in *relation to the fire at the Tregathick farm were involved in the shooting incident on the moor this afternoon. In an exchange of gunfire, two police were injured and a number of dogs were killed. The two fugitives, who have been identified as Alan Drenner and his oldest son, Derrick Drenner, are both dead, killed in the shooting. A third man, also a son of Alan Drenner, Ryan Drenner, is still missing, but the PPU have widened their search as they now believe he may have left the vicinity of the moors....*"

I sank back into the shadows, feeling the horror creep over me. *Dead.* Father and Derrick, shot by the PPU. Maybe it's what father wanted, but it was still the worst news. Mother and the kids in custody. But she'd said they would be okay. Aggie and Jerome – what about them? Who'd look after them? Not me, I'd likely never even see them again.

"Put some music on," one of the kids near me said and they shifted the channel on the radio. None of them had taken any notice of the news. It might as well have been in another world to them. They didn't connect me with it. Their world was this place. They lived like animals, on the run. Like foxes, maybe, scavenging. Picking up scraps, they'd said. No way to live.

I was one of them now. Hunted. These kids didn't know I'd left the moor, but the PPU would. Their trackers wouldn't find out how I'd done it, but the PPU would guess. And someone out in this city would spot me. There wouldn't be any photos, not that I knew of. Someone would do a drawing. They were good at that. I had to get to London. It would swallow me up.

"Tomorrow," I said, so that they all looked at me, "I want to get away. I don't want no bus, or train. I need to get into a lorry. London, that's where I'll head. You going to help me?"

The others all looked to Dyl. He was nodding. I reckon he would be glad to see me go. I was a threat to his leading this pack. They were like dogs and only one could run them.

"What about the body?" he said. "You told us you'd know how to hide it."

I unsheathed my knife and one of the others. "First job is to cut it up. Don't worry, I'll take care of it. We don't want any mess. The PPU will trace it to here, even if they can't find it. They'll find blood in the end. But you boys can be across the city by then, in a new hideout."

Dyl nodded. He didn't look happy, but he knew I was right. I

98

went to the body and undid the plastic, making a sheet on the floor that would catch the blood as I worked. I did the same as I'd done with Jed Tregathick. I took the head off and bagged it up. Then I did the limbs, then last I quartered the rest. The kids watched me from the fire, all of them too terrified to interrupt.

I took a slice of meat off part of the body, white as chicken, and held it up so they could see it. "You boys want food? You got plenty. Here, try this."

It was like I'd told them the worst thing in the world. They all cowered back in disgust, too horrified to speak. I put the piece of flesh into my mouth and bit off a smaller piece, chewing. Then I ate the rest. "It's good meat," I said. "You're all starving. Eat! Cook it if you want. It's like pork. Go on, try it."

Whether they did it because they were shit scared of me, or whether it was because they were so hungry, two of them came forward as I sliced off some more meat. They looked at it, shaking their heads, but then they tried it. They chewed it, pulling faces. Then they tried more.

"You've eaten bacon, chops, beef, chicken, all that stuff? Maybe not regularly," I said, given that they'd probably never been near a farm. "So what's the difference? Food is food. You can die if you want. Not me."

Dyl and the others wouldn't try it raw, so they made a rough spit and cooked some of the flesh. That did it – it smelled amazing, just as good as anything in the shops. Pretty soon we were all pigging out on the stuff, fit to bust. The juices ran down our chins and we laughed. Survival. The basic rule. I'd opened up a new world for them. They'd just been sitting outside its door, not realising.

"We can't eat all of it," said Dyl.

"No. Take what's left when you go. Just be careful not to leave any traces. Always use bags, or sheets, or anything that you can burn, or better still, bury. Deep, mind. The dogs can always find stuff that's buried too shallow."

"What about the head?" one of the kids said.

"Put it in a sack, weigh it with stones and drop it out in the harbour. No one will find it. Use a boat if you can. Further out the better. That water's deep, isn't it?"

Dyl grinned. "Yeah, you're right. Very deep."

"Deep enough for the bones when you've done," I told him.

*

I slept okay in a bed of newspapers and stuff and woke up early. Dyl had promised to take me to someone called The Pole, who he said was a contact man for people using lorries and other transport to get into and out of the country. It was risky, but a lot of them, people from Poland and places like that, paid money for a place on the lorries, to get here. The Virus had been worse in Europe. People had more chance of surviving here.

Dyl said The Pole wouldn't give me to the PPU. He was their enemy. But he'd only help me if I paid him. I didn't like taking risks, but I knew the PPU would soon work out that the guard I'd killed was missing and they'd find traces. I had to get away while I had time. I didn't give a fuck about Dyl and the kids.

We met The Pole in a car park. He was a big bloke, with short hair and a scar down the side of his face, like he knew about knife fights. He looked about as hard as anyone I'd ever seen, not the sort of guy to cross. His hands were even bigger than father's and looked like they were used to labouring, as if he'd been on a farm like me, or in a quarry. He had tattoos and scars over his knuckles and when he spoke it wasn't easy to understand him properly. There were three other guys behind him, watching, and I reckoned they were his guards.

"You want to get to London?" he said.

I nodded.

"You got money? You show me. I get you to London."

I didn't have no choice. I took out my envelope and showed him. I hadn't counted the money. I was going to need to keep some, so I held a few notes back and handed him the rest. I waited while he thumbed through it, his face scowling. I thought he would just take the money and say no.

"Okay. When you want to go?" He gave me some of the money back, which surprised me.

"Now."

Again I thought he'd say no, but he nodded. "Come."

I went with him and his three mates. I didn't bother to wave to Dyl. The Pole led me through the car park, down a narrow staircase and out into an alley way. I had one hand on one of my knives, just in case. I didn't want to have to take these guys on.

They'd kill me easy. The morning was still early enough to be grey and we kept to the shadows. We got to the back of some wide buildings and I could hear men shouting and machines. Engines roaring. Rows of lorries.

The Pole pointed. "They load and unload here. See the big lorries. Some park all night. Driver sleep. Some in cabs. They eat soon." He pointed to a smaller truck, a big van with its side open. A man was working inside, cooking food. Pasties and stuff. Drivers and other men were buying stuff and standing around eating and drinking from tin mugs. It made me feel very hungry.

The Pole said something to one of his men and the guy went over to the van. The Pole said, "You eat before you go." He patted me on the shoulder. "You pay good money. I look after you."

His mate got a couple of rolls and a plastic cup of tea and brought them back. We'd kept out of sight of anyone and no one seemed bothered about the guy buying food. A lot of people got stuff from the van. I scoffed the two fat bacon rolls and drank the hot tea. Then I was ready.

"Listen," said The Pole. "You go under lorry. I show you which one. Near axle – you know front axle? Yes? You swing up there and there's place you can get in. We made it, secret. Squeeze tight. Careful, huh? When engine start, you hold on. London a long way. Driver has breaks. You get down then and wait. Get back up before start again."

He led me into the lines of trucks and we moved like a couple of ghosts, making sure we weren't seen. The Pole must have known which lorries were due out and when. He chose one – a huge one that you could have put three tractors inside easy. I thought it would be easier to get inside, but maybe it wasn't safe. I didn't want to be caught – I reckoned the PPU would be checking everything more closely now. Lorries leaving the city might be opened. I just did what the Pole said and swung up above the axle into a sort of boxed cubby-hole that had been fitted pretty well. There was enough room to get into and lie flat, just above the fat, greasy metal. Mind you, when it span, it would be inches away from me.

I had to wait a long time before anyone came. I heard voices, right beside the lorry. Three men were talking. Drivers, preparing to leave and go out on the road.

"Where you off to, Jack?" said one voice.

"Midlands. Early finish, mate. Wife's birthday coming up, so I've got a couple of days off. Staying in our place up there. I've stashed enough guns for a regiment."

They laughed and made crude comments about their women. I just wanted them to get a move on and leave.

"I'll follow you," said a third man. "I'm heading north. Overnight in Liverpool. It'll be a bastard. You heard about the food riots? Going on all over the North. The PPU are having a hard time keeping control. If I can avoid trouble, I'll be on up to Edinburgh tomorrow."

The first voice was a local man's. "I'm to London. Fucking Thursday run. Traffic's just as fucking bad as the weekend these days. Only a few roads are open. More and more are getting clogged up with discarded vehicles. Far less people about. Lot of gang wars going on. I never get in on time. They'll moan like fuck, but it's tough shit. What can you do?"

"Keep your eyes open," said the second voice. "You been listening to the news? Heard about that farm up on the moors? All to hell up there. Eight people burned alive. PPU reckon it's deliberate. Even the farmlands are starting into the riots."

"Fucking maniacs," said my driver. "It weren't no kids, neither. The PPU caught up with two men on the moor. Bloody gunfight. What sort of fucking nutters were they? Can you believe that? Got all the food and supplies they need and they still end up killing each other."

"Fucking hillbillies, weren't they? Inbred. Like in that old banjo film. Jeeze, they must have been crazy."

"You hear what happened this morning?" said my driver. "One of the boys they took in got free and grabbed a knife. Used it on one of the PPU women. Killed her."

"You're fucking joking! So what happened?"

"They cornered him. Ended up shooting him. Reckoned he was as mad as a dog. Don't suppose there was much else they could do."

"They're well rid of him. I'd have done the same."

"You watch out," said the second voice. "They reckon there's still one of them on the run. Come down off the moor. No telling what the bastard'll do next. Don't go picking up no hitchhikers. Likely to have your head blown off."

"Shit, has the fucker got a gun?" said my driver.

102

"Don't know. Police said he may be armed. Don't take no chances. Run the fucker over if you see him."

My driver laughed. "Take it easy, Mick. How the hell you going to know if it's him?"

"I ain't stopping' for no one. They'll get the bastard. He ain't got a snowball's chance in hell. I hope they shoot him, like the others."

"So what's going to happen to all them kids? There was young girls, and a baby. Suppose they'll all go into Social Control. That's a fucking joke. Nasty lot of bastards."

"They'll be split up. Saw it on the news last night. PPU are trying to work out who was involved in the fire. Not the women, but there's two boys left, both teenagers. They think they was involved. They'll do time. Better off dead."

I shuddered at that. I knew what the men meant. My brothers would be sent to prison, or some sort of place like it. Not the big place on the moor. They weren't old enough. But it would be bad enough. It would drive them mad.

"Anyway," said my driver, "the whole fucking family must be raving. They ought to put the fuckers down. Take 'em out and shoot the buggers. We're too soft these days. They ought to send the Militia in and clean out the whole area."

I felt the anger burning me up, but I had to keep as still as a hunting dog. I heard the men exchange a few more remarks, a few coarse jokes, before they split up. I heard my driver climb up into his cab and the door slammed. The engine came on and we moved. I got a good grip and tried to close my mind off to everything. We swung this way and that as the big lorry worked its way through the city streets.

I was going into darkness. My family were gone. Three dead and the rest about to be split up for good. It had all happened so quickly. Fucking Tregathicks. They were to blame for this. At least we'd sorted those bastards out. We'd paid, though. I thought about my sister, Aggie. I always wondered which one of us had sired Jerome on her. Aggie said it was me. I said, how can you tell? She just used to smile and say, I know. And Jerome always liked me to hold him and fuss him. The others used to take the piss out of me, but they wouldn't have harmed Jerome.

Now it seemed like everyone else had one word for us – scum. *Better off dead.* That's what these men had said. No better than rats in the corn stocks.

I cried for a long time on that journey out of the city and on to the big road they call the motorway. When I finished crying, my face wet, I knew I'd done with feeling sorry for myself, like I'd kind of crossed some sort of private bridge. No more crying. If I was going to survive, I would have to get a lot tougher. Maybe the old gods would look after me. I didn't have much money now. Okay, so when I got to London, I'd steal what I needed. Maybe not money – money was just something to buy stuff with. All I needed was food. I could steal that.

Or kill.

*

The Pole had been right about the driver taking breaks on the journey. I was able to get down and slip out from my hiding place a couple of times. I saw the driver go into a big café place. There were some small stands outside in the car park, selling cheap stuff, junk really, so I was able to use some of my money to buy food and a hot drink. No one was a bit interested in me. We were a long way from the moors now. I suppose I was just like any other traveller. I was scruffy, but no more than a lot of others on the road. Since the Virus a lot of people roamed backwards and forwards, trying to keep going, dig out some kind of life. No one paid the travellers much attention. More scum, I supposed.

We got to the outskirts of a big city in the evening and we stopped and started over and over again. There were lanes of traffic on either side of us. I couldn't see them, but I knew by all the noise. It was terrifying, so many cars and trucks! I had to stay put. My arms were like lead, my whole body cramped up, but I was used to it now. I wasn't going to give up. The worst of it was the fumes. They came from everywhere, and I coughed like fuck. Luckily there was no way the driver would hear me.

In the end, I'd had enough. It was dark now, apart from the glare of the headlights of all the cars and that, so I decided to make a break for it. I picked a time when the lorry stopped. In the jam it would be held up for a while, engine ticking over. I dropped down and swung out from under the fat wheels. It was raining, vision difficult. There were cars close up beside the lorry and I could just about make out people inside them, but they were either too pissed off with the jam to notice me, or they couldn't see out properly. I threaded between two lanes of cars to the side of the road.

There was a grass bank sloping away and I slid down it and jumped over the trench at the bottom. I had to climb through some fencing, but there were trees here and I went into them and out of sight. I dropped down, hidden from the road above and waited. No one had followed me. I waited, a knife ready. Still no one came. I moved off. The trees didn't cover much of an area and there were buildings beyond them. Not houses, but probably factories, like I'd been told. There were lights on here and there. I got to a road and it had signs. I didn't know any of the names, but I knew which direction London was in. I started walking.

It was much quieter than the motorway. A few cars passed me, but none of them stopped. It was night now, though the sky ahead was a weird colour, lit up by the city, I guessed. I'd heard London went on for miles and miles, big as the moor, or even bigger. I didn't know what to do. Should I just keep going, or should I find somewhere to hole up? I thought travel by day might be more risky, even though everywhere was lit up here at night. There were enough shadow places to keep me covered.

In the end my mind was made up for me. I saw this long building, with a sign that I recognised, a red circle and the word "Underground" written across it. I remembered mother's words, when she'd told me to get to London. She'd said I could go underground. This must be what she'd meant. I'd seen this railway on the TV at school and the teacher had talked about it and how it still worked. Once there had been a massive network of these train lines, like a spider's web, but since the Virus there were just a few main lines left. This must be one of them.

It was supposed to go right into the city, burrowing down into the ground like a big worm. I thought it was mostly bullshit at the time, but now it made me wonder. I guessed it worked like any other train. I would have to buy a ticket, like you did on a bus.

I went into the building, wrapping my coat tight so my knives were out of sight. There was an old black guy in a jacket, a sort of uniform. He was sitting in a sort of cage, protected, and he looked at me, but didn't seem suspicious. I stood there for a moment, not sure what to do. I could see a platform the other side of some metal gate things.

"You want a ticket?" said the black guy, leaning forward.

I nodded. The lights were bright and I felt exposed, trapped.

"Where you goin'? Into town?"

"London," I said.

He grinned, his teeth very white. "All the trains go to London, son. You want to go all the way in. Paddington?" I could just about understand him because he had a funny sort of voice.

What he'd said sounded right. I didn't want to argue, or show him that I was clueless. I nodded. He turned to some kind a small machine next to him. I wondered if he knew who I was and was going to report me, so I went closer, a hand on one of the knives. There was no one else about. Maybe I'd have to try to break into his cubicle and kill him.

I couldn't tell from his face if he recognised me. He was smiling, though he didn't seem interested in much, yawning. "Here you go." He slipped a small piece of card through a hole in the bottom of the cage. A ticket. I took out what I had left of the money, a few notes, and pushed them through to him. He took most of it and gave me back a note and a few coins. I shoved them in my pocket and held the ticket tight.

"Go on through," he said, pointing to the metal gates. I went to them, but I couldn't get past. I started to panic. The black guy was watching me and I felt myself tensing up.

"Just push your ticket through there," he said, smiling. He pointed to a slot in part of the machine beside the gate. I did what he told me and the gate swung open. I pushed through quickly.

"Hey, hold on, boy! Your ticket! You got to take it with you. Keep it all the time until you leave the station at Paddington. You won't have long to wait. Last train will be here soon. Take it easy."

I snatched the ticket back from the machine, my face wet with sweat.

"Your first time? You go carefully, son. Got someone to meet you?"

I nodded. He wouldn't know it was a lie, but I didn't want anyone interfering.

"Good. Don't let people know you got money. Keep it safe or they'll take it off you." He turned back to whatever he was doing and again I wondered if he'd recognised me, if I'd been on TV. They do those pictures, drawings. The PPU would look for me all over the country. At least he'd been helpful. Hadn't swore at me or called me vermin. Maybe it was a trick.

I went on to the platform and found a place of shadows to hide in. There was a young guy and girl further down, but they were huddled together. They wouldn't be interested in me. I kept thinking, what if the guard calls the PPU before the train gets here? He'd have a telephone for sure. I was listening out for footsteps. I held one of the knives inside my coat so hard it hurt my hand.

Then a train came out of the darkness, slowing down, very quiet, not like the trains I'd seen on TV. It was grey and lit up inside. About five people got off it, further down the platform. None of them saw me. They just went out the way I had come in. I went to the train – its doors were still open – and got on. There was nowhere dark to sit, but no one else got on, not in my section. I sat down, holding the ticket.

Nothing happened. The train stayed still. Had the guard called the PPU? Maybe I should get off and make a run for it. I got up, but as I did, the doors closed. They shut tight and I knew I wouldn't be able to open them. Then we moved. The train was going back the way it had come. So I was going to London. I knew the bit of money I'd got left was enough to buy some food, a coffee and not much else. I was hungry. What was I going to eat tonight? Or tomorrow, or after that? I'd have to steal.

The motion of the train made me sleepy and I must have dozed off. When I came to, there were a few people in the carriage, some reading papers, others talking. No one seemed to notice me. The train kept stopping, people getting on and off. The further we went, the more it filled up. Mother had told me once that these trains got so full that everyone was jammed together, really tight. She'd said *millions* of people used them. I couldn't imagine it, and anyway, if too many people had got on, I'd have lost my nerve. Even these few silent strangers were frightening.

Outside, the lights had gone and it was mostly pitch black. There were stations, and a voice – like a radio – kept saying their names, but I didn't know any of them. It didn't say London, but it did say we were going to that place the guard had said, Paddington. It seemed like a long journey. I knew we were underground and it scared me even more, as if we were heading for the Jesus people's Hell. Maybe that black guy trapped people like me and sent us here.

"Got any change for an old man?" The deep voice sounded

right in my ear. I must have dozed off again. This old fucker was sitting next to me. He stank. He wore a thick, black coat, stained and with tears in it, like one of the vagrants that sometimes wandered around the edge of the moor before we moved them on, usually pelting them with sheep shit. His shoes were falling apart. His face was really old. He needed a shave and his white hair was all straggly. "Just for a cup of tea?"

"I ain't got no money," I said, shrinking back into the seat.

"You must have something, sonny. I only want a few coppers." His breath smelled rotten.

I couldn't do anything to shift him, not with other people on the train. If we'd been alone, outside, I'd just have smacked him one and beat it. I was trapped here. I shoved my hand in my pocket and pulled out the last of the money.

"Here," I said. "Take it. Take it and fuck off. It's all I've got. Leave me alone."

He stared in amazement, but took the money in his filthy hand. Didn't look like he'd ever washed, his skin grimy, his nails all blackened. "That's very kind, son. More here than I need."

"Keep it."

He put the money away and sat in silence for a while. We went through more stations, but the voice still said we were going to Paddington. Maybe the old man would know how far it was. I asked him.

"Not far. You got somewhere to go?"

"Yeah," I lied.

"First time in the city?" he said. "I can see it is." He was talking quietly, so no one else could hear. I don't think anyone else gave a shit about us, though. Especially him. They were avoiding him. "It'll be hard for you if you don't have any contacts. Not a good place for loners. Never was."

I didn't say anything, just looked out at the darkness.

"You were kind to give me the money, son. I know where you can get some grub. Won't cost you. Maybe a place to kip for the night. Won't be special, but it's dry and no one will bother you. It's up to you. I'm getting off soon. If you want it, follow me. If not, well, good luck to you." He said nothing else after that.

I was weighing it up. Whatever I did from now on would be risky. I was going to have to fight and steal my way to survival. Maybe one night in some kind of shelter would be a better way to start, just to get me on my feet. The old guy seemed like he was glad of the money. Maybe most people just told him to fuck off. I didn't want to trust him, or anyone, but there was nothing else.

I reckon we must have been close to Paddington when the old man got up and went to the door. I still hesitated, but when he got off, I followed him. I kept a few steps behind him. He knew I was there. He moved slowly, like he was lame, so it was easy to keep up, even though there were more people about now. They all seemed to be smartly dressed, clean, and they all had some kind of work to do, or definite plans. I'd never been in a crowd like this, people jostling and pushing for the exits. There were stairs up that moved. I knew about them, but they scared the shit out of me. I clung on to the sides to steady myself. No one paid any attention. I saw other guys with coats and hoods – the hoods up – but it seemed normal, even though we weren't outside.

At the top of the moving stair, the old man turned to me and took me to one side. "You got a ticket?" He knew I had – he'd seen me clutching it. "Okay. You go through – there, that gate on the end. Farthest from the guard. When he's looking the other way, I'll jam up behind you and we'll go through together. I don't have a ticket. Don't worry, I do it every day."

I didn't like the idea, but I didn't have a choice. I did what he told me and put my ticket into the slot. It only took a moment and we were through, part of a small stream of people. It was so fast that no one knew anything was wrong. So he was a clever old bastard. Maybe he would be useful after all, especially if he knew the tricks of surviving without money.

We got outside and I was glad of the cold night air, even though I felt suffocated by the buildings that rose up like fucking mountains all around us. So this was London. Massive, stuffed with people, even at night. Cars, taxis, horns blaring, lights dazzling. Shops the size of factories, all lit up. How did anyone live like this? It was like the rest of the country had poured in here. Even the other city I'd come from seemed like a town compared to this.

"Come on, son," said the old man. I knew now he wasn't going to turn me in to the PPU. He was living rough. He was a tramp, a city tramp. Lived on his wits, I guessed. I followed where he led. He stopped at a kiosk where papers were sold – something else I'd heard about but not seen before – and bought two cups of coffee with some of the money I'd given him. We edged back into the doorway of a closed shop, glad of the shadows, and sipped our drinks. I could see a board next to the kiosk. It said: PPU STILL HUNT LAST OF DEVON FARM KILLERS. I almost dropped my coffee. I watched the tramp's face, but he didn't take any notice of the board. I guessed he couldn't read. At least there was no picture of me, but I wanted to get away from there.

We made our way through the streets and down side alleys until I was dizzy. The tramp knew where he was going, like a rat in a maze. He came to a tall fence, overgrown so thickly that there was no way through it. There was a sheet of rusting corrugated iron fixed up to it and the old man checked that no one was about and tugged it enough to make an opening. He told me to go inside. I trusted him enough now to do it and he followed me. We went through the tall bushes inside that made a tunnel. There was still enough light to see by. We came out into a wider area, but it was overgrown. I could see gravestones sticking up from the grass and brambles.

Ahead of us was a tall building with a bust-up spire. A church. Like a bigger version of the one in the village nearest our farm at home. Its windows had all been boarded up and what I could see of the roof was damaged. Looked like it was about to fall down. There was a board that said "Saint" something, but the paint was flaked off. No one could have come here for ages, apart from the tramp and any mates he had. There was a big wooden door, with a smaller door set into it. The old man opened it and we went inside. I had one hand on a knife.

There were fires burning and that was the only light. The main inside part of the church had had all the chairs taken out – probably used for firewood – and the ceiling was mostly gone. I looked up at the night sky. It still had that weird pinky-orange city glow. Around me there must have been a couple of dozen people. They were cooking stuff on spits and had coffee pots going. Made me hungry again. The old man spoke to a few of the people – they were of all ages, and everyone was dressed in rags. I could smell them. Like they'd always lived outside. I wondered if any of them were on the run, like me.

"Here, have some grub," said the old man. I found out his name was Gaz. He pulled a bag out from his big coat that he'd been hiding. It had fruit in it and vegetables, which he handed over to one of the groups by a fire. Must have been a sort of payment for food because they gave him and me a bowl each. The bowls had a thick sort of stew in them. The meat was tough and fatty. I didn't ask what it was, dog probably. I just ate it. We had coffee with it. Tasted sour, but okay.

"You can stay here for a while," Gaz told me. "But you'll have to be seen by Father O'Mara. He likes to meet everyone. Not everyone is allowed in. The city is full of tramps and derelicts, homeless people that only sneak out at night to find scraps of food, enough to get by. Must be thousands of them. There's a lot of old places like this, since the Virus. We can only cope with a small amount of people. But I'll get you in. Father O'Mara will be here in a while." Gaz pointed to the raised area at the far end of the open area, which had several long tables on it, pushed together to make a kind of stage. We used to have a small stage at school. Beside this one on a tall stand was a big cross, a relic from when the church had been working I guessed. I didn't say anything about the old gods. I wondered if they were watching me – through that huge hole in the roof. They'd got me to this place, anyhow.

"No one's going to ask you where you're from, or who you are," said Gaz. "But if you stay, Father O'Mara will want you to get stuff for us, to earn your keep. Food mostly. Okay?"

I nodded.

"I can show you parts of the city, if you need help. I know you're new here. It's no problem, lad. We live as we can. The citizens – they go on like they always have. The systems are still in place for them. We're outside all that, but no one bothers us. This place may as well be a thousand miles away. There's old tombs under us. Dry places to sleep. We've even got toilets that drain properly. All the comforts of home. Father O'Mara is the law. We all do what he says, or we get punished. Best not to defy him."

He was grinning, but I felt uncomfortable, thinking about home. Father, Derrick and one of my other brothers, dead. Murdered by the PPU. I'd be killed, too, if they got me. I thought again about Aggie, and baby Jerome. Where would they be? Mother said they'd be okay. How could they be okay, split up from everyone?

A while later there was a buzz among the people and I saw movement up on the raised area that Gaz called the dais. He said

111

the table was the altar. Two men were up there and everyone had turned to watch them, going very quiet. Gaz got me to my feet and we went slowly forward, joining the small crowd that had formed. On the altar, the man called Father O'Mara was watching everyone, nodding and smiling. He was quite old and wore a long black robe and he was just like a priest I had seen at the village church. None of my family went to church, but we'd seen it. Father O'Mara waved his hands about and said something, which I guessed was a prayer.

I said my own prayer under my breath – to the old gods, apologising to them for being here with the hated Jesus people. Next to the priest was a very different man. He was much younger and looked like a hard case. Even harder than The Pole. He wore a leather jacket with chains and had a shaved head. His shirt looked clean and where it was open at the chest, I could see tattoos. Derrick, my brother, had always gone on about getting tattoos and having an eagle on his chest. I said I'd have a raven. Ravens are the old gods' children.

Gaz pushed me forward so that the priest would see me. I didn't like it, but I waited. Father O'Mara and the hard-looking bloke, who Gaz said was called Maul, both looked at me. The priest smiled but Maul stared like he wanted a fight. I could see he didn't go short of food, he was too muscled, like one of them boxers.

"This is Ryan, Father," said Gaz. He told him as much about me as I'd let on, which wasn't much, but the priest liked that I'd given Gaz all my money.

"Well, this place is a haven," said the priest. "Blessed by God. I am sure he welcomes you. Will you promise to serve him and us, by helping us? In return we will find a bed for you." He held out a small cross on a chain that he wore round his neck.

"Kiss it," said Maul, standing over me.

I drew back. I wasn't kissing no fucking cross. Over the priest's shoulder I could see up through the smashed roof and the moon came out, bright as gold. If the old gods were watching me now, they'd be angry if I touched that cross.

"What's wrong?" said the priest. He frowned.

Maul glared at me. "Kiss it," he said, sharp like. "Or I'll break your fuckin' arm and throw you back out on to the streets."

Father O'Mara didn't seem bothered that Maul had sworn. He

just waited for me to kiss the cross, holding it out again.

Gaz put a hand on my shoulder, but I shrugged it off. This was a trap! "What you waitin' for, you fuckin' little scumball?" snarled Maul, jumping down off the dais, meaning to grab me, but I was too quick for the bastard. He shouldn't have called me that. Not the same as the PPU. He was no better. I already had a hand inside my coat and I pulled out the biggest of my knives and as Maul came for me, I shoved it hard up under his rib cage. It was easy because all he had on was the shirt and he wasn't expecting to be attacked. I felt the blade go home, deep, and I twisted it, pulled it out and rammed it back again. It would have sliced into his heart.

Maul screamed in pain as blood started to leak fast down his tattooed chest. I used my elbow to drive backwards into Gaz's face and the old man was flung away, toppling over. I pulled my knife free of Maul and he made another grab for me but all he could do was double up in pain. I thought he was going to spew up. I stepped away from him and leaped up on to the dais beside Father O'Mara. He looked completely freaked out, his face white in the moonlight. My knife was dripping blood. Down below us the people were all making a noise, some shouting. They all sounded angry. I thought they'd go for me and tear me to bits, like a lot of mad dogs.

Father O'Mara backed away, letting the cross slip from his fingers so it dangled. "What have you done? This is God's house." He held up his hands as if I was going to stick the knife in him.

"Fuck your God," I said. "I didn't come all this way to be one of his slaves. The old gods look after me. They're watching me right now." I pointed with the knife up at the moon. It just seemed like the right thing to say, to make them understand.

The priest looked even more shocked and the people in the church stopped making a noise and watched us. None of them moved much. I reckon they were scared of me, like I was some kind of demon. Maul had collapsed at the foot of the altar. Those knife cuts would have done for him. He wouldn't last. Sometimes when I killed a big pig, it would last for a while, but never long.

Father O'Mara bumped up against the bigger cross on the stand. He grabbed it and pulled it free. It was quite long, made of metal. It had been painted gold once, to make it look expensive, but the paint was coming off. It was just metal. But it would make a good weapon. The priest swung it and I dodged back. He saw that I was wary of it and swung it again.

"Kill him! Kill him!" shouted some of the people at the front. The priest nodded, though I could see he was shit scared. He wasn't used to fighting. I got my knife ready. I watched the big cross as it swept back and forward. It was easy to dodge: it moved slowly, too heavy to use like a proper weapon. The longer it went on, the more the priest started to panic. I reckoned his arms were already getting tired.

"You must leave," he gasped. "They'll let you go, I promise." The moonlight was kind of pouring over him now and I knew that the old gods had a plan here. That's why they'd brought me. All this way, to this place. To show the people here that they still existed.

Father O'Mara knew I wasn't going to run. He swung the cross again, as hard as he could, in the hope that he'd hit me and drive me off the altar to where the people could grab me and trample me, kick me to death. He overbalanced and dropped to one knee, the cross banging flat down on the altar.

I looked again at the people below the dais and that's when I saw the girl. She was about Aggie's age, and she was holding a baby. Just like Jerome. I remembered. It made me more and more angry, like I was going to explode with all that hate for what had been done to us.

So, as Father O'Mara looked up at me, I shoved the knife hard into his right eye until it ground up against bone. He screamed and twisted away, pulling the knife free as he fell half across the altar. His feet were kicking the floor and he went on screaming.

I grabbed his hair and yanked his head up. Blood was pouring from the eye and everyone in the church was shrieking and shouting like mad. Moonlight gleamed on the blood. I swept the blade across the priest's throat and held the severed flesh open until the black robe was drenched in it. When I knew he was dead, I let him fall back across the altar. I could feel the eyes of the old gods on me again. I could hear them laughing, pleased at what I'd done.

It wasn't just the old gods who were pleased. The people were shouting, but they weren't angry. Some of them were laughing, or cheering. Father O'Mara wasn't the law any more. He wasn't going to punish anyone. Nor that muscled freak, Maul. I looked down on his carcass. He was dead. The people nearest him lifted

114

him up and swung him on to the dais, next to me. Now that I knew they weren't going to attack me, I had time to think clearer. I started to understand what the old gods had planned.

I went to the body of the priest and dragged it right across the altar and spread-eagled it. The people were watching. They were all scared as hell. No one made a move to stop me as I started to strip the clothes from the priest until he was naked. I cut his head off first and I went to the tall stand that had held the cross. I rammed the head on to the top of the stand so that it seemed like it was looking at the crowd. Everyone was silent. Next I went back to the body and opened up the chest. It would have been long and messy work for anyone who didn't know what they were doing, but it was easy for me. I cut out the heart and held it up, letting the moonlight bathe it.

"This is what the gods want!" I shouted. "Not the Jesus god – he lied to you. He always lies! That's why you're all hungry. That's why you hide in this dump!"

There was a long moment of silence. Maybe they thought I was a madman. Then someone shouted, "Yeah!" or something like it and others started doing the same, cheering again. I lowered the heart and bit into it, tearing a bloody bit free and chewing. I put the heart on the altar and went on to cut out the priest's liver. No one made a move to stop me and some of them were shouting encouragement, like when kids are having a fight.

"These are for the gods," I said. I pointed to Maul's body. "And that's for them, too."

"Yes, yes!" they shouted.

"You don't need to eat bowls of soup and stolen vegetables," I told them. It quietened them down. "Why should you grub about in the dirt? You're all half-starving, I can see that. Why should you go hungry? It's time to change all that. Gaz told me this city is full of people like you, hiding away, sneaking out at night. Those others, the ones who live like they did before, they don't give a fuck about you. No one notices when you die. Your Jesus god doesn't."

I went over to the priest and sliced off a length of flesh, holding it up. Now I would really test them.

"Give the old gods their share, then *eat*." Again I chewed the flesh. I cut more of it and flung it out at them.

There was only a small pause, then they were fighting over the

115

meat.

"Eat!" I shouted.

The noise they made came back like an echo. "Eat! Eat! Eat!"

I felt a great surge inside me, like something really big had grabbed hold of me. It felt so good. So good.

That's how it all began.

A SMELL OF BURNING

I woke up and I thought everything was normal, I mean like any other time. Took a while before I knew it wasn't. Something was different. I thought I had a hangover, but I didn't remember drinking. Well, I didn't remember anything. That was the problem. Mind you, I wasn't that bothered. I was comfortable. I was in a bed.

I didn't feel like moving, never mind getting up. Like I wanted to go back to sleep, or just doze. Yeah, comfortable. I did ache a bit. All over. Like I'd run a marathon or something. Couldn't remember. If I tried to stretch my brain and think about it, it made the headache a bit worse.

Okay, so I just stayed put. I didn't recognise the room, but it wasn't right. Didn't know why, just knew. Funny smell. Not a bad one, just strange. Like disinfectant. Medicine? Yeah, that was it. Bits started to fit. I could just about move my head on the big fat pillow and see on either side of me. Restricted vision. One side had a cabinet, with a metal dish and the other side there was a white cupboard. I didn't recognise any of it.

Strip lights overhead, off for now. It was day. There was a window behind me. Couldn't see it, but plenty of light came in from it, so it must be pretty big. There was a door opposite, with a small window in it. Fire glass, with the wire net inside. I recognised that. I did doze again.

When I came to, there was a nurse standing at my bedside. She was a very large black lady, with a brilliant smile. And she was wearing a very white uniform, and had her name on a little tab. It said 'Julie'.

"How are we feeling today, Mr Andrews?" I knew from her voice she was West Indian. Funny that I should know that, but not remember anything about me. She fussed about the pillow and sheets.

I said something and smiled back.

"You've had a tough time," she said, standing back and looking at me like she was trying to decide if I was okay. "You just rest, darlin'. You'll be fine."

117

She was gone before I had time to think of anything to ask her. Like if I needed the toilet. I couldn't tell if I did. Couldn't feel anything below my neck, apart from a sort of all-over ache. Perhaps they'd fixed a tube or two so that I could go automatically. Weird. It didn't seem to matter. Same with grub. I didn't feel hungry.

I must have gone back to sleep. I could hear background noises. Don't know if I was dreaming or just dozing. It kind of merged. You know what I mean.

Later, when the sunlight was fading, so I knew evening was coming on, things started to get a bit weird. I was awake, definitely awake. No change in my condition, still aching and with a slight pain in the head. I could hear distant voices, outside the room. I guessed there was an open ward out there. Maybe the walls were very thin. Plasterboard.

I tried to fix on some of the voices and that's when the weird stuff kicked in. It's hard to describe. I sort of – got up. Not physically. It was like I was standing over myself, looking down at the bed where my body was lying. It was in complete shadow, just a vague shape under the sheets, but I knew it was me. I thought, *fuck it, have I died? Is this my spirit, separated from me?*

Now I couldn't feel anything at all. This was just mind. It didn't feel like a dream, though. It was like I was alive, only floating about, above things. Freaky. It was okay, though. I sort of liked it and stopped panicking about maybe having died. I hadn't, I knew that, somehow. It was kind of fun. I tried to direct myself, you know, move about. A bit like a fish in water, I suppose.

Next thing, I went through the wall. One minute I was in the room, the next I was outside, in a corridor that led to the ward where I'd heard the far off voices. They were quiet now. I drifted towards them and into the ward. I think everyone had been fed and they were settling down for the coming night. I was hovering, up above the rows of beds. I thought someone must see me. I mean, I felt exposed. But I didn't know what they would see. Did I have a body? Or was I just a – what, a ghostly shape? A cloud? Whatever, as I moved down the middle of the ward, just below the high ceiling, no one showed any sign of knowing I was there.

It was fucking brilliant! I remembered then that there was something called an out-of-the-body experience. Someone had told me about it. Said his old man had been dying and had left his body and looked down on himself. Again I worried about it – was my body dead? But the thing was, I *knew* I could go back to it when I wanted to. So I just went on enjoying myself, because that's what I was doing, you know?

One of the people below me, a bloke of about sixty, was fast asleep. And I could see his mind working. Don't ask me how. It was a bit like listening to a radio, turned down. I fixed on it and suddenly I could see the guy's thoughts. He was either dreaming, or thinking about his past, something that had happened to him recently. I just floated around it, watching it, like some weird kind of 3-D TV, right there in the middle of it.

The guy was in a kitchen, a smartly decorated place, fiddling about with the sink taps and talking to this woman. She was his wife. They were nattering on about holidays, going abroad, what they'd read in the papers or seen on the news, stuff like that. It was boring crap, but I was just enjoying the experience of being able to be right there. I could even hear what these people were thinking. It was more confused, jumbled about, but it was amazing to be able to do it. They had no idea I was there. I got flashes of war in Syria, something about rail prices and a fire where several people had died.

I pulled myself away, easy as a bird winging it back up into the sky. The patients were all starting to prepare for lights out. Some were watching TVs on those wall extension arm things. Others had headphones on, listening to music or whatever. As I tuned in, I could hear vague sounds further afield – other wards. Hell, the whole hospital was open to me. I could go anywhere and listen in to anyone!

I must have started to get a bit tired, because I felt myself drawn back to my private ward, like I was being pushed by an invisible tide. I sank down into my physical body and next thing I was lying in the bed, looking up at the ceiling. I was alive, all right. Obviously I was not very strong, but I was okay. The night thickened about me and I must have dropped off.

The next morning the nurse fed me – well, I say fed, but she had to give me liquid food through a tube. I had to suck it up from a plastic beaker-thing. It tasted okay. I was too weak to resist, so I just got on with it. She smiled and told me I was a clever boy, all that bollocks. If I'd had any energy, I'd have felt a right pillock. After she left, saying I needed to rest, I tried to think about what must have happened to me. But when I wanted to remember stuff, my head started to hurt, like it was too much effort. Sod that. I just lay there.

Before long I had the urge to send out my thoughts again, you know, the astral thing or whatever it was. It was easy to do and I felt like I was getting good at it. I sent my mind out into the corridor and hovered there, listening. Just like before, I could hear the babble of voices, but this time my senses must have been a bit more acute, because if I stretched my mind, I could hear even more voices, further away. A lot of them were clearer. It was the same kind of stuff, chatter, news and that.

There was one thing that was different. Hard to explain it – it was like a dark spot. Like someone hiding. I was curious about it. So I tried to focus and move towards it. Not a good idea. I could sense something in that cloud, something fucking nasty. It was like I'd put my hand into a dark place and there was a poison snake in there, invisible but poised to strike. Gave me the shits, I can tell you. I veered away. It was somewhere in the hospital. It was even weirder because I could *smell* that darkness, just as I could hear it. There was a faint smell of burning, a bit like an old one bar electric fire.

I glided along to the open ward and blotted the other thing out by listening to a young guy in a bed below me. He'd broken a leg playing football on a local park. Sunday football. The lads took it too seriously. Never my scene. I didn't care for sport. The memory just struggled into my head, triggered by the young guy's thoughts, but it faded almost at once. His leg was in plaster and he was re-living the game, mentally wincing as he went over the clash that ended with him here. He nudged the thought away and replaced it with a vision of his girlfriend, who was due to visit him later. She was quite pretty. They were having sex together, but he knew he wouldn't be able to do it for a while. His imagination started getting lurid, so I pulled away.

I listened in to the thoughts of a few more people, but the novelty was wearing off. Nothing exciting. Some of it was grubby, sordid, but I didn't want to bother with it. The news from the outside world was not much better. Terrorists and politics. That fire. The police thought it was arson. Some nutter had started it deliberately and there was a big investigation going on. Seven people dead and a lot more injured – some of them here in this hospital. Maybe I should try and find out where they were. I might be able to find something out about what happened. Mind you, I didn't want to get involved with the police – that was another thought that just popped into my head. Avoid the police. I tried to figure out why I should want to do that, but it gave me another headache.

I went back to my body and slept for a while. I wasn't aware of having any dreams. One minute I was asleep, the next I was awake again. Only darkness in between. Physically I was drained. It was easy to doze on and off. There was a TV, on an extending arm, but I didn't want it on, or the radio. Just intermittent sleep. I had no idea how long I was going to be like this, but I didn't care. Too knackered.

It would have been boring as fuck, but for the mental trips I could make. I explored further afield, but each time I went out, that darkness was there, hovering somewhere at the edge of things where I couldn't see clearly. It gave me a kind of sick feeling in the guts, a real terror. It was like I'd had a brush with death, which must be why I was in this place, and death was stalking me, like I'd cheated it and now it was out to get me. That sounds like a fucking film, but I tell you, it felt nasty. Especially as I couldn't share it with anybody, and anyway, they'd have told me not to be an idiot, wouldn't they?

I tried not to think about that darkness, but it nagged and nagged at me. In the end I decided, fuck it, I'll sort this out. I'm not going to be a victim. Strike first. Yeah, that was it. If someone had it in for me, I'd have them. The thought brought a stab of pain. Another memory, trying to squeeze into my head? I shook it off. Not now. I wanted to concentrate on what I was going to do.

It was in the early hours of the morning, the hospital in close to total darkness. Well, they don't switch off all the lights, for obvious reasons, but the wards were silent. Wherever this darkness was hiding, it was likely in a dark place, too. When I sent my mind out, I didn't need light – I just kind of latched on to some sort of energy. Like radio waves – can't see them, but they work.

I wondered if this darkness was someone like me, someone who could send his – or her – mind out. No reason to think I was unique. I was going to have to be sneaky. I didn't know what I had to do to shield myself – you know, hide my mind as it went through the wards and that. I just thought of a mental shield and hoped maybe it would protect me. I went out, ready as I could be for some sort of attack. Hell, I was enjoying it. Scared, but not shitless. Not this time. I was ready to kick arse if I had to. Bring it on, pal.

I found him. It was a bit like coming round a corner and stumbling across a kid playing with his toys, oblivious of anything else. I did the mental equivalent of ducking behind a wall so I could watch. And I saw into that mind. Saw and felt his emotions, what he was thinking about. It was a young boy – well, what I mean is, it was a bloke, but thinking back to when he was a young boy.

He was in some kind of old building, derelict, with a broken roof and just a bit of light coming in, the place mostly in darkness. The kid had a box of matches and some paper. He'd twisted the paper into a rough figure, no bigger than his hand. I knew from his thoughts that it was supposed to represent his old man. I could feel the boy's hate. It was part of what had made the darkness that boiled around him, I'd felt first. His old man had treated him really badly. There was no mother. Just the two of them in a shitty old flat. The old man drank and beat the kid, like he wished he hadn't wanted him around at all. There was worse things. The old man had some sick friends, drunks like him. They'd been allowed to do things to the kid. It was hard to listen in on those thoughts, but something made me stay.

I could feel the kid's anger, like the fire he wanted to start up. He struck a match and watched its flame, holding it up close to his face so that he could feel its little bit of heat. He ignited the paper thing and held it as long as he could, watching it burn, loving the effect as it slowly disintegrated. He was imagining he was burning his old man, I could feel that. It was very powerful. It was also weird, because I could smell the flames and the smoke, the charred paper.

There was a period of calmness after that, like the kid had withdrawn into himself, and although I still sensed his thoughts, they were jumbled and random and I couldn't make any sense of them. He still didn't know someone was listening in. Just as well, because I got the idea that if he'd known he'd have sent something after me, some kind of mental attack. I could feel that sort of black power coiled up inside him there, part of the hatred that fuelled him.

More images started to assemble themselves in his mind and he was older, about twelve, still with his old man, but no longer abused or as mistreated – the old man was a wreck and hardly able to look after himself. The boy tolerated him, got money off him for food, but had to fight to get it because the old man would have spent the lot on booze. The kid's hatred hadn't abated. He wasn't muscular, but he was physically fairly strong. He needed to be. Other kids bullied him, taking the piss out of him because his clothes were shoddy and he looked scruffy and dirty. The water in the flat wasn't always working, nor the electricity.

The boy relived an incident, again with fire, when he'd gone to a local dumping place near a canal. There was a broken-down fence and a narrow plot of overgrown land where tippers had had their fill. Old stoves, bits of machinery, chunks of timber, window frames, doors, and bags and bags of rubbish, just dumped in a great heap, fly-blown and neglected by the Council. They knew if they cleared it up, it would only come back again. The boy had dug himself a tunnel into one part of it, a secret retreat. There were a couple of gangs of kids who hung about the place and the boy realised they'd cottoned on to him, so he decided to quit the place, but not before he'd scared them shitless.

He siphoned some petrol out of a couple of cars parked in a cul-de-sac near the tip and sloshed it about inside his tunnel den, soaking the old planks and broken kitchen units. Then he set fire to it and scuttled away along the canal bank, crossing a footbridge and hiding among the trees of the park that backed on to that side. He was able to watch without being detected. Several of the kids in one of the gangs were in the tip, and they came out of there like rabbits, terrified. For a few glorious minutes it looked like one of them had been trapped and was going to be incinerated in the tip. It had become an inferno, smoke pouring into the night sky, flecked with scores of glowing embers. Things popped and cracked dangerously, especially the aerosol cans that went off like bombs, a couple doused by the murky canal waters.

The boy was ecstatic. I could feel him reliving that joy. It was like a sexual thrill. He had a hard on. Especially seeing as how he thought he'd snared one of the other kids. He hadn't, because the kid came flying out of the smoke, coughing his guts up, then spewing. They all ran away, frightened that the Fire Brigade would find them and blame the fire on them.

The boy headed home and when his old man got back from the pub, too drunk to speak, the boy was ready to defend himself if he had to – he *wanted* to. He was glowing, like the fire had filled him with a new energy. The old man just collapsed into bed. No one ever suspected the boy of starting the fire.

Or the others he started afterwards. It was easy to find old places, more dumps, broken down houses, empty factories and warehouses. There were enough shit heaps in the city to provide him with targets. He didn't always stay to watch – too risky. He had to stop for a while because the newspapers reckoned there was a pyromaniac on the loose, so the police and everyone else were on the lookout. The boy just kept to himself. I could feel his smug satisfaction. Also his frustration. The burnings really had become like a sexual drug now. Abstention got harder. The craving got stronger. I could feel that cloud of darkness, swollen with malevolence.

I went back to my private ward and slipped down into my body. Although I'd got a kinky thrill from what I'd shared with that twisted mind, I was scared. I was sure that if the guy got any kind of hint that someone had peered into his world, he'd come looking and fuck knew what he was capable of. Yet in spite of that, I knew I'd be drawn back for more. I wanted the rest of that story.

The next day I remembered some of the things I'd heard other minds sharing, out in the main ward. Things from the news. There'd been a fire. Seemed like it hadn't been too far away from the hospital. Seven people had died. Arson suspected. Shit, it couldn't be –

Had I stumbled across the fire starter? Was that his mind I'd looked into? Maybe he'd been a victim of the fire he'd set and that's why he was here in hospital somewhere. Did anyone know? The police?

I still couldn't move. I'd seen the full extent of the tubes and wires plugged into my body. Hell, I was still pissing and shitting through a system of tubes. The West Indian nurse, Julie, changed my clothes and washed me, helped by another nurse, not that I felt anything. They jabbered on a bit and I tried to speak, but couldn't. I wouldn't have been able to write either, so there was no way I could do anything about the contact I'd made.

That night I went out again. I couldn't stop myself now and I was even more drawn to the darkness, like I was being pulled.

124

Luckily I was still outside the guy's radar. While I went outwards, he must have gone inside himself, going over his past. I could watch it, carefully, without him knowing, but I was still afraid of him. He had it in him to cause real pain.

His old man had died and he was put into care. I could feel his relief and the way he still felt pleased with himself because the home that he was sent to was staffed with people who felt sorry for him and did nice things for him, at least, better than his old man had done. It was easy to pretend to be a quiet kid who didn't cause any bother. What was a problem was that he didn't have the freedom he'd had living in the flat. He couldn't go out any time and worse, there was no chance of any fire games. He went to a new school, where he mixed with some other kids who'd had more or less the same kind of life he'd had and that's when he'd got his next fire going.

One of the kids had got some matches and there was an old shed at the edge of the playing fields, full of sports stuff, a lot of it made from wood. Old desks and chairs, too. The kid showed the others how to get petrol and in the end they set the shed alight. Caused a riot with the school staff. Fire Brigade, all that. Some twat snitched, though, and the kid and his mates were rumbled. They were all split up.

He knew he was being watched after that. He had to keep to himself and forget about using fire. They'd stick him in a remand home if they caught him. It was frustrating, but he was patient. No more fires until he was old enough to quit school. I got a lot of very jumbled stuff after that, as if the guy wasn't particularly focusing on his past. It seemed like it was all balling up, creating that congealed darkness that brought me to him. I wasn't getting anything worthwhile, so I was about to go back.

He must have jumped forward in his thoughts. Like me, he had been listening to the patients in this hospital and their conversations about the fire. It really got him going again and I could feel that sexual excitement, like he was burning up with it. He *had* started that fire! It was in a row of terraced houses, about a mile from the hospital. He'd been living there, with a small group. I saw them, their faces. They were a bunch of losers, dossers the lot of them. Some were on drugs, others made their way thieving and there were two girls who were on the game.

The guy had sort of shacked up with one of them, Stella. She had a pimp, some older bloke who came to the house every now and then. He was okay for money. Ran a chain of these girls and creamed off most of the money. He owned the house and what he said went. And he didn't like the guy messing about with Stella. Warned him off. Had him beaten up. The guy and Stella still had a thing going, so the pimp chucked him out. Threatened to kill Stella if she saw the guy again. When the guy was thinking about that, his darkness boiled up and it was like I was suddenly caught in a cloud of thick, choking smoke. It really freaked me out. Anger into fire. The fire of Hell as far as that pimp bastard was concerned.

The guy planned things carefully and I could see it now, all that work, putting paper and wood and inflammable stuff under the floorboards, into old cupboards. No one had a clue that he was doing it. There was an old gas cooker in the house. It would never have passed an inspection. Leaking gas, a wonder it didn't go off. The guy knew all about that. He waited for the right moment. He knew that the pimp and his shitty mates liked to use the house sometimes for a party. They'd bring a group of other men, men with a bit of money to spend, and Stella and the other prostitutes would have to take part in the entertainment, whatever the men's sick minds could dream up.

One night, when a party had been planned, the guy and the other ones in the house had all been told to fuck off for a day or two. The guy warned Stella to keep away. She was frightened because she didn't think she could do it. She was expected to be there when the pimp's people arrived. It was going to be tough slipping out. The guy didn't tell her what he'd planned.

He'd sneaked in and run a trail of oil under the kitchen floorboards and out into the yard. It had been easy to do, the mess outside covered up with rubbish and other crap that no one ever bothered with. The pimp and his mates wouldn't be coming out here anyway. The guy ran the oil down a broken pipe in the yard right to the back gate, blocking its escape into the drain, so that it just congealed, invisible in the night.

The night of the party, the guy waited beyond the back gate, hidden in the alley. He'd arranged with Stella that she'd get out of the house just after one in the morning, just for a fag break and some air, something that wouldn't make the customers suspicious. It would have gone well, but for one thing. Stella hadn't got out of the house. She was supposed to go out the front door and he didn't realise she hadn't been able to do it. So when he ignited the oil, she was still inside.

He watched as the oil flared, right up the broken drain to the pile of rubbish, which caught and then sent flames inside the kitchen, under its floor, beside that old gas cooker. When it went, it went like a fucking volcano. Even just listening in and watching the guy's thoughts, I could feel everything, like I was there. Coupled with his ecstasy – man, he was so worked up, so amazingly high on excitement as the fire roared into life in the house. Then he saw a face at an upstairs window. Stella. Trapped inside.

I felt his terror. Knowing she was going to be torched along with the pimps and the others. He ran to the back door, which was already hanging off its hinges. Smoke poured out from the wrecked kitchen and flames licked at everything. He tried several times to get in, knowing that he was risking his life doing it. He was coughing his guts up and his skin was so hot he thought it would just boil off him. In the end he was forced back and he collapsed in the yard. The building had quickly become an inferno. His last vision of it as its roof fell in and walls started to collapse was when someone dragged him away, still screaming, both in frustration and searing agony.

I must have let out some kind of mental cry in sympathy with him as he recalled the nightmare events, because now, in the hospital, he had become aware that someone was listening in, watching him, studying the images he was sifting in his mind. I felt his attention swivel towards me, like the beam of a lighthouse. It hit me, hot and angry, like those flames. It was like I was going to be scorched, burned up just like the pimps and that girl Stella and all the others in the house. Seven had died, it had said on the news.

I withdrew. If I'd been in my body, I'd have run like fuck. Like something out of Hell was after me. I was surrounded by darkness and I could smell that thick smoke now, clouds of it and it seemed to get into my lungs. It must be what the guy was sending. I told myself it had to be my imagination. No way was there a fire in the hospital. It stopped me from seeing and I was just blundering about. I knew he was after me. I could feel his hatred, like a hot knife in the guts, twisting, barbed and pulling me back.

If I could just get to my body… But then I thought, *what if he sees me, where I am, who I am? Is he like me, bed-bound, or can he move his physical body?* If he could, then he could find his way to me physically. And if he could do that, what would stop him doing something nasty – shit, this guy was that screwed up, he could kill me. Sure, that's what he'd do, to protect himself. Christ, he might even start another fire. He wouldn't care about the consequences, I knew that from what I'd touched in his warped mind.

I veered away from my single ward. What I should do was find him. If I could do that, I'd see whether he could move. If not, that was okay, I could at least get back and feel a bit safer. If he could move – but I didn't want to think about that, not yet.

So I twisted this way and that inside the hospital in my mental form, slowly easing out of the thick shadows that were trying to stream around me and drag me into the guy's personal darkness. The smoke thinned and I got to another big ward that I hadn't seen before. I was able to move faster. I could still feel the guy pursuing me, the intensity of his raw hatred closing in, just out of sight, screened by that mental blanket. I felt like I was just inching ahead of him, a claw's length from being snared.

I got a bit further away, straining my head, my own blanket. Maybe I was better than him at this. Maybe he'd only just learned the trick. Whatever, I was just glad to avoid him grabbing me. I reckoned his touch would be like fire, like he could scorch the flesh off me.

I hunted through each ward, looking for a clue that would identify him before he got me. I realised that it was impossible. There were hundreds of patients, on several floors. It could take all night.

In the end, I got lucky. I twisted and turned into a corridor, free for a moment, when I heard two nurses talking to each other. They mentioned a man who'd been badly burned, in a ward on his own, who they were keeping an eye on, given his condition. I followed one of them. I knew it would soon be dawn and I wanted to be back in my body by then.

I followed the nurse into a small room and I knew at once I'd found the guy. It was dark and the nurse used a very low lamp to study the patient. Of course, he was still out of his body, looking for me, maybe just an eye-blink away behind me. This was my one chance of seeing him without being discovered.

There was no way the guy could move. The nurse checked his

128

arms, which were bandaged up and I guessed the rest of him was swathed like a mummy. He wasn't going to be able to get up and physically hunt me down after all. I could go back and shut myself into my body, where he couldn't harm me. Somehow I'd find a way to alert people about him, who he was.

I moved closer, mentally listening for anything beyond the room that would warn me his mental form was returning. His head was bandaged up, only his face showing. I could see it in the wan light, that ravaged, fire-burned face. Terrible, ruined, that mess of a face. But I knew it. I knew that face.

It was mine.

NOT IF YOU WANT TO LIVE

It is evident that if we are to run our Redeemer programme successfully, we will need to exercise proper control over its components, while at the same time, allowing them enough freedom of choice to be able to function efficiently. After all, they will have been chosen because of their own unique skills, traits and reactions to any given situation. These are their essential tools and we would be falling short of our expectations for the Redeemer programme if we were merely creating corporate clones, no matter how pliant we made them. To this end we have developed the selective memory treatment, a process that is chemically introduced into our Redeemers at the time of transfer from their primary lifetimes to their next level of existence as Redeemers. It goes without saying that they are completely unaware of the treatment.

Part One

You have to die several times before your mind is able to adjust itself and accept the radical concept of surviving the experience. Shifting from life to death and back again eventually does become routine, but it takes a bit of getting used to. It's understandable: we're born with a survival instinct that conditions us to avoid death at all costs and we're conditioned to think of death as final, the end of life and its freedom of choices.

I suppose it can be. Well, as I've come to understand things now, it can be that simple. There's always the Great Beyond, in its many guises, and I'm sure that's not life as we know it. I've not been there, so I can only speculate. It could be the best fun you ever had, or then again, something very, very different. For me and others like me death has become a transition. For the time being, anyhow.

The first time I died, I didn't think I had. Hell, I *thought* I must have, given that I had been pumped so full of lead I'd have sunk to the bottom of the sea if they'd dumped me in it. They probably would have, if we'd been anywhere near it. So – I woke up in a bare room, clean walls, just one very moth-eared armchair in which I was slouched. The springs had gone and the stuffing was hanging out of it in places where a succession of previous tenants had pulled at it, probably nervously.

There was a light bulb, no shade. A hundred watts, judging by the harsh brightness. A door, newly painted, white. So what was this, a hospital? Two dozen bullets, some lodged in or passing through vital organs, including my heart, and I was *alive*. That would be a miracle, if not several. I tried my fingers: all in working order. Arms, legs and so on. The same. And no pain. Maybe I'd been filled with anaesthetic.

How long had I been here? My watch had stopped. I was wearing the same suit I had died in – that is to say, been shot-up in. No bullet-proof vest or armour of any kind. I pushed my jacket lapels aside and undid a couple of shirt buttons, slipping my hand inside and poking around my chest and upper body. My last memory had been those bullets hitting and the pain that had gone with it. Not a scratch. Weird. Surgery had made great strides, but there were always scars. Not on me, it seemed. I was even more surprised when the realisation hit me that the suit was undamaged, too.

I stood up. Felt fine. No dizziness, no reaction. I walked about, did a few basic exercises. Inevitably I started to smile. This was pretty damn cool. Alive and kicking. I did wonder about this being some way-out kind of death-dream, but my basic instinct, also intact, told me that was bullshit. This was no dream. This was reality. I had survived the impossible. Two dozen bullets at almost point blank range and I had survived. So now what? Mephistopheles would show up and say, you owe me?

That's not quite how it works, but it's a variation on a theme.

When the door opened, I stiffened. I was expecting a man in a white coat with a needle. It was a guy in a suit. Expensive, stylish, but otherwise there was nothing about his habiliment to explain the situation. He waved me back to the prediluvian armchair and as I sat in it he folded his arms. He had a nondescript, pinched face, eyes sharp, sort of military cut hair. I guessed he was in his late twenties.

"How are you feeling?" The tone of his voice suggested he didn't really give much of a damn about how I was feeling.

I would have said, *like death warmed up*, but actually I felt pretty good. I said so.

He nodded. "This will be a fresh start. A new life. In a manner of speaking."

"Where is this place?"

"It doesn't really have a name," he said, as though that explained everything. "Think of it as a way station. Or a base. The place you always come back to, now that you're here."

I got the feeling I could have thrown a dozen questions at him and all I would get back would be conundrums. If he wanted to explain anything to me, he'd do it. I let it pass – at the moment I was still feeling relieved. Presumably that would fade.

"There are a number of ways you can leave this place," he said. I had the impression he had had this conversation with others like me. People who should have been dead, I mean. "You can either go on to the, shall we say, Afterlife, or you can remain here and make yourself useful. For an unspecified time."

"By Afterlife, you mean either the Elysian Fields, or the place where they spend most of their time tending the furnaces?" I was still feeling light-headed. Flippancy came easily.

"That's a very simplistic summary, but it'll do. There are so many variations. But they're not your concern right now. If and when you do get to move on, it will be dealt with by another department. Here, we are only concerned with our own specific duties."

"And do I get a choice?"

"You do."

"That's settled, then. I'll take the Elysian Fields. Or whichever one of the variations is most desirable. Is there a brochure?"

"I'm afraid it doesn't work like that. You can choose the Afterlife, of course. But which of its many destinations you are sent to is out of your hands."

"No doubt that depends on whether I've lived the life of a saint or a sinner." Which would mean the slag heaps, for sure. If Saint Michael was out there somewhere, running a performance management review of my life, I would have missed all the targets. Dismissal on grounds of incompetence.

"You're catching on," he said, condescendingly, I thought.

"And if I stay here, how do I make myself useful, as you put it?"

He nodded, as though assuming I'd made my decision. Let's face it, the decision had been made for me. This was all bizarre anyway, so I just played along. He was very convincing in his role, I'll concede that. If the lunatics had taken over the asylum, he was making a more than passable job of disguising his part in it.

"We have it in mind to make you a Redeemer," he said. I waited for him to expand on this. "It will give you certain powers. And a significant amount of freedom of movement, within the parameters of your duties, of course. There's no contract of employment, but you will be bound to us. If you – overreach yourself – we'll set you back on the path."

"The straight and narrow?"

"Probably not. More likely to be devious and convoluted. But we'll always be there to keep an eye on things."

So I'll be on a leash, I thought. "When do I start?"

He smiled, but it was a cold, official smile. Perhaps he was a cybernetic organism, or whatever they called them here. "With immediate effect. If that's acceptable. Or if you want more time to weigh your options –"

"No. Let's do this."

"You'll need a name." He meant a new one, which was fine by me. I would be glad to drop the old one. As it happened, I couldn't remember it anyway.

"How would Razorjack suit you?" he said.

I would have laughed, but he was quite serious. No hint of a smile. Okay, I'd play along. Razorjack it would be, although I couldn't recall anything about using blades. This whole vagueness of memory didn't bother me, though. A hail of bullets had sent me here and I wasn't so sure I wanted to relive all the gory details. I think someone called it blissful ignorance.

"So, who do I redeem?"

*

I began my training. I thought of this place as Purgatory, though no one tried to cleanse my soul or review my past sins and help me to expiate them. It was simply a way station, like the man said. I saw him and no one else. We never called each other by name – I never knew his. While I was here, I didn't eat, excrete or do anything other than communicate. I didn't sleep – day and night didn't exist. I just learned what being a Redeemer meant. I fell into my new incarnation – another convenient but inaccurate word –

almost at once, accepting it and getting on with it. If I'm honest, it was fascinating and beat the crap out of where I'd been before. Most of that had become increasingly vague, like a retreating train. It suited me. Evidently my life had been a mess, from what little I could recall.

They gave me some basic stuff to begin with. The weird part was the transition from base to field. By field I mean the world as I had known it. Same place, same time, same people, I assumed. And likewise getting back to base after fieldwork. That could mean a number of things, the strangest of which was a kind of re-death. Mercifully painless, but not entirely comfortable. Then I botched one of my jobs and got killed again. Woke up back at base.

"It happens," said my ubiquitous mentor. "Very few get it right every time in the early days. Redeemers tend to think of themselves as immortal. In a way they are. But in the field it is important not to get careless. Or arrogant."

Maybe that was a clue to the old me, but if I'd started out here that way, I damn soon had it knocked out of me. I got wise. More proficient. More difficult to kill in the field. I took the view that Redeemers who kept on being rubbed out would eventually be considered inefficient and then they'd be moved on. I wanted to move on when I was ready and not before.

So what does a Redeemer do? It's a kind of rescue mission. Most people who die simply move on to the Afterlife. There's no way station, like there was for me. Death is generally a straight transition. For a small number of people, it's not that simple. They go into limbo and they're on hold until a decision is made about whether they go on or back. We're not talking about reincarnation. I suppose you could call it resuscitation. It takes unusual circumstances, but when you think of the millions who die all the time, there's bound to be a few glitches.

If you get blown apart by a bomb, or burned alive or die any one of a hundred nasty, comprehensive ways, you're not going to be revived. If you get riddled by bullets like I was, you're not going to be revived, but you could be pulled out of the stream of things and used. Otherwise, condition permitting, you could be Redeemed. I have no idea who decides about Redemption – like my man tells me, that's controlled by another department. And we don't have inter-departmental meetings. All I know is that when a subject is fit to be Redeemed, I'm called upon to undertake the necessary procedures. I go back and tend to the details.

They gave me an easy one first time out. Young guy, in his late teens. Not long qualified, bright future. Car accident that left him with minor injuries, but also put him in a coma. He died after three weeks. I was there within minutes, did what I had been trained to do and *voila*, he came round. There was a bit of fuss among the medics, but the dust settled and the kid got up and walked. Got on with his life. As for me, I could have been a ghost, which would be appropriate.

"So where does that fit in with the Grand Scheme of Things?" I asked my mentor.

"If such a thing exists," he said, dryly, "it's not our concern here."

"That would be another department, yes?"

"You learn quickly, Razorjack." He didn't use my name very often, but when he did, he made it sound like a minor rank, rather than a personal cognomen. I knew my place. I was getting used to it.

Out in the field, in the world I had known, I enjoyed the pleasures of the flesh just as I must have done in life. I wasn't profligate with them. In fact, I was pretty restrained, whatever I'd been inclined to in my original life. More and more, though, that life was almost lost to me, though I felt no sense of loss. In my new role, I kept to myself. I had a gut feeling that I'd always been a loner and now I was almost aloof from society. And I was sharp. I mean, at surviving. I had occasional glimpses – visions, memories maybe – of being in the Army, fighting in the desert, which would toughen anyone up – you learned how to stay alive. Now I was quicker, slicker and if anyone was going to kill me this time around, they were going to have to be exceptional. I liked to think that, as far as Redeemers went, they didn't come better. Maybe it was the arrogance my mentor had warned me about, but to me it was just part of surviving.

*

I didn't have much notion of time, except when I was in the field, when I lived by everyone else's clock. So I had no idea how long I'd been at my new role. I'd been back several times and Redeemed a number of people, but it soon got to be run of the mill.

136

I had this feeling that there was more to the Afterlife than this. Maybe I was being groomed for something a bit more – interesting. Apart from that clumsy early outing when I died for the second time, I came back by the less dramatic route, a kind of deep sleep process, waking up at base in my favourite battered armchair.

I was used to prompt meetings with my mentor, but there came a time when it was a different guy watching me reviving. He was older, had a tougher demeanour and wore a similar bland but expensive-looking suit. And he'd brought a chair. Not an armchair, just a simple wooden thing, like something out of a cheap kitchen. The furnishings department here must be running on empty.

"Razorjack," he said, pronouncing it like a sentence. His neutral gaze met mine as though he was sizing up a piece of machinery. Maybe he was. "How do you rate your performance so far?"

As I said, my memory of my original life seemed to be pretty sporadic, but obviously I could go back into what I will call for convenience, the live world, and I was required to. The world itself was familiar, if not my old life in it. This new guy's question had a familiar ring to it. It must have been the sort of thing I had been used to hearing, on a par with such things as risk assessments.

"The work's not a problem in itself," I replied. "Tedious, now that I'm used to it. But I do it well enough. It's difficult to excel at stacking shelves, if you get me."

My bluntness slipped off him like water off a duck's back. His expression remained impassive. "Yes, I'd come to that conclusion. So it's time for something a little more challenging."

"I'm up for it."

"Good. The Powers that Be have asked me to set things in motion. Your new task will be far more complex and there's a good chance that it could go wrong. That would not be desirable. A lot will be depending on you."

"So you're taking a calculated risk in sending me on this new mission?"

"Yes, I think that frames it very succinctly. A calculated risk."

"Can I ask a question?"

"Of course."

"Why don't the Powers that Be just organise things to suit

themselves? Divine power, ultimate power, doesn't it just – act? Why use middle men who could screw things up?"

"Life and death are not that simple. There has to be an element of chance, even here. Let's just say, if everything was pre-ordained and free will didn't exist, well, things would be excruciatingly dull, wouldn't they? In the same way that complete randomness would lead to utter chaos – everything would soon collapse. Existence needs to be balanced."

"And we adjust the scales."

"Your perception is flawless. Thus, whenever you are sent on a task, you will always have the capacity to succeed or fail. Should you fail, the problem and its consequences will have to be re-addressed and solved in another way."

"But not by me?"

"Quite. Your time with us would be at an end."

That wasn't an option I cared to contemplate. "Okay, so what's the brief?"

*

In the live world they set me up in an office in a part of the city where the world in general would pass me by. My front was an agency that specialised in looking for missing persons. Pretty dull stuff, but I had three members of staff who ran the business. Surprisingly to me it was busy. I let them get on with it. No questions, either way. I kept to myself. No one consulted me unless they had to, which was hardly at all. I was a free agent.

"You'll be sought out," my new mentor had told me as part of my briefing. "The man who will want to hire your services is called Silvio Fellini. He runs something of an empire and is very powerful. His influence extends from the lowest levels of society to government itself. He is probably as dangerous a man as you could meet."

"He'll want me to find somebody?"

"Oh yes. But he will know what you are. He'll want to utilise you as a Redeemer."

"He knows about such things? How come?"

"He's being groomed by our Adversaries. They see him as a useful tool in their own aspirations. He's prepared to make his entire operation available to them in exchange for what he wants."

138

"Sell his soul to the Devil?"

"That's a very medieval way of putting it. But if it helps you to understand the situation, it's an image that will suffice, if a crude one. Silvio Fellini had a young wife, whom he adored. Recently, she died. An overdose. She can be Redeemed. Fellini is obsessed with her. He wants her back. He will seek to engage you for just that reason."

The logic of all this was yet to make itself apparent to me. If Fellini got what he wanted, the Adversaries got what they wanted. How did that help my side?

"You will be dealing with one of our Adversaries. It is very unusual, almost unprecedented, for one of them to enter the world and expose himself this way. It gives us an opportunity to capitalise."

"You want me to rub him out."

He almost smiled. I could feel it behind that mask. "Your use of imagery is very colourful. Nevertheless, there is something in what you say. The Adversary cannot be eliminated in the sense that you mean, but he can be brought to us." His eyes momentarily lit up at the prospect of capturing an enemy. Obviously it was a big deal.

So there I was, sitting in my live world office, waiting. From time to time I left it, establishing a pattern of coming and going that Silvio Fellini and his nameless master would be able to observe from a distance. The business of a Redeemer, moving between life and his base, would apparently be known to them. As far as they should be able to see, I wasn't doing anything that they would regard as suspicious. Just a regular guy getting on with his work. Ripe for an approach.

Fellini sent one of his minions. I played the game. I made a fuss about not being for hire and so on, but in the end capitulated in what I hoped was a convincing way. If I made it too easy for them, they might smell a rat. I got into the Bentley, a very flash, extremely expensive auto and was driven out into the plush end of town. Fellini's place was like a palace and it was guarded like a fortress. More guns than a barracks. He could afford it. He probably had shares in the military.

I waited in an annex, studying the paintings and antiques that were on display. Everything reeked of money. I reckoned that Fellini was the kind of man who bought whatever he wanted, no matter what it was or what it took. I looked out through a huge window. It was night but floodlights washed elegant lawns that stretched away across grounds that were more park than garden. A door opened and I turned to meet the calculated gaze of a man who looked perfectly at home among the ostentatious surroundings.

Silvio Fellini was in his late sixties, of medium height and with a bald, shining pate. There were dark bags under his eyes, his face grim, as though smiling was alien to him, for all his wealth. He wore a dark suit that would have cost what some people earn in a year. It fitted him well but did not completely disguise his bulky figure. I could see he liked rich food as well as all the other pleasures of an expensive lifestyle. He came into the room and stared at me, not quite openly hostile, but there was no love lost in that glare.

My attention was taken by one of the three men with him. Two were, I assumed, body guards. Athletic and lithe, good looking young men, doubtless armed and dangerous. The third, however, was in a different league. My mentor had prepared me for this meeting, but even so, I was struck by the nature of the Adversary. He was very tall and imposing, his skin an unusual tan, his features perfectly proportioned, his eyes as bright as crystal. I suppose you would say he was extraordinarily beautiful, but in a masculine sort of way. His hands were long, like the delicate hands of a musician, but there was nothing soft about them, as if they could become claws at a moment's notice. His hair was silver, or as near as dammit, falling like silk around his ears and on to his neck.

I waited for someone to speak. The air was warm, but the atmosphere very taut.

"You have been told why I asked you to come here?" said Fellini. He seemed to be forcing the words out, almost reluctantly, as though speaking to me was beneath him. He was a man who didn't like being beholden to anyone. He needed my services and he didn't like to be at a disadvantage.

"I told your man I'm not for hire, but that I'd listen to what you wanted."

Fellini's scowl deepened, mirrored by that of his two hired guns. I paid no attention to either of them, looking at the fourth man instead. The Adversary was smiling, as though approving my mild show of bravado. He lifted his hand as if to say, *I'll take it from here*, like he was conducting an orchestra. Fellini's teeth were barred against his anger.

"We know who you really work for, of course," said the Adversary. He had a strong voice, an accent that could have been almost anything European. It was deceptively warm, designed, naturally, to soothe those he met. I nodded slowly, waiting.

"The nature of your work makes it exclusive to them. It is not something to be hired out or made light of. We quite understand that. But if you were to undertake an assignment for Mr Fellini, you would be compensated accordingly."

I said nothing, ignoring Fellini's animosity.

"I would like to think that what we could offer you would be far more satisfying than your current employment. All that tedious commuting, those wearisome errands. How long will it go on for? I imagine you'd like to break the chain. Stretch yourself a little."

"That's not for me to say."

"Oh, but it is. There is so much more. In your current capacity, you are a retriever. We are well aware of the arrangements. And we know who controls you."

"What is it you want of me?"

"Mr Fellini would like you to Redeem his wife. She died recently. In rather unfortunate circumstances." He walked across to an ornate writing desk. On top of it there were a few framed photographs and he brought one to me and held it out.

I took it and found myself looking at the face of a particularly beautiful woman. She was about thirty, her expression amused, slightly coquettish for the camera. It was the sort of face you'd see on the top fashion magazines. Maybe she had been a model, or a film starlet. Certainly she had the looks.

"This is Mrs Fellini, I take it?" I said.

"It is," said the Adversary. "In the flower of life. That was taken a few months ago." He put the picture back carefully. Behind him, Fellini was staring out at the lawn, again holding in his emotions.

"So what were the circumstances of her death?" I saw Fellini's fists bunch like hams. But he didn't otherwise move.

"She was having an affair with one of Mr Fellini's employees. Mr Fellini discovered this. You have no need to know the details, or what happened to him. Mrs Fellini, saddened by his removal, committed suicide. She took an overdose. As you will know, in such cases, the body can be Redeemed. We have preserved it against damage. It is not too late."

"I'd have thought people like you would have had the power to do it yourselves," I said.

"Of course. However, there would be a different set of consequences." He smiled again, but there was nothing remotely pleasant in his expression.

Fellini turned and favoured me with another scathing look. "Can you do this thing?"

I nodded. "I'm capable of it, yes. But are you able to protect me from the reactions of my masters? If I step beyond my brief, I'll be in hot water. And I do mean hot."

The Adversary laughed softly, as if he appreciated my little joke. "Your sense of humour does you credit. But you are quite correct. Failure to adhere to your brief would indeed bring disastrous consequences. However, it does not have to be so. There are many powers. I have powers invested in me. I am not a Redeemer, but I do have the power to recruit. Do this thing and you can have what you wish."

"You mean I'd have to switch sides?"

"It would be so much more rewarding. There would be no reprisals. You'd simply be one of us. A conversion to our faith. We are all used to winning or losing. We don't bear grudges. We just – adapt."

"And if I don't accept?" I smiled insouciantly.

I could feel Fellini's eyes burning into me but I ignored him and looked at the Adversary. He was smiling himself, but there was undeniable steel in his own gaze. "We can offer an alternative incentive."

"I'm guessing it would be more painful."

"Surely we don't need to go down such a path. Of course, now that we have approached you and shown our hand, as it were, we need to be circumspect. We should hate your superiors hearing of this discussion. That would not be in our interests at all. We would need to rely on your discretion, indeed – your silence."

"So you'd kill me?"

"You're not thinking this through. If we killed you, you'd go straight back to your base. That wouldn't do at all. No, no. We would have to do something far more – let's say, soul-destroying. A kind of imprisonment. Entropy. You'd be completely isolated, immobile, totally de-activated. Can you think of anything worse?"

"I'm warming to your offer."

"We don't have a lot of time," said the Adversary, suddenly becoming more brisk. "We need to show you something." He turned on his heel and led the way from the room. Fellini fell in step beside him and the two young men got behind me. They would have had orders not to kill me, of course. Maim, perhaps, a shot or two in the legs. But not kill. Fellini didn't want me sent back to my base.

We moved to lower levels of the amazing building, into a long vault, its far end lit by dimmed strips. This area reminded me of a hospital, clinical, sanitised and minimal. I was taken to a long, metal table. It was fed by tubes and thin, glass pipes and in the background I could hear the muffled drone of motors and machines. Lying on the table, under a transparent cover was who I took to be Fellini's wife, wearing a simple dress and flat-heeled shoes, seemingly asleep. She was dead, of course, but this bio-system was here to provide a kind of stasis, a unique means of preventing her from moving on. There would be a time limit on that and ultimately she would simply decay.

Her face was serene, eyes closed. I was struck again by her remarkable beauty. Ironically, given the manner of her death and her condition, she was the sort of person that I was usually commissioned to Redeem.

"She's dead," said the Adversary superfluously. "Matters will be taken out of our hands all too soon. We've been able to suspend things temporarily. It's up to you now."

I nodded. "Okay."

We left the sleeping princess and went back up into the building above. Fellini and his henchmen disappeared, leaving me to sit in another plush room with the Adversary.

"There are a number of things I can offer you. For example, if you want to spend some time in this world, alive and well, before taking up your new post, I can arrange it. You can live a long, protected life, let's say, until you're sixty? How would that suit? Or you can cut to the chase and begin working for me with immediate effect, once you've Redeemed Mrs Fellini. Either way, there will be substantial opportunities. You probably don't remember much about your life?"

"They scrub the slate pretty clean. They just leave the essentials. I guess the rest would be inconvenient."

"It would be of no use to you now. You should start anew. It is bound to be a lot more satisfying. We have some very interesting things planned. You have everything to gain."

"And my current employer is just going to write me off?"

"The fact is, you're a very small cog in their wheels. They will simply replace you."

"The Afterlife goes on."

He smiled again. "That's the one thing you can be sure of."

*

The Adversary – he went under the name Villefranche – was alone with me, looking down at Mrs Rebecca Fellini. Her husband and his toughs had not returned. It suited me. I didn't much care for Fellini's withering looks, though I was impervious to his moodiness.

"How long does the transition take?" said Villefranche.

"It depends. Usually not long." I looked at the watch I was wearing. "The switch across usually brings me out somewhere close by the subject. I reach out and bring them back. But if we get separated on the other side and it takes me longer, we could end up some distance away from here. In which case, you'll have to wait for me to re-route." I tapped my watch. "Time over there doesn't relate to time here. If I leave now, at best I could be back with Mrs Fellini within a few minutes."

"And if not?"

"At worst I'd end up back here but anything up to twenty miles away. If that happens, it's not a problem, but I'd suggest Mrs Fellini gets some rest overnight and I bring her back to you in the morning at, say, eight am. She may be a bit confused – they often are. I can have her relaxed and adjusted by eight."

"And if you don't get back here by eight?"

"Let's worry about that if and when it happens. It's not likely."

He nodded as though prepared to accept what I'd said – I had nothing to gain by lying. I motioned for him to step well back and began the working. It was very straightforward. I lifted the transparent lid and set it aside. I took each of Mrs Fellini's hands in mine. They were very cold, almost icy.

Transition was instantaneous. Villefranche would have simply seen me and Mrs Fellini fade out quickly like figures on a movie screen, leaving him alone.

I knew from recent experience that there were a number of possibilities on the other side, in the limbo between the live world and Beyond. I would have hardly any time to adjust and act. There are various transport arrangements for delivering those who pass over to their ultimate destinations, of which there are many. On this occasion, we were on the rail network that runs underground, although that's my own rationalisation of what it is, the best comparison I can make. I was relatively new to Redeeming, so I still used familiar imagery from my garbled memories. It gave me a basis to work around, given that there was no other immediate support.

I came out of transition alone, which often happened. If you were lucky, the subject was either still holding hands or close by. All it needed was a touch and they would be back with you in the live world, mission accomplished. It was that simple. In most of my retrievals, I had had to do a little work finding the subject before making the transition back. The main problem was not the timing. Time here meant nothing, frozen in relation to the live world.

What you had to look out for and avoid were the Androgynes. They were run by yet another department and had their own strict code of practice. Generally they were on board to ensure that everything ran smoothly, namely all the travellers got to their assigned destinations with the minimum of disruption. I thought of them as glorified baggage handlers. They were necessarily sexless and loveless, automatons and didn't give much of a damn for Redeemers. Redeemers were an affront to the services provided by the Androgynes. Redeemers *stole* passengers and returned them to the live world, passengers who the Androgynes saw as their sole responsibility. They held on to them possessively, determined to see them to their resting place.

On this particular Hell-forged train, rattling through the maze of tunnels, passengers were bound for the darker retreats, their designated afterlives shaped by despair, the bitter fruit of lives spent contrary to the demands of Piety, amen. Well, let's call a spade a spade – they were the damned. And Mrs Fellini was one of them.

I took in my surroundings in an instant. Not very crowded carriages, running ahead of me like the inside of a wriggling metal worm. The people were silent, many with heads bowed, some muttering prayers – fat use that was at this stage – others gazing at the windows, which were pitch black. Between whatever passed for stations there was nothing to be seen, other than solid stone or the void of interstellar space. Who knows? The light in the carriages was perversely bright, throwing the passengers into garish relief, highlighting their misery. No conversations blossomed; no one took out a paper or book and read it.

Yes, they were the damned and they were resigned to it. From time to time the train would stop, the doors would open and a fresh batch of travellers would board. The Androgynes appeared like ghosts, ensuring that no one got off at these stops, though as far as I could see, no one tried to leave the train inappropriately. At other stations, people did get off. On these occasions, no one was allowed to get on. Again the Androgynes were present to supervise the process.

I couldn't see my charge. Mrs Fellini was not in the immediate carriage. I craned my neck. There were more people further down in the next carriage, all seated with their backs to the windows. One might have been her, head drooping so that the hair obscured the face. That hair was dark, the right colour.   There was an Androgyne standing between carriages, motionless, morose, lost in its own thoughts, if it had any. Its job must have been a variation on hell, monotonous and endless. Its robe was grey, its skin pallor much the same.

I moved very slowly along the carriage. No one paid much attention. The air was heavy with a kind of mournfulness, as though this were a funeral cortege, which I suppose in a way it was. Feet shuffled as I passed. As I got to the Androgyne, it came to life, its mundane, starched uniform crackling slightly.

"I should sit down, sir," it said in a soft, emotionless voice, gently barring the way ahead.

"I'll go and sit in there," I said, equally as quietly, pointing to the next carriage. But it wasn't going to be that easy. Perhaps the Androgyne sensed the potential for breaking the drudgery of its watch. It put a thin, white hand on my chest.

"I should go back and sit down," it said. I took its wrist and pulled the creature closer to me so that we were almost chest to chest. No one in either carriage paid any heed. I had made my mind up. I needed to act quickly and without drawing the attention of any other Androgynes. My superiors had elected to call me Razorjack. They had equipped me accordingly.

In one very swift movement, I slipped a long, wickedly sharp razor from inside my jacket and ran it up under the heart of the Androgyne – oh, yes, it had such an organ. After all, it was only a man in a different guise. I put my free hand over its mouth to stifle any cries and watched its eyes register pain, the light in them already starting to drain away. It tried to struggle, but I was that much stronger. I had been trained well; I twisted my blade expertly, each terrible laceration a joy, a fuel to my resolve. This is what my new masters had put into me, this overwhelming desire. With my weapon carving up its vitals, the Androgyne couldn't sustain its resistance. The body sagged and then slumped. I put the weapon away and held on to the Androgyne. Carefully I walked it back into the carriage.

"Excuse me," I said to the passengers, some of whom were staring listlessly at us as we waltzed in slow motion down the carriage. "My companion isn't well. Excuse me. Thank you." I got to the far end of the carriage. It was the last one. There was a narrow area beyond a door and I let the dead Androgyne slide down on to the floor, sitting up against the outer door. I looked back down the carriage. It was as though we had never been there.

I waited. The next stop was an embarkation point. I held the Androgyne upright so that when the door automatically opened, it had its back to the platform. No one attempted to board here, so we were ignored. I could see other Androgynes on the platform, but their bland faces expressed no suspicion, all their attention focussed on the boarders. We moved off once more.

The next station was for disembarkation only. Again I held the dead Androgyne upright as the door behind it slid open. And again there were Androgynes on the platform. I timed my movements carefully, delaying as long as I could before I pushed the dead Androgyne out on to the platform. As it fell, two Androgynes were on it almost immediately, looking up at me through the open door. It slid shut before they could get to me. I watched them, their furious eyes uniquely animated by my act. The train sped away.

I had no idea whether the Androgynes on the platform had any means of communicating with those on the train. I knew I had to locate Mrs Fellini as quickly as I could. I moved down the carriages much faster now, stepping over the occasional leg, watching ahead for any more Androgynes. The woman I had seen was not Mrs Fellini. She drew back from me in fear as I stared down at her. I went on along the carriages and at last saw my goal. She was slumped down in a seat, flanked by two men who appeared to have fallen asleep.

I wanted to shout out to her, but knew that would be foolish. Even so, two Androgynes materialised, seemingly from nothing, though they must have been blending in with the rest of the passengers. They studied me and my abnormally fast progress down the carriage as though they could read in my face what I'd done, the killing written there in plain sight. They were between me and the woman. And they were armed. Each of them had pulled out some kind of baton, a long, black instrument that resembled a baseball bat.

There would be no time for subtlety. I had to finish this before we reached another station. Our conflict would be seen from the platform and it would mean reinforcements.

"I think you need to sit down, sir," said one of the Androgynes. "The journey will soon be over. No need to distress yourself. Here, have a seat."

I nodded, my long razor out of sight, moving forward slowly as if I meant to take up its offer. I bent down to the seat but as I did so, I gripped the Androgyne's wrist and swung it towards me. It tried to lift the baton, but we were too close for it to do it effectively. I ran the weapon across its neck and used my shoulder to shunt it into its companion. Blood leaked from the long gash – still the passengers looked on emptily, as though all this was taking place on a screen or somewhere else. No one moved to intervene.

The wounded Androgyne dropped to its knees, uselessly trying to stem the flow of blood, inadvertently hampering the movements of its fellow, which swung a blow at me with its baton. I evaded it easily but the fallen Androgyne grabbed my legs, both arms wrapping my knees in an embrace that almost had me over. Its energy was being sapped as the blood ran more freely through its impotent fingers and over its uniform. I avoided another swipe

148

from the second Androgyne and pushed the fallen one away.

Once free of it I was able to time my next thrust, into the midriff of the second Androgyne. Its hands automatically clasped its gut, exposing its head and neck, allowing me to finish the job with another clinical slash of the razor. I kicked the Androgyne aside and made my way down the carriage. Mrs Fellini and her immediate companions had paid no heed to the scuffle, all of them locked into their own private thoughts. All I needed to do was reach her and take her by the hand and we would be back in Fellini's private realm.

Before I got to her, the train slowed and stopped and all those around me got to their feet in unison, suddenly electrified. It was a disembarkation point and they were all about to get off. So, too, I saw, was Mrs Fellini.

I called out to her and she looked up, her eyes frightened. When she saw me, as I tried to grope my way through the sudden surge of humanity separating us, her expression changed to one of horror. She must have thought I was another Androgyne or another official here to abuse her in some way. Frightened, she shook her head and turned back down the carriage, making for the nearest door.

I muscled my way past the outgoing mob and almost reached Mrs Fellini's shoulder with my outstretched hand, but she was on the platform before I could claim her. I followed, jostled at once by a stream of disembarking passengers. This was a major station on the route. The only exits from here would be down. None of them would return to the live world. I had to catch Mrs Fellini.

She had already put some distance between us, determined to avoid me. She kept looking back over her shoulder. I dare not call out again, not here, given that there were several Androgynes about, this being such a busy place. The bodies flowed strongly, a human current that was becoming impossible to resist. I could not bridge the gap between me and my target.

She had reached the top of a side tunnel that led steeply down into darkness. There was a horrifying finality about that darkness that chilled my every bone. I knew I couldn't enter it. Raw terror prevented me. It was a like a solid wave, a terrible threat of horror beyond imagining and my entire being revolted at its power. I fought my way to the side of the tunnel and the ongoing bodies, hitting the wall and holding my position. I craned my neck to see

Mrs Fellini. She was about to begin the ultimate descent, lost to me forever in that repellent pit.

Around her, people began to fan out, away from her. Two Androgynes had thrust themselves into the mass and they both gripped one of Mrs Fellini's arms. They pulled her back and away from that frightful maw and returned up the tunnel, unhampered by the crowd that swept around them like water flowing past boulders. I moved along the wall, less easily, but not caught up in the crowd. I was able to get back to the platform, which was devoid of people at last. The train had gone.

Mrs Fellini was being escorted, unresisting, along the platform. The Androgynes led her through a door and I followed. Beyond it was a narrow brick stairway, lit by a single, dull bulb. I climbed up after the Androgynes, who for the moment hadn't noticed me. At the top of the stairs was a door, its paint flaking, the word "office" barely readable. The Androgynes pushed Mrs Fellini through it and closed it behind them.

I stood outside, listening. There seemed to be no one else in there. I looked back down the stairs, but no one had followed me. Silence had fallen everywhere, and the last of the travellers had dispersed.

One of the Androgynes was speaking. "Three of our colleagues have been murdered. What do you know about it?"

After a pause, Mrs Fellini's voice answered. I could hear her panic. "Nothing! I was about to go. This was my stop. I don't know anything about the man who was following me."

"*Following* you? Why should anyone be following you?"

I eased the door open. The two Androgynes had their backs to me. Mrs Fellini was sitting on a rough, wooden chair, her eyes downcast. I closed the door and slid its single bolt. The two Androgynes swung round, their eyes meeting mine. They knew what I was, of course.

"Redeemer," hissed one of them. They were armed, but made no attempt to slip their batons from their belts. I, on the other hand, had taken out my razor. It still dripped blood.

"Indeed," I said. "I'm here for the woman. Don't waste your existence. Go and get on with your business and let me finish mine."

I was anathema to them, their worst kind of nightmare. They were here to oversee departures, to ensure that their wards got to their destinations. Nothing should be allowed to interfere with that. Least of all my kind. The powers that ran me were not those who ran the Androgynes. They were not my Adversaries, but they were absolutely opposed to me and my work. Go away? Not a chance. They would expire first.

Mrs Fellini shrank back on the chair, even more horrified at the unfolding events. I knew that I would have to deal quickly with these two Androgynes – there had been more down on the platform and they might come up here at any moment. One of them in front of me made a move to pull out its baton. I already had my hand on another of my weapons, a long dirk and this time I chose to throw it. It was far too quick for the Androgyne to avoid and it plunged into its right eye. The creature catapulted backwards with the combined shock and pain, its baton falling to the ground.

The second Androgyne had pulled out its own baton and rushed me, thinking I was now unarmed, but it had miscalculated. In fact I had three blades sheathed within my jacket. I raised my left arm and took the blow from the baton on the elbow. Pain shot through me like fire, but I refused to let it govern my movements, ducking down and bringing up my second blade, driving it hard through the robe and into the soft gut of the Androgyne, twisting it viciously. It gasped and tried to raise its baton for a second strike. If it had fallen, it would have smashed against my unguarded head, but all the strength went out of the Androgyne and the baton tumbled from nerveless fingers. The Androgyne doubled up as the stomach wound racked it with agony.

I pulled out the blade and plunged it home a second time. The Androgyne gasped, falling face to the ground. The other was holding its ruined eye. Quickly I used my razor to finish the business with two clean cuts to each of their necks.

I turned my attention to Mrs Fellini. Her eyes were brimming with tears, regarding me and my hands, both slick with blood, with revulsion, as well she might. What she had witnessed could hardly have enamoured me to her. I reached out for her but she drew back, utterly repulsed.

"No! Don't touch me. Let me go. *Get away from me!*"

Part Two

The party to celebrate the merger between Silvio Fellini's conglomerate and the Ganymede Company was an overtly lavish affair held in the most expensive hotel suite in central London that Fellini could commission. Spread through a suite of rooms that would have graced a royal visit, the proceedings were a monument to wealth and prosperity, a union of some significance in the City, from which many of its magnates benefited triumphantly. Fellini circulated like an ancient Mogul, dispensing his goodwill and blessings to the gathered financiers, stockholders and politicians from his position of unprecedented power. Many jealous eyes regarded him, but few would have admitted their desires to unseat him. Better to woo him and enjoy the fruits of his rise.

His wife, Rebecca, a tall, extraordinarily beautiful woman, drifted quietly through the throngs, ignoring the food, carrying a champagne glass from which she sipped occasionally, as though it were something she was required to do, rather than something she did for pleasure. Fellini had given her explicit instructions. She must mingle. Play the good hostess. Stunning creature that she was, the guests must be made envious of the great man in all ways. Everything he had – his empire, his power, his wife – must be objects of the green-eyed goddess.

As she moved among the fawning sycophants – she saw them all in the same light – she came across the man. Most people here were either in pairs or in groups, but this man was alone. He stood at one of the over-laden tables, a cocktail glass in one hand. He looked up as she approached and nodded. He regarded her coolly, almost indifferently, which was unusual in this company. His manner suggested he was as unmoved by all the preening around him as she was. She liked that.

"Mrs Fellini," he said.

She was slightly tipsy, only her eyes betraying the fact. She took a breath, as if steeling herself to her duty and offered him her hand. He took it and raised it somewhat gallantly to his lips. For once she found that it did not irritate her. She smiled thinly. "And you are?"

"Krane. Jack Krane. One of Ganymede's crew. Or should I say, one of your husband's crew, as he's just bought Ganymede. He owns me now."

"Welcome to the club, Mr Krane." She drained her glass and set it down unsteadily on the table. In spite of his expensive suit and careful grooming, she could see that he was not at home here. A kindred spirit, perhaps. "And what do you do?"

"I run Ganymede's security." He said it casually, not for effect.

"And what does that mean?" She was prepared for the usual glib answers. He was not a handsome man, but lean and with an air of confidence, independence perhaps. The merger had probably not been to his liking.

He smiled wryly, looking around him as though the gathering was comprised of aliens. "A mixture of computers and people. Hardware and software, if you like."

She nodded, trying not to slip into the *ennui* that so often claimed her.

"It's okay," he said, reading her perfectly. "I'm sure you're bored enough without listening to a *résumé* of my job description."

It made her smile. She helped herself to another glass of champagne from a tray held by a hovering waiter, sipping it slowly. "I'm sure it's very important. To my husband, anyway."

"He's very successful."

"Oh yes, today Ganymede, tomorrow the world. Whatever he wants, he takes."

Krane looked around him discreetly to see if anyone else had heard her remark. He had sensed the element of resentment in her tone. She seemed to be including herself in the comment. He knew her background, of course. It was very public knowledge. She had burst on to the scene ten years ago, at eighteen, a tall, leggy model who was soon plastered across billboards and the television screen in a number of perfume ads. There had been a flirtation with the cinema, but she was no actress, her roles limited to eye candy. Adored by the public, a leading icon, she had been wooed and wedded by Silvio Fellini, a man forty years her senior, who caught her up in the meshes of society and fabulous wealth. A goddess, revered by the world, though if she had a personality of her own, it had been buried under the deluge of praise and worship. A construct, a supremely beautiful piece of porcelain.

Krane could see from her face and its minute, well-concealed hairline cracks that the days of glory were going to change. There had been rumours of drugs, the usual sad extravagances associated with her type of existence. Fellini provided everything. His business affairs were entrenched deep in the dark side of commerce. He had never rid himself of his dubious roots. Roots that had spread their shoots high up into society. Cut him down and too many public figures would topple with him.

"Ever wish you hadn't started all this?" said Krane.

She flashed him a look of surprise. He had struck right into the heart of things. But she laughed softly. "You think I'm unhappy?"

He looked as if he'd decided he'd gone too far. "I'm being impertinent," he said.

She leaned closer. "And you, Mr Krane? Are *you* happy? I'd rather you were honest, even if it means being rude. If you can be that, you would be a very singular man."

"When in Rome," he said with another smile. "And when you're in the Senate itself, discretion rules."

She laughed a little more loudly, but naturally. Something she had not done for a long time. They moved away from the table and the crowd, standing instead by a tall window and balcony that afforded a wide view of the cityscape.

"I often wonder," she said, her eyes on the intimidating array of buildings outside, "what life is like out there, beyond my ivory tower." She glanced at him, as if it were a challenge.

"Different kind of rat race. No guarantee of winning," he said, slightly guardedly.

"You're a winner, I expect."

"I'm a survivor." He saw the unmistakable figure of Silvio Fellini approaching and inclined his head towards his employer.

"There you are, my dear," said the host to his wife, eyes fixed briefly on Krane. "Are you entertaining our guests?" he said casually to his wife, putting a large hand on her bare shoulder and there was no reaction. She turned to him and switched on a smile that had no perceptible warmth in it.

"This is Mr Krane, Silvio."

The two men shook hands automatically, both grips firm. "Forgive me –" said Fellini. He studied Krane as though he had no idea who he was, but Krane felt sure that was feigned.

"Security, sir. I ran Ganymede's security."

"And are you going to run mine?"

Krane smiled diplomatically. "You have an excellent system in place, sir. But they've found a role for me. I think I can make

154

myself useful."

"Well, you can never have enough protection, Mr Krane. Glad to have you aboard." Fellini said something quietly to his wife and then was gone as suddenly as he had appeared. She turned her attention again to the skyline, her mood changing. Krane sensed the tension in her, the resentment of her husband and his touch.

"Is my security part of your brief?" she asked him.

He nodded. "Of course."

"Does that mean I'll have even more people following me around? Making sure I don't step out of line?" She was looking out at the city again, as if drawn to it. "There's a lot out there I've never seen. When you're in a cage, your vision is limited."

He wondered if he was being tested. Was this Fellini's way of checking up on his new man? And yet he had seen her reaction to him. There had been no mistaking her change of mood when he'd appeared.

She looked directly at him, her eyes searching for something. He held her gaze, waiting.

"You don't trust me," she said, though she smiled.

"Does your husband?"

She shook her head. "Silvio's arrogance leads him to believe that I would never disobey him. In his eyes I am completely docile. There's nothing in me to fight him with. He has me watched all the time, but it's simply in case some rival decides to abduct me and demand money. I know how his mind works. I am part of his valuable art collection, that's all. I'm tired of moving from one luxurious hotel to another."

"Where would you go – out there?"

"I don't know. Anywhere. Where no one would know me. Where I could eat a simple meal. Sit in a park. Go to a zoo. There must be a zoo out there?"

He looked around him. No one appeared to be taking any notice of them, the crowd absorbed in its own business. Whoever among the bodyguards had been assigned to her today were well out of sight in this place, a safe haven.

"I would have thought," she said, "that someone as important as you, Mr Krane, would be able to arrange a visit for me. No one else need know."

And so it began.

He watched her wrestling with the huge plateful of food – the biggest portion of cod and chips on the menu of the cramped restaurant. She speared three chips and held them up on the fork.

"What?" she said, seeing his amused expression. "*What?*"

He laughed. She was like a kid in a sweetshop. She'd pulled her hair back in a tight bun and eschewed make-up, wearing a cheap dress and jacket that she had managed to get from somewhere. It had been enough to fool the goons who were supposed to be her shadows. She and Krane had been away from the hotel that was her temporary home for two hours and so far no one had recognised her.

"I can't believe you're going to fit that meal into your skinny little frame," he said.

"I'm going to try," she replied, defiantly. Then, putting down the fork, she relented. "Actually, I think I'm going to burst." She looked around, sniggering. The place was crowded, but everyone here was totally engaged in demolishing their own food, chattering away, lost in their personal worlds. They ignored her. Occasionally someone would look her way, but not in recognition, more in curiosity. Krane, who was dressed as casually as she was, drew a few glances. There was a hardness to him and people here liked that.

"So you won't want a sweet?" he said.

She frowned. "God, should I? What have they got?"

"Maybe just a coffee," he suggested, laughing again.

She pulled her lemonade to her and sipped it through a straw. "No, no. I want a sweet. No cheating. You promised me a meal."

"The apple pie and custard is the best there is. Or if you really want to test your taste buds, there's the bread and butter pudding. But I warn you – it's a killer. Eat that and you won't move for a day."

"I want one!" she said, pushing the plate of fish and chips aside. "Come on, Krane, I want bread and butter pudding."

He shook his head. She had become a different woman. The fabricated goddess, the immaculate, cool icon that the world knew, was gone. Instead she was a tall, skinny kid, almost plain. There was a blob of tomato sauce on her cheek and he wiped it off with a deft swipe of paper tissue. She was adorable.

She gasped when the pudding arrived. Three layers of sliced bread, cooked in milk with currants, it overhung the dish, dripping with butter. There was a jug of custard, thick as whipped cream. She dug into the pudding, chewing on a mouthful.

"Unbelievable!" she said. The rest was lost as she attacked the food.

It wasn't long before she stopped and gazed across at Krane, who was grimacing. "You don't think I'm going to be able to eat all this, do you?" she growled.

"No, I don't think you're going to be able to eat all of that." He was shaking with subdued laughter.

"What are you, my mummy?"

He leaned forward and dipped his own spoon into the pudding, taking a bite. "I'll help you."

She giggled, pushing the plate closer to him and easing her chair right up to the little table. She fed him a spoonful of the pudding.

"When you've had enough," he said, "where do you want to go next? There's a good market near here. You can go and haggle."

Their heads were quite close. She took a handkerchief and wiped her mouth, her eyes fixed on his. "No. I want to go somewhere quiet." She put her hand over his. "I want you to make love to me."

*

He had access to a number of flats in the city and he'd chosen the most discreet of them. Lying naked on the bed together, they looked out at the afternoon sun as it began to slip down towards the city skyline. She snuggled closer, her fingers stroking his chest, her lips brushing his shoulder.

"So how did you come to get mixed up with him?" he said. Her fervour – and his own – had surprised him.

"It was a combination of things. I was caught up in the lifestyle. It was pretty wild and we were all stupid, really. I was in a relationship. Tony Vincent – you know, the actor. All conceit, no brain. He liked to spread himself around the ladies and by the time I came to my senses, the damage was done. We had an ugly break-up – you must have seen it in the media. I was pretty cut up about it. Silvio had appeared on the scene, bombarding me with charm and everything that goes with it. I suppose part of me was hooked on the wealth that went with the fame. And boy, is Silvio wealthy."

"You were into the drug thing, then?"

"Not as much as I could have been. Not like some. I lost friends to drugs. I took coke for a while. Who didn't? I was an idiot. Probably just ripe for Silvio to pluck. And he knows how to control people. I was manipulated into loving him – so I thought. I hate him for that now." She shuddered and pulled herself closer.

"There was one other thing," she said and he felt the sudden tension in her. "Silvio is a catholic, as you'd imagine. He goes through all the motions and does everything the church would expect of him. He puts a lot of money into the church. It's all calculated, part of his control. I don't think he has a real faith. He's too preoccupied with himself and his own power. If God criticised him, he'd want to start a fight with him."

"So are you catholic?"

"No. My parents were Jewish, actually. Another kind of control. I rebelled, of course. A headstrong bitch like me was never going to stick to all those rules," she laughed. "No one was going to tell me what to believe and how to behave. It caused any number of rows. I wasn't very nice."

"All kids rebel."

"Modelling was my escape from all that. I left home after another battle and hardly saw my parents at all. I was angry. But I missed them. Silvio learned about all this and used it to his advantage. When I was at my most vulnerable, he fixed it for me to see them again. My relationship with them was never perfect, but at least I had one."

"You still see them?"

"They're both dead now. They had me quite late. My father died of a heart attack two years ago and mom followed him soon after. I guess she couldn't bear to be without him."

"I'm sorry."

"My life is a mess. It's my own fault. I have everything I want, except what I really want."

"And what do you want?"

"More trips to the zoo. And bread and butter pudding *every day*."

"Have you any idea how fat you'll get?"

"Yes!" she laughed, rolling over on top of him. "I want to get *fat*. Fat, fat, fat!"

*

The boardroom was full. Fellini sat at the head of the table, the focal point of all attention. Today he appeared to be in a mellow state of mind, not necessarily a common thing for him. His usual tyrannical brand of management wasn't in evidence and he seemed more prepared to listen to his people. No one questioned it. They were just thankful that whatever advice they had brought to the meeting was considered less destructively than they would have expected.

Mahlmann, who until the merger with Ganymede had counted security among his responsibilities, fidgeted with the file in front of him until he was invited to speak.

"I've reviewed our overall arrangements," he said, tapping the file. "All the major service providers have submitted costed proposals." He went on to enlarge upon the operation he had conducted with his team, which now included Krane, who sat opposite him, listening quietly. There were nods around the table, mostly polite acknowledgements as Mahlmann was not a gifted public speaker, his material dry. Fellini, however, listened attentively, his eyes fixed on the speaker as though drilling for flaws in the presentation.

"In conclusion," said Mahlmann, looking not at Fellini, but at Krane, "I would recommend that we continue with our current arrangements. That is, we run the human resources ourselves and the systems will be provided by Lieberfeld Industries." The fact that they were owned by a cousin of Mahlmann's was well known, but since they provided a good service, no one saw any reason to rock the boat and call for a change.

Fellini turned his attention to Krane. "Mr Krane, you've joined us as part of our recent merger." All eyes swung round to Krane. "Gentlemen, you may not be aware, but Mr Krane was in charge of security at Ganymede. Their record over the last three years was exceptionally good. No doubt you had something to do with that, Mr Krane?"

Krane allowed himself a smile. "I'd like to think so, sir." Any information Fellini had accessed on that score would have confirmed it.

"So what do you think of Mr Mahlmann's proposal? Do you have any reservations about Lieberfeld Industries?"

Krane looked directly at Mahlmann. The man was glaring, willing him to agree to what had been presented, but Krane wasn't here to be intimidated. "Lieberfeld are one of the top people. Their hardware is as good as anybody's. I would say there are about three companies whose equipment is state of the art and Lieberfeld are one of them."

Mahlmann relaxed a little.

"Their software programmes," Krane went on, "are also top notch. I'm familiar with them. Ganymede used them at one time."

Fellini frowned. "But not now?"

"We shifted over to a British company, Ultracom. Their integrated telephony system and overall data streaming is unusually effective. Some of the big American corporations are taking them on board."

Mahlmann said nothing, but his expression had changed, his suppressed anger not quite hidden. Krane noted it but he didn't flinch. This was conflict and there were rules that went with it, just as there were in any arena.

"Well, Mahlmann, what do you know of Ultracom?" said Fellini.

"They are very good, of course. Software develops so quickly. It can vary from month to month. And often when some companies fall behind, they go out of existence. That can be embarrassing. I build long term reliability into our contracts. With respect to Mr Krane, I don't think Ultracom have been around long enough for us to feel sure we could get that from them. And, I have to say, they are very expensive."

"Krane?" said Fellini.

"Ganymede had them for the last two years," said Krane. "And they've just secured Government funding for further developments." He was pleased to see that this had come as a surprise to Mahlmann, as he had planned. "I wouldn't want to pre-empt anything, but my money would be on Ultracom landing a few very tasty Government contracts over the next few years. This is all highly confidential, you understand."

Fellini grinned. "I see. No doubt you have reliable sources, Mr Krane."

"What sort of developments?" said Mahlmann.

Krane had been ready for a challenge. Mahlmann wasn't going to let his share of the family empire go without a fight. "Satellite communications."

Fellini looked impressed. "I like the sound of this. And Ultracom's price?"

"They aren't cheap, but I have some useful contacts on their board. I'm sure, if we were interested, I could negotiate a favourable price for their services. It occurs to me, sir, that it could be of mutual interest to us to explore a partnership."

"Aren't we getting ahead of ourselves?" grunted Mahlmann.

Fellini shook his head. "Get me a full report, Mr Krane. I'll meet you in two days. You will join us, won't you, Mahlmann?"

"Yes, of course," Mahlmann said, though testily.

Krane could see that he'd made an enemy, but he shielded his own feelings on the matter. This would simply be the first step to moving Mahlmann out of security altogether.

*

Later, deep in the heart of the main office complex, Krane was interrogating his computer, when he felt a presence at his side. It was Monahan, one of the men he had brought across from Ganymede with him.

"There's a rumour going round that we might be bringing Ultracom in," Monahan breathed, his eyes looking around him to see if any heads were turned their way.

Krane grinned. "Is that so?"

"I got it from Atterby. He's part of the Mahlmann hierarchy. We play squash together. Listen, boss, watch your back."

"Goes with the territory, Nick. I knew from day one that Mahlmann didn't want our little gang fused with his. Spoiling his little family business. He'll do his best to pour poison in Fellini's ear. But I've put a big carrot Fellini's way."

"It's not that," said Monahan. He looked doubly uncomfortable. "Mahlmann knows about you."

Krane sat back, studying the younger man. He had used him as his own right arm for a long time. He knew he could trust him implicitly. Indeed, in the matter of Rebecca Fellini, he had done so. Was that it? Had Mahlmann got hold of something?

161

"He's had her watched," said Monahan, as if reading his thoughts. "We've been more than careful, getting her in and out of the hotel. No one has paid any attention. I don't know what put Mahlmann on to it. But he knows the people who run the hotel. Easy enough for him to access whatever part of the security system he wants to see."

"What about beyond the hotel?" said Krane, his mouth drying. "Has she been followed?"

"I don't know. Do you want me to find out?"

Krane was thinking frantically. If Fellini got hold of this, it was curtains, for him and Rebecca. He could handle being fired. But Rebecca – there was no saying what that bastard would do to her.

"Shit," he said and for the moment it was as much as he could come up with.

*

Rebecca Fellini was towelling herself down, coming into the bedroom to look across at Krane. He was standing by the side of the window, his cell phone to his ear. She looked askance at him, but he gently shook his head.

"You were right," said Monahan on the other end of the line. "Mrs Fellini was followed from the hotel. My man saw two of them working the watch – Mahlmann's goons. I doubt that they recognised me in the car. It's an old Vauxhall, so they probably thought it was a cheap taxi. I kept my head down, but I'm sure someone was following me."

"Here? They followed you here?"

"I got rid of them. When I dropped Mrs Fellini off, I didn't see anyone. She may have got in without being seen."

"Where are you now?"

"Not far. If anyone turns up, I'll let you know."

"Who was that?" said Rebecca as Krane put the phone down on a sideboard.

He told her and she frowned. "Followed me? So our little deception hasn't worked."

He put his arms around her and kissed her forehead. "Monahan's good. He shook them off. But we can't risk staying here. I'd better get you back."

"But he'll know. Silvio will know."

162

"Only that you've been out. You can bluff him. Say you wanted some freedom and just went out for some air. The only way you could do it was by using a bit of subterfuge."

She hugged him more tightly. "I'm scared. You don't know what he'll do to me."

"I won't let him hurt you."

"That's all very well, but how will you stop him! He's a monster. Once I'm back in that hotel, I'll be on my own. He'll beat it out of me."

The cell phone beeped and Krane snatched it up. It was Monahan again. "Sorry, boss, but they're here, watching the place. At least three of them. I don't like the look of it, boss. This could get ugly."

"Okay. If they start to come into the building, stall them. But don't take any risks. You don't know what these bastards will do."

"What about you, boss?"

"Ring me again in half an hour, but only if it's safe." Krane put the phone down again and turned to Rebecca. "Get dressed. Quick as you can. We have to leave."

"Where are we going?" She did as he told her and he did the same.

"You can't go back. Neither of us can. There's a place further afield we can go to for now."

She smiled, but her fear was evident. "Are we on the run?"

"Do you want to? Run? Run and hide, at least for a time. He'll come for us, but we need time to prepare."

She pulled him to her again. "Maybe I should just go back and take what's coming. Better for you if I do. He's too powerful."

"Is that what you want?"

"No, of course not."

He grinned. "Then let's get going." He pulled open a drawer and lifted a shoulder holster, a gun and a silencer, strapping the holster on. "I won't use this unless I have to."

She shook her head. "This is mad. You can't use that –"

"They'll be armed. They'll be relying on frightening us. That's all. But I don't scare easy. So what's it to be? We have to go now, if you want to. Are you completely sure?"

She nodded, but she was shaking with fear.

They took the stairs, slipping away as quietly as they could, she pulling her coat collar up around her neck, holding the front closed up to her chin. They had to go down a dozen flights. He paused before they reached the last section that would take them to the underground car park and his vehicle.

"What's wrong?" she asked him.

"If they've blocked off the car park, we'll be trapped down there. We'll have to go out into the streets. At least they won't expect that."

There was no time to deliberate and he tugged her through a service door and down a narrower staircase to a fire exit. He dropped the bar and eased the door open into bright sunlight. There was a yard beyond and a dozen large dumper bins. They went outside and across the concrete to the gate beyond. It was bolted, not locked and he slid the two bolts aside slowly.

"You got any loose change?" he said as they went out into the street, under the shadow of some trees.

She shook her head, baffled.

"Okay. There's a shop at the end of the street. I'll get some change. For the bus," he grinned, seeing her mystification. "They won't expect us to be jumping a bus to get away."

He checked to see that no one had come out of the building behind them, then pulled her along the narrow street towards its end and the general stores there. The front was almost buried under boxes of fruit and vegetables and the windows were covered in advertisements and posters. Inside it was all shadows, uncomfortably cave-like, the walls piled high with tins and bottles.

She pressed close to him, afraid of this alien world, which had suddenly ceased to become amusing. He had pulled a couple of newspapers from a rack and gave the shopkeeper, a cheerful Indian, a ten pound note, pocketing the change. Then they were outside again. He looked up and down two streets that met at the nearest crossroads and saw a bus stop, just visible in a space between two parked cars.

They crossed the road and made for the bus stop, shielding themselves from general view by another tree. He checked his watch. Monahan should be ringing soon.

"You okay?" he asked her.

She wasn't, he could see that. She was still shaking. He put his arms around her and pulled her close in to him. They waited in silence. Apart from an occasional passer-by they saw no one. Ten minutes later – it had seemed like an hour – the double-decker ground its way through the parked vehicles and he flagged it down. He dropped a few pound coins into the slot and got a couple of tickets, guiding her to a seat near the front of the bus.

"Keep your head down," he whispered. "I'll sit two rows back. You're less likely to attract attention if you're on your own."

Her eyes were wide with fear, but she nodded. She stared at the floor, hugging the coat tightly to her as if she was freezing, not daring to look out of the windows, certain that if she had done, she would see Silvio's people out there, closing in.

Krane sat two rows back on the opposite side of the bus and pretended to read the paper. There were a few passengers, but they were all preoccupied with their own worlds. The bus stopped to drop and pick up more.

His cell phone vibrated in his pocket and he took it out.

"Where are you?" said Monahan's urgent voice.

"Away," Krane said. "What's happening at your end?"

"I did my best to hold them up at the front doors. But they pushed on through. Are you in the car? Only – the car park was covered, and the back of the building. Fellini wasn't taking any chances. He knew you were in there. Both of you."

"Yeah, I guessed as much. Where are you now?"

"In the foyer. Fellini's men are searching the flats. They may not know you've got away."

"Can you get out?"

"Not without being seen. They suspect I'm shielding you."

"Assume it, Nick. When they realise I'm not there, they'll be focusing on you." Krane looked around him casually, to ensure that no one could overhear him. "Nick, you need to get out of there."

"Sure. Are you in a car?"

"No, but I'm going to get one." He gave Monahan an address in the east of the city. "It's a safe house. I'll pick up a vehicle there. Get yourself away, Nick. Don't try and contact me again. I'm closing this channel."

He got up and went to Rebecca. She flinched as he took her arm, but rose and went to the front of the bus. They got off without a backward glance.

"Where are we?" she said, her face even paler than usual.

He nodded across the road. "There's the Tube," he said.

"Another short journey. We're in north London, heading for the outer suburbs. Don't worry. If they're after us, they'll be looking in the east. There's a place there I use sometimes. They'll go there." *Once they've dragged it out of Monahan*, he thought. It was a pity to have betrayed his loyalty, but this was about survival now. Fellini wasn't going to take prisoners. It would be the law of the gun.

*

The place was a nondescript bungalow, owned by the company, one of a number used to house its new employees temporarily when they were making arrangements to relocate to London and their new work bases. Krane knew it would be empty and that there would be a car in the garage, also for the temporary use of new employees. He had master keys to the premises. He used them to switch off the surveillance system so they could enter without blowing their cover.

Inside, sagging down on to a settee, Rebecca undid her coat. She looked frail, exhausted.

"You don't have to do this," he said, kneeling down in front of her and taking both her cold hands in his. "Maybe you should just go back."

She shook her head. "I'm scared, but going back now would be a nightmare. What are we going to do? We're not staying here. Are we?"

"No. But we've got time for some coffee. Yes? Good." He went into the kitchen, which was supplied with basic food and drink. He emerged a few minutes later with two mugs. She took hers and warmed her hands around it, sipping slowly.

"I've got a place out in the country," he told her. "I bought it before I joined Ganymede. No one knows about it. It's always been my private retreat," he smiled. "I don't go there very often. We'll make our way there for now."

"What are we going to do?"

"Well, I guess I'm washed up with Fellini. But that's okay. I can always get work. I'm not short of money," he laughed. "Most of it's tied up, but I can access enough to tide us over. Fellini will just have to accept the situation."

"What is the situation? I'm a kept woman now, am I?"

He laughed. "I suppose you are. We'll live comfortably, but it can never be like it was. Everything you knew, the high living, the glamour, the friends – that's all in the past."

She shook her head. "I'm glad. I don't want that. I hated it. I don't know how much longer I could have stood it. But I'm scared."

"Fellini? He can only do so much. He may think he owns you, but he doesn't. You have a mind of your own. If he comes on heavy, we'll involve the police. Or the press. He has enemies. I'll use them, if I have to."

"You don't understand. If he doesn't get me back, he'll kill me. Or you, at least."

His eyes narrowed and she saw something in them that she had not seen before, something that made her flinch for a moment. But it passed as he laughed it off. "No," he said. "We're not gangsters. In the end, even he has to behave like a responsible adult."

Soon afterwards they got in the car, after he had done a brief inspection for what he called "bugs." He understood enough about surveillance to know that it would have been a simple matter for Fellini's people to have tracked its movements. He found what he was looking for and disabled it before switching on the engine.

They drove twenty miles out into the country.

*

3.00 am.

The bedside phone rang. Krane reached over blearily and lifted the mobile handset. Rebecca, worn out from the tribulations of the day, remained mercifully asleep.

Monahan was on the other end of the line. It acted like a douche of icy water. Krane came fully awake, sliding silently from the bed and moving away from it into the shadows next door to the bedroom. How had Monahan got this number? Only a few people knew it. This country retreat was supposed to be off limits. Krane had been particularly careful to make the arrangements.

"Nick, I told you not to ring me. Where are you?"

When Monahan replied, his voice was strained: something was wrong. "I'm sorry, Mr Krane."

Mr Krane? It was a warning. Monahan wouldn't use the form

of address unless he was being monitored. The line fell silent for a moment. Then another voice came on the line.

"You know who I am," it said coldly. "And you have something of mine, Mr Krane."

"I don't think so, Mr Fellini. Not any more."

"Make this easy, Mr Krane. Just send her out. I'm all around you."

Krane had no reason to doubt Fellini's words. "Spare yourself the embarrassment, Mr Fellini. The local police have been detailed to watch the house. They're probably looking at you right now."

Something that sounded vaguely like muted laughter came from the other end of the phone. "I don't think so, Mr Krane. I'm sure your local contacts are very good. But mine are better. There's no one out here but me and my boys. *I've* arranged that the whole area won't be disturbed until our business is concluded. And your alarm system will no longer serve you. I've had that seen to as well."

Krane said nothing. There was no reason to believe that Fellini was lying.

"I say again, send her out. You have five minutes to get her dressed and out here. After that, I am going to have your house burned to the ground. Look out of any window, Mr Krane. You'll see the torches are already lit."

Krane wasn't going to fall for that. But he guessed that Fellini did have the place ringed. Krane switched the handset off. He felt a movement at his shoulder. It was Rebecca, a sheet wrapped around her.

"It's him, isn't it?" she said.

He nodded, but put his finger to her lips. "He's full of crap."

"What about the police? They're supposed –"

"He's bought them off. We're on our own. He's threatened me, but he dare not try anything. He wants you alive. He's not going to risk hurting you."

"Let me go out to him," she said quietly. "It's no use fighting him –"

"If you go out to him, he'll have what he wants. And he won't spare me. No one will see me again. I've got one chance."

Her eyes widened. "What?"

"The car. I can get to the garage from the house. Make a break for it. They may have guns, but I'll take my chances. You stay here until he comes for you."

She shook her head. "I don't want him near me. I'd rather die."

"Don't be crazy," he said, gripping her arm. "There's no need for that. Your time will come. He can't hold you against your will indefinitely."

She kissed him urgently. "I won't stay behind. If he thinks I'm in the car, he won't shoot." There was no time to discuss it. They got dressed in the dark. Through a crack in the curtains they could see the wavering glow of torchlight. Fellini was mad enough to carry out his threat.

Krane embraced Rebecca. "Are you sure you want to do this? If I can slip away, I'll find a way of getting you free of him."

She nodded. "Let's just go."

"Once we're in the car, keep your head well down. And hold on. It's going to be one hell of a ride."

She tried to smile. Then they were through the house and out into the garage. Krane slid into the driver's seat of the car and she dropped down beside him in the passenger seat. It was a low, sleek machine, built for speed. He put the key in the ignition and took up the hand control for the automatic garage door. She nodded at him and he flicked the ignition, opening the door at the same time.

The door hummed open smoothly, but the ignition failed. He tried it several times before he realised the truth.

"What is it?" she gasped, seeing his expression.

"They were ahead of me. They've wrecked the engine. Must have done it when they deactivated the alarms."

"What do we do?"

He looked out through the windscreen to the grounds. There were figures moving in the torchlight, waiting. "You have no choice. You have to go to him."

She struggled up into the seat and leaned over to kiss him. "Not on my own. Come out with me. I'm frightened for you. I can't go out there alone. Put your arm around me and take me out."

For a few moments more he thought it through, then something seemed to snap into place. "Okay," he said, opening his door. They stood side by side and he slid his left arm around her waist.

"Whatever happens, I don't regret any of it," she said.

169

"No. You just hold on to that."

They walked out slowly into the darkness, the smell of smoke from the torches acrid. They could hear muted voices, among them Fellini's. Krane eased his right hand inside his jacket, his palm closing round the grip of the gun.

I'll take you with me, Mr Fellini. God help me, I will.

*

The bedroom was sumptuous, the central bed extravagant. Money had been lavished on the place, some of the furnishings antique and priceless. The curtains were drawn, the lighting subdued. There was a huge fireplace and a mirror above it that would have fetched a king's ransom. The carpet pile was deep, its weave of the highest quality.

In the midst of all this splendour, Rebecca Fellini sat on the end of the bed, her hair dishevelled, her make-up smudged, as though she had made no effort to remove it before getting into the bed the night before. The sheets were crumpled, thrown across the bed. She had snatched at sleep as she had done for days now, but mostly it had evaded her.

The door opened and two men entered, speaking in hushed tones, like conspirators plotting a *coup*. The first of them, Silvio Fellini, came over to his wife and studied her gravely.

"You're still not sleeping," he said, his tone shaped as much by anger as concern.

Slowly she looked up at him, her expression blank.

"My darling, you cannot go on like this," he told her. "What is past is past. You must move on. Life has so much to offer you."

She looked away, then her head dropped and she sat stiffly, as though the world was far away. Fellini stepped back and turned to his companion.

Villefranche put his arm on Fellini's shoulder, a familiarity no ordinary man would have been able to enjoy. He spoke very softly. "Let me talk to her, my friend. I am sure that I can provide something that will not only bring her out of this, but also enable her to regain her strength and be as she was when you once knew her."

If Rebecca Fellini heard the words, she made no show of having registered the fact.

"Call it a test of your faith in me," Villefranche went on.

Fellini grunted and watched as the tall man bent down to the slumped woman.

"Mrs Fellini?" Villefranche knelt and looked into Rebecca Fellini's eyes. "You must get some proper rest, my dear. I can help you. A few simple sedatives. All the unpleasantness of recent days will recede for a while and allow you to recover your strength. You are confused now, drained of energy. We can put that back. Give you the power to rebuild yourself."

She nodded dumbly.

"Good," said Villefranche, standing again. He withdrew, standing once more beside his host. "I will have the sedatives brought to you."

"I would give much to have her as she was," said Fellini.

"And you will, my friend. Now – have you thought anymore about our conversion?"

Fellini frowned, apparently uncomfortable. "I have, but I am not a religious man."

Villefranche's smile was predatory. "Nor am I, Silvio. My masters are well outside any religious spheres. And well beyond their trappings. You must think of the power that attaches to such a pact as I am offering. What you control now is significant. But it is nothing to what you will be if you accept our gift."

"I need a little more time."

Villefranche nodded. "Of course. It is a momentous decision for anyone. In the meantime, I will provide what you need for your wife."

*

A few days later, Rebecca Fellini rose from sleep. The pills she had been given had allowed her to sleep and she felt stronger in herself than she had since Fellini had first brought her back to their home. However, they had also served to fuel her disgust and her fury at what had happened.

Krane was dead, she was sure of it. Buried somewhere in a remote grave where he would never be found. There would be no trace of him. If she ever had an opportunity to speak to the police, Fellini would have every angle covered. Nothing could be proved and people like Monahan would either have been paid off to keep silent, or moved well out of the way, with the threat of execution hanging over them. She was trapped, back in the gilded cage, only now the locks were tighter.

For the moment there was consolation in the fact that her husband was becoming more and more involved with the strange Villefranche. As far as she could tell, he was the driving force behind a major pharmaceutical company, one that was about to link itself very closely to Fellini's empire. There was more to it than that. She had heard them speak of a pact as though it were some ancient ritual, a rival of the freemason movement maybe. As long as it kept Fellini occupied and away from her, it was fine with her.

She looked out of the window at the cityscape. Somewhere down there, in one of the less salubrious quarters, there was a small, untidy restaurant, where packed bodies would be fuelling up with cheap food. And bread and butter pudding.

Her throat thickened as she thought of it, tears forming in her eyes. *I want to be fat*, she had told him. She remembered his laughter. He had been a hard man. She never really found out what had made him that way, but for their short time together she had softened him.

She straightened. Tonight. It would be tonight. Villefranche had unwittingly given her the means of escape. There were enough sedatives in the bathroom. Enough for what she intended. She would be free of Fellini and this artificial life.

Part Three

I watched Mrs Fellini, momentarily drawing back from the intensity of her horrified reaction.

"Get away from me!" The walls of the tiny office shook to the sound of her fear. Beneath us I could hear another train rumbling alongside the platform.

"Mrs Fellini, it's okay," I told her. "I'm not here to hurt you. I'm here to take you back."

She shook her head violently. "No! I'm not going back. Not there. Don't you see, it's no good any more. I want to go on."

I thought about the darkness that she had been about to descend into with revulsion. "I can't leave you to go down into that place. You've no conception of how vile it is. Nothing could prepare you for it."

Her eyes were filled with tears. They coursed down her cheeks. She looked utterly wretched, shrinking further back into the room. She kept shaking her head.

"There'll be more of these creatures here in minutes," I told her, trying to coax her gently to me. "I can't take them all on."

Her shoulders suddenly sagged. "I can't," she gasped, but I could see the fight draining out of her. Quickly I moved forward and took both her hands in mine. They were icy, as though she had been out in a blizzard. Behind me there were steps on the stair, the sound of angry voices. The door burst open, but when the Androgynes flung themselves in, they found nothing.

The transition was instant. I was standing with Fellini's wife back in the live world outside a drab building in the city, the night rain falling heavily. In moments we were soaked. I pulled her aside into a doorway and watched the road. It was a side road, a branch off one of the bigger city thoroughfares. Beyond it the traffic blared and roared. Here only an occasional vehicle drove past, lights probing the rain.

"Are you okay?" I asked her.

Bedraggled, her hair hanging like wet string across her face, she looked very young and very pale, as if I had been too late and she really was beyond this life. But something fired her up. She shook her head, bemused by her surroundings.

"You should have let me go. I can't do this anymore. No more running." Her face flashed lividly, lit by an on-off neon sign that made her ghastly in its glow.

I was looking around, trying to figure out where we were. We must have been a good distance from Fellini's place, as I had warned Villefranche we might be when we re-emerged. The journey on the train had lasted a while. Abruptly she put her arms around me and hugged me tightly, burying her head in my chest. I could feel her sobbing. This was too much for her.

Instinctively I held on to her. "Hey, it'll be okay, Mrs Fellini. Really. You're better off here, believe me."

She looked up into my face, her own puzzled. "Why do you keep calling me Mrs Fellini? You act as if we're – strangers."

Something in the way she said it made my mind spin, as though I only had part of the picture, as if I was groping about in shadows. I gaped at her, dumbly, I guess.

"Jack?" she said. She shook me. "*Jack?* What's wrong?"

The name inserted itself like a needle into my mind. A hot shaft of memory. Yes, I was Jack. Or I had been. Before.

"What's going on?" she demanded. "How is it you're here? I don't understand." She gently smoothed my face with her hand, pushing away droplets of rain. The sensation was disturbing, igniting more memories.

"I'm a Redeemer," I said. "I bring people back," I mumbled. It must have sounded banal to her, but she was nodding, trying to understand.

"Don't you know who I am?" she said, her eyes searching my face.

"Mrs Rebecca Fellini. He arranged for me to bring you back."

"We were lovers. Don't you remember? What have they done to you?"

We were still holding each other. The rain poured around us. We barely had enough shelter from it. But at that moment we were like people on a distant moon.

"Listen," I said. "We have to get away from here. I'm supposed to deliver you to your husband."

"No!" Her reaction was violent. "There's no way I'll go back to him. You *can't* mean to do it. Surely you remember what happened?" Her whole manner warned me off going back to Fellini. I sensed that it would be dangerous.

"Okay, there's a place we can go to. But we have to work fast. If I don't get you back, Fellini won't be the only one after us."

"Who? Who else is after us?"

"Not the people I work for. Something much more sinister. Come on, I'll get us a taxi."

I hailed a cab and in the back she pressed herself up close to me again. Piece by piece, memories were jabbing at me like shards of broken glass.

"Where are we going?" she said.

"Protected house. We've got a few hours yet. As soon as Villefranche realises I'm not bringing you back, he'll be out looking for us. He'll go to my office first. He'll draw a blank. I have a place set up by the people who run me. They won't find us there."

"Jack, you're frightening me. Who is running you? You've never said anything about them before."

I stroked her hair and again felt something inside me twisting, more memories struggling to break free of their shadows. "I'll tell you when we get there."

Fifteen minutes later the cab dropped us off in a side street. I paid the driver and watched him pull away indifferently, already focused on his next fare. In a side alley, at a doorway, I pressed an intercom. After a few minutes a voice said, "Yes?"

"Razorjack," I said, looking up. I knew that the lone occupant of the building, one of my office staff, would see my face on the CCTV. He would assume Rebecca was a client.

The door hummed open and we went inside and up the narrow staircase. There was a flat above and the occupant, whose name was Pendle, let us in and secured the place.

"I need the top flat for a few days," I told him. "Absolute shut down."

"No problem, sir. Everything you might need is up there. I've just had the larder stocked."

I took Rebecca up to the flat and we locked ourselves in. "This is about as secure as it gets," I told her. "But I don't know how long we can hold out here. There are clothes in the bedroom wardrobes. Get out of those wet ones, get dried off and sort something out."

She was only too glad to do it. I did the same, putting my weapons down on a low table. Three knives, wrapped in blood-stained cloth. She looked at the cloth, guessing what it contained. She'd seen me dispose of the Androgynes. But she didn't comment.

We sat by the gas fire, sipping coffee. She looked very frail, younger than her years. "Tell me now," she said. "What is happening? What are you?"

"They call me a Redeemer," I said.

"I thought you were dead. Christ, Jack, I thought *I* was dead."

"They've wiped part of my mind. Tell me everything. About how you know me. How we were – lovers."

So she did, slowly and haltingly, sometimes close to tears. How we'd met at that party to celebrate the Ganymede merger. How she'd coerced me into sneaking her out from under her bodyguards' noses and taken her to visit the city outside. How we had become lovers and ultimately victims of her husband's wrath.

"When we emerged from your cottage that night," she ended, "Silvio was waiting. He knew you'd be armed and made sure you never got a chance to use your gun. They shot your legs out from under you." She put her hand up to her mouth, stifling a sob. "I couldn't do anything. I just watched as they –"

I sat beside her and held her again. I remembered it now. Ironically it was her near-hysteria that acted like a key. What had been screened from me was unlocked, an open memory. They had pumped bullets into my legs and then my arms. I was sprawled on the gravel, writhing like a maimed spider while others dragged her away. Somewhere in the darkness I had heard Fellini laugh. I was manhandled into one of the waiting cars and driven out into the night. I lost consciousness. When a vague, grey light came again, I was lying on my back, looking up from some kind of pit. A rough grave. Fellini himself stood over it with a clutch of his men, one of which was Mahlmann. They were all armed, a dozen weapons directed at me.

The rest was all noise and pain.

"Make no mistake," I told her. "I died in that pit and my corpse was buried in it. And you?"

"He took me back to the house. There was no way of getting free. I wanted to kill myself, but he made sure I had no means to do it. I hardly slept. I don't know if I would have had the resolve to starve myself to death. But I was a total mess. In the end, they slipped up."

"They?"

"Silvio and that reptile he's teamed up with."

"Villefranche. What about him?"

"He's something to do with pharmaceuticals. Another merger with Silvio's empire. I heard them talking about a pact. Villefranche promised my husband something – I don't know what. Silvio for once was uneasy. As if he sensed a trap. Villefranche persuaded me to take some pills. He was determined to do something to win Fellini over completely. Fixing me would have done it. I played along. It seemed to work. They were off guard when I chose my moment and swallowed a whole bottle of them."

"And died," I said.

She nodded. "I thought I must have done. The next thing I remember was that tube train. But I wanted it. When it was my stop – I knew it was my stop – I wanted to go. I knew that Silvio could never reach me again. When I saw you I thought it was some kind of trick. It terrified me."

We both fell silent for a while. Something had occurred to me. Villefranche wanted Fellini badly. My masters knew that – it was why they had sent me here, their chance to snare Villefranche. The Adversary had been determined to convert Fellini by means of this pact, whatever it was. And I knew now what the lever was.

Villefranche had deliberately enabled Rebecca to commit suicide, so that he could then reveal to Fellini that he could have her returned to him through the use of a Redeemer. Fellini had bought it and been duped. The Redemption of his wife would bind Fellini to Villefranche – to him no price would have been too high for such a prize. The Adversaries must have valued Fellini's soul even more highly.

Rebecca broke into my thoughts. "You said you are a Redeemer."

I explained what it meant. "The people who run me – I've only ever seen two of them – set me up here in the live world with the office and this protected place as my bases. When I first came to, in limbo, I couldn't remember much. I knew I'd been filled full of lead and killed. Then it emerged that I'd been recruited.

"My people and whoever runs them, have enemies. They call them Adversaries. They work for some other power."

"Are you trying to say – Satan?" She was perfectly serious.

"That's just a label. There are powers, that's all. Somehow I don't think they're all good or all bad. Maybe some are darker than others. Maybe the whole thing just balances out and it's a constant war for control. But the Adversaries don't seem like the Good Guys to me. Villefranche, whatever the hell he is, is our enemy. If he gets control of Fellini, it will mean a major spread of their influence, more power to the Adversaries. That's as much as I know.

"I was sent here this time to play along with Villefranche's plan. To bring you back to Fellini. You see, until you reopened my memories, I had no idea that your husband and his men had killed me. Maybe it was Villefranche's sick idea of a joke. But the job should have been routine. My real task was to kill Villefranche. By doing that, I would be delivering him into the hands of the people that run me. Here, in the live world, Villefranche is subject to the same laws that govern normal people. He's had to make himself vulnerable to death, just as anyone else is."

"But you're not going to take me back to Silvio?"

"No. That's not going to happen."

"I told you – I'd rather go back to that place on the tube journey."

"That's not going to happen either."

"You mean, we're on the run again. Like before. Or are you just going to let me go?" She studied my face. No doubt it was colder and harder than she remembered it. Maybe what drove me now was uglier, less compromising.

I kissed her softly. "No. But running isn't the answer, not for me. This has to be resolved quickly. I have no idea what resources Villefranche has with him, or what powers he can call upon. I have the means to kill him." I leaned forward and picked up the cloth containing my knives. I unwrapped it and exposed the three weapons. One was a long razor, another a dirk and the final blade was a knife that looked to have been cast in pure silver, with a long bone handle.

Rebecca shuddered at the sight of it, as though it were a live thing, eager for work. I held it up to the light. Its cutting edge was equally as sharp as the razor. I knew what needed to be done. First, I had to lie to her.

I was going to kill Fellini. Maybe a few of his mob along with him. But by doing it, I would remove the need for Villefranche to remain here. Revenge would be of no use to him. Killing me here would simply send me back to my masters. And there'd be nothing here for Villefranche, so he would return to his own. I would have failed in my mission.

Unless I killed him. And I had to do it as soon after I killed Fellini as I could. It would mean my return to my masters, but Rebecca would be free to live a life without Fellini. She could create a new world for herself. I couldn't be part of it, not unless I could rebel against my masters, but they had all the aces. I had nothing to challenge them with. I didn't think sympathy was part of their brief.

"So what are you going to do?" she whispered.

I put the long dirk on the table. "That is for Mahlmann." Next I put the razor down. "That's for Silvio Fellini." Finally I held up the silver blade. "And this is for Villefranche. An unholy trinity."

She shuddered in my arms. "What if it goes wrong?"

"It won't." I looked at my watch. "We've been back here for

just over an hour. As far as Villefranche knows, I am still working for him. I told him when he commissioned me that when I Redeemed you, I would not necessarily be able to do it quickly. I told him I might be some distance away from Fellini's place. I've got until eight am."

"But Silvio knows you! He knows what we did. How could he have trusted you?"

"The Adversaries know how the Redeemers are set up. They know we have our memories all but wiped. Only the necessary means for basic survival and operation in the live world are retained by Redeemers. Villefranche will have told your husband that I have no memory of him, of you, or of what happened. It was true. When I was with Fellini and Villefranche, I remembered nothing of our past together. Of course, it was all still fresh in Fellini's mind – his hatred of me shone through their subterfuge like a beacon. He must have hated having to employ me.

"What they didn't know was that you would re-open my memory. So my trump card now, if I act quickly, is to make them think I'm still working for them."

"You said you wouldn't take me to them." Again the implications made her tremble. She really would have preferred to take her chances in the pit.

"No – you'll stay here. By morning this will be over."

She knew what that meant. She might not see me again. I knew she wanted to say it, to plead with me not to go, to run after all. But she knew it would be no use. I was torn, I admit it. Seeing her again, realising who she was and what she meant to me, the only oasis in what had been a desert of a life, almost turned me away from the path I had been directed to follow. It was a dream, though, just not possible.

If I ran, we might both lose everything, both pitched into an Afterlife that was beyond contemplation. This way, if I took out my targets, she, at least, would have a chance at some kind of true redemption.

*

Mahlmann was easy.

Now that my mind had been reopened, I remembered a lot of stuff. Like the fact that Mahlmann worked long hours and went

179

home at 10 pm every night. You could set your watch by his movements. He would come out of the building – a multi-storey office block in the centre of the city – and get into his sleek, state-of-the-art Mercedes. It was all I needed to know. I had access to the underground car park, a leftover from my former life and parked up, waiting. At this time of night there were only a few stragglers quitting work.

I saw Mahlmann emerge from a stairwell and make for his car. It only took me a few seconds to follow him. He wasn't aware of me until he had opened the driver's door. Standing behind him, I put the gun I had brought to his temple. "Open the back doors and get into the driver's seat."

He'd stiffened, but otherwise made no attempt to disobey. He used his remote to unlock all the doors and slid into the front seat. I closed the door and got in behind him, again pressing my gun to the back of his neck. I think he was about to say something like, "You're a fool if you think you can get away with this." But he looked in the mirror and I let him see who I was. Instead of speaking, he gasped.

"You remember the last time we met?" I said.

His eyes betrayed his terror. Not just because of the gun, but because he knew I should be dead – riddled with bullets in a murder I could not possibly have survived. He tried to speak but his voice had dried up.

"Jack Krane, back from the dead," I said. "You won't be."

My grip on his head was vice-like – one of the things a Redeemer possesses is an additional strength – and he was unable to move. I put the gun away and took out the long dirk. He was shaking, tears dribbling down his cheeks.

I let him watch in the mirror as I opened up his throat and let the blood seep, ever more quickly, into a flow as his life ebbed away.

When it was over, I locked the car up. By the time anyone found his corpse, I would be long gone, one way or another. I left the car park. If the surveillance cameras had seen me, no one checked me out. I drove across the city to Fellini's. It was close to midnight when I arrived outside the main gates.

I used my cell phone to call up the Reception area. I knew there would be several night guards on duty in this fortress. Fellini was paranoid about security – who knew it better than me?

"Silvio Fellini's residence. How can I help?" The voice was cool but wary.

"I need to speak to Mr Fellini, as a matter of urgency."

"I'm afraid he's retired for the night. He won't be available until the morning. Try again at about eleven am."

"What about Mr Villefranche? Could I speak to him?"

"Mr Villefranche is not here. Who is this speaking?"

"Jack Krane."

There was a pause. He'd told me what I needed to know – Villefranche wasn't in the house. Evidently he wouldn't be here until our appointment in the morning at 8 am. It suited my purpose fine.

I had guessed that Fellini had left word with his guards that if I showed up, I was the one person he *would* want to see. I wasn't wrong. The next voice on the phone was Fellini's.

"Krane? You're early. Is there a problem?"

"No. It took me a little longer than I would have liked, but your wife is fine. Resting."

Again there was a pause. I could hear his deep breathing. It was not in his nature to be trusting. Especially when he was talking to a man – a dead man, at that – who he'd had pumped full of lead. "Where are you?"

"Outside the front gates."

"Is my wife with you?"

"No. Like I said, she's resting. The whole thing scared the shit out of her. You can imagine, I guess. I'll bring her here in the morning. She'll be okay by then."

"So what do you want?"

"I've been mulling over Mr Villefranche's offer. If I convert. I need to talk to you about it. I need you to set my mind at rest on a few things."

"He won't be here until 8 am."

"That's okay. You and I can talk first." I was gambling that he wouldn't want to risk pissing me off, not while I still had his wife.

"Sure, Mr Krane. Step out of the car and stand by the gates so I can get a good look at you. I'm a cautious man, eh?"

I did as he asked, satisfying him that I was alone and as I got back into the car, the gates swung back silently. I drove up into the grounds and parked discreetly off the main gravelled area in front of the house, leaving the car I was using – an anonymous four-door – in the shadows. Anyone else arriving wouldn't have necessarily associated it with me.

Two guards were waiting at the main door to the house and admitted me. They didn't frisk me for weapons – I assumed Fellini would have expected me to be armed as part of my role. There was no reason to think that he knew I was anything but a robot, my past life shielded from me. Villefranche would have impressed that on him.

The guards led me up into the house and to a suite of rooms where Fellini was shut away from the world. They closed the door behind me and as I entered I could see Fellini standing behind a huge writing desk by the long curved window that led out on to his gardens: he was silhouetted by the floodlights out there. I crossed the room – the floor was sprung, made of very expensive wood and a few exotic rugs were scattered around.

Fellini turned as I came in, his solid form wrapped in a dressing gown. There was only one light in the room, a discreet table map. His features were barely picked out in its glow. It didn't disguise his resentment of me.

"So, Mr Krane, you have brought my wife back. She is alive? As she was – before her accident?"

"Sure. I don't know how these things work, Mr Fellini. I just carry out my instructions. But I understand that if the transition back is undertaken reasonably soon after death, the subject recovers very quickly. Your wife was a little distraught when I recalled her – it's to be expected. But when I left her, she was asleep, quite relaxed. When she wakes up, I'm sure she'll be excited about the prospect of rejoining you."

"You recall how she died?"

"Yes, Villefranche explained it to me. However, her memory is very cloudy. A lot of what happened, especially at the end, is more like a dream to her. Some of the people I bring back hardly remember anything."

His eyes were fixed on me, his hatred barely under control. I never flinched. I played it dumb, really dumb. And of course, I gave him nothing to suggest I remembered anything about my part in his wife's death. As far as he was concerned, I was very relaxed, proof that I wasn't hostile.

"You want to talk about – conversion?"

I nodded. "Villefranche gave me two options. My life back,

whatever it was. Or conversion. Work for him. And you, I guess, Mr Fellini." As I had been speaking, I was moving slowly towards him, my movements gradual, as though they were a natural part of my conversation. I was fairly sure he would have a gun, either inside his dressing gown or more likely close at hand on the writing desk.

He was nodding slowly, waiting.

"What does it entail, this conversion?" I said. "Have you undergone it yourself?" I was up close to the front of the writing desk. We stared at one another.

"If you're worried about offending those you serve as a Redeemer, you should set your mind at rest, Mr Krane. Villefranche offers remarkable power. We are damned, men like you and I. What difference will it make to go further along that dark path? Perhaps we shall savour it all the more. I am sure your life of before was a small thing compared to what you could experience working for Villefranche."

I had been right about the gun. There was one on the desk top, inches away from his reach. If he used it on me, he could send me back to my base. If he'd read my mind, he would have done.

"Maybe you could ring him," I said. "Ask him to come now. Then we can finish all of our business."

His eyes narrowed, his reservations obvious. "You are suggesting new terms?"

I shook my head. "I'm just looking for protection, Mr Fellini. You and Villefranche are the least of my worries at the moment. My masters are the unforgiving type. They weren't the ones who endorsed your wife's Redemption. Right now, I'm a sitting duck. I need to be reassured this is all going to pan out okay for me. Surely you can understand that?"

He seemed to weigh it up, straightening. "Perhaps you are being reasonable." He picked up the handset from the desk top and punched the keys. In a moment he had Villefranche on the line. He turned away and spoke softly to him, explaining that I was here, looking for a discussion – talking about conversion. After a few moments he grunted and put the phone down.

"He will be here in half an hour," he said. "Pour yourself a drink while I get changed." He reached down for the gun automatically, frowning when he realised it was no longer on the writing desk. He looked up but I had already moved towards the drinks cabinet. While he sweated it out, I poured myself a brandy. I turned to him with it in my hand.

"Good health," I said, toasting him. I tossed the drink back.

I could see the deep suspicion in his eyes. He remained behind the desk, knowing that I had taken the gun and slipped it into a pocket of my suit. I put the glass down and walked very slowly towards him once more. I could see the beads of sweat glistening on his brow. I knew this was the one part of the mansion that was not covered by surveillance, his one haven of privacy. None of his guards would be watching us.

I took my own gun from its shoulder holster and held it so that its muzzle lined up with his chest. The movement confirmed his worst fears. He looked as though he'd been punched.

"You'll achieve nothing by this," he said, rigid now, terror surging through his body, a cold sluice of it.

"Do you love your wife, Mr Fellini?"

"Of course. Why else would I want her brought back?"

"I wonder about that. You don't like to be defied. Everyone must be obedient, even her. So what has Villefranche promised you? Eternal life? Infallibility, absolute power? The oldest bargain in the world. What has your wife got to do with it? What is she – Helen to your Faust?"

"You can be part of this. Think carefully before you throw it away, Krane."

"Oh, I have." I lifted the gun a fraction. "So you love your wife. Is she the most important thing in the world to you? Do her hopes and dreams mean anything to you? Does she come first?"

"I have given her everything."

"Material things, yes. How about your own uncompromising love? Even when she defies you?"

"I cannot live without her." He forced the words out through gritted teeth as though at great cost.

"She doesn't love you, Mr Fellini. She doesn't want to be with you. She would rather die."

"No!" he snarled, almost coming at me, but the gun was too much of a threat.

"You're deceiving yourself. Whatever it is you feel for her, it isn't love. It's part of the greed that drives you. You want to play God and have the world worship you. You say you can't live without her. Okay. That makes this so much easier."

I put three bullets in his gut and watched him crumple into the chair behind him. I knew it would be a slow, agonising death. His face had gone grey, his mouth working like a landed fish's. His hand groped for the phone on the desk but I brushed it aside easily as I stood over him. He tried to speak through his pain, blood beginning to trickle from his mouth. I suppose I should have felt elated, but I was about as cold and practical as I'd ever been.

I took the long razor from inside my jacket. Time to begin the real work.

*

Villefranche arrived shortly after I had finished my preparations. I had taken both my gun and Fellini's – I had found two others in the suite of rooms – and shut them away. I had no reason to expect Villefranche to be armed: whatever powers he had would transcend something as mundane as guns. When he entered, the room was still illuminated by the single desk lamp. The floodlights outside were turned off, so we were in near darkness. I was sitting in one of the armchairs, having cleaned myself up in the bathroom.

Fellini was in his chair behind the desk, head sunk on his chest as if he was asleep. He had taken a while to die, but I'd have dragged it out for a week if I'd had the time.

"Mr Krane," said Villefranche. "I take it your mission was successful? How is Mrs Fellini?"

"She'll be fine," I said, not getting up. "Asleep."

"Good." He walked towards Fellini. "Silvio, too, I see." He smiled, rounding the desk and putting a hand on the dead man's shoulder. He shook him. Fellini's head lolled back to reveal his throat, which I had opened up in a neat line, not quite ear to ear, but close enough. There was a thick coagulation of blood. His front was stained with it and it'd pooled in his lap and run down the bare legs that protruded from his dressing gown.

Villefranche drew back, nonplussed. He swore crudely, knowing at once I was responsible. His eyes flashed murderously. "What have you done?"

I remained seated. The question had been rhetorical. I didn't answer it.

Villefranche studied my face, although he could see little of it. "So you know who you are, and what you were in life. Strange –

this is not something that happens to you Redeemers. You would be no use to your employers if it did. How did it happen? Oh, no, of course. The woman told you. She would have remembered, then. And this is your revenge."

"He told me he couldn't live without her," I said laconically. "And there was no way he was going to be with her again."

Villefranche swore again. "You've done a thorough job."

"Sure. I didn't want some smart-ass trying to Redeem him."

"Such a waste, Krane! You've no idea what you've done. All over a woman! How ridiculous you are. You had an opportunity for something beyond the dreariness of normal mortal life. For you, that's over. Go back to your masters and run their errands, if they'll have you. It will be just as wearisome as the life you knew. Probably more so."

"Maybe I'll be leaving a cleaner world behind me."

He laughed derisively. "You imagine Fellini's death is more than just petty vengeance? That you would overturn *my* intentions?"

"What exactly were they?"

He smiled arrogantly. "I have been working towards merging some of the biggest conglomerates in the world, Krane. Fellini was one of a number of pawns in a much bigger game. At the heart of it all – a new type of drug, far more stimulating than anything previously discovered and completely addictive. Nothing could control the lice of the world more effectively. My people are the next phase of power. It's not the mad dream of a lunatic – that's a human tendency and history is littered with such things. No, this is a simple evolution. There's nothing mystic about it.

"Fellini's empire will have an heir. He has a big family. His death is a setback, but in the end, it won't matter. Time is not important, only to those of you who think in human terms. The Fellini family will turn to me for guidance." He was standing over me, the initial fury that had welled up in him when he realised that Fellini was dead had either receded or was held under control.

"You needn't worry about my extracting some hideous revenge upon you for your interference," he said. "That sort of thing is beneath me. Go back to your masters and I'll go back to mine. Although I would strongly suggest that you make no attempt to interfere in my affairs again."

"I don't anticipate meeting again after tonight," I said.

He nodded – a curt dismissal – and walked towards the door. He'd closed it on his way in, of course. So it was only now, as he reached for its handle, that he saw what I'd set there. Yes, I'd been busy all right. I'd learned something about power, and magic – and talismans. Hooked to the back of the door was a severed head – that of an Androgyne. Its blood still leaked from the precisely cut neck. Blood that contained unique powers. After I'd set it there, I'd used Fellini's blood for paint and my fingers as paintbrushes, and daubed a symbol under the head, one of four specific ones given to me by the people who controlled me, as part of my protective armoury. Villefranche backed away from it as though facing something menacing.

I got up and went over to the large window. There was a mechanism beside it for opening and closing the long, velvet curtains. I had them close. They were of a light coloured material, with no pattern. Except for the second bloody symbol that I had put there, under the detached head of another Androgyne.

Villefranche flinched as if he had been scalded. He swung round to the wall on his left. It was in darkness. I walked over to it and flicked on a wall light that threw into sharp relief a third head and a symbol from both of which the blood had run thickly down the wallpaper. On the opposite wall I had set the fourth and final head and symbol.

I had been warned that setting this trap would only be the initial part of the work ahead of me. I had in effect locked myself into a cage with a dreadful power – call it a demon if you like. Villefranche was no human. Okay, neither was I. A Redeemer is more than that. But he was dangerous, never more so than now, like a trapped rat. Or a potentially rabid dog.

If he had been angered by my disposal of Fellini, he was livid now. His eyes held an almost volcanic fury, his whole being infused with it. He stood in the centre of the room, glaring at me. "You have an opportunity to undo this," he said, his voice raking over me. "Do it quickly and I'll spare you yet."

I slid the silver knife from its hiding place close to my chest. Even in this poor light it gleamed. He knew then that I meant business. He had come to the live world and by so doing had taken a risk – he could die here, but not in any conventional way. It would have been a waste of time my trying to shoot him. Easy enough to put bullets into him, but he was immune to them. But this knife could kill him and send him back to *my* people, not his.

Slowly he nodded, as though recognising that this could only be ended with a fight. He seemed to be considering something, walking across to the drinks cabinet, though his eyes flicked up to the nearest of the bloody symbols. If I had been sceptical when my people had instructed me in their use, I wasn't now. Villefranche was afraid of them, the dead eyes that gazed fixedly at him. He poured himself some of the brandy.

I moved slowly and easily around the desk, careful not to trigger any sudden movements in him. He eyed the silver knife with the same deep unease as he did the heads and symbols. He'd be ready if I tried to rush him. I watched him edge around the room as I moved nearer to its centre. One of the luxurious rugs, a circular Arabian carpet, was under my feet and I was careful not to trip over it, standing in its centre. It had a circumference of about six feet.

"You are adamant?" he said, sipping the brandy. "You would throw away all that I can give you? Power beyond anything you've known. Deep fulfilment, lasting success. Control of everything you touch. You would reject all this?"

"You're full of crap," I told him.

He casually tossed aside the brandy glass. It skidded across the polished floor but I ignored it. He became very still, his body tense, his eyes seemingly focused on some far off point. I watched his lips moving and imagined this was an incantation, part of his ritual of self-protection. He looked vulnerable, but I had been *warned* not to attack him at this point. There would be a moment for that.

The air was changing. It was colder and it was – thickening, like a live thing. The knife was warm in my hand and its warmth spread protectively. I won't pretend I wasn't afraid. This whole thing was designed to scare the shit out of me. Outside the window, the night was uniquely black, utterly devoid of light. We might have been at the bottom of an ocean's deepest abyss.

I sensed movement and looked across at the desk and Fellini's corpse behind it. Energy seemed to be coalescing around it, invisible but palpable. It was as though something was exuding from the ruined neck, a vapour, grey and smoke-like. Three of these clouds manifested themselves and became parodies of human figures, half the size of a man. Hunched and crudely formed, they stood in silence. Fellini's corpse jerked, as though a massive electric current had been sent through it. It flopped down, motionless, a finality about the movement.

The light was poor, but I realised that each of the three grotesque figures were taking on more substance. They were drawing flesh and blood from the withering corpse, converting it into energy like batteries powering up.

It was as much as I could do to stand my ground, but I did, waiting until the three *homunculi* were complete. They had no faces to speak of, just the suggestion of features, and were hairless, their grey skins glistening as if they had just emerged from a womb. As I watched them, they moved out from behind the desk, lifting their stocky legs woodenly, as if pulling them up from a bog with each step. Their arms were long and ape-like, their hands disproportionately large, thick fingers groping the air.

Villefranche's eyes were wide open now, looking upon the things he had conjured and his expression was one of unholy glee as he contemplated whatever havoc his spawn were about to unleash. The first of them stretched, shook itself like someone coming awake from a deep sleep and regarded me from sunken eyes. Something like a mouth, a dark gash, opened and emitted a sound like steam being released from an engine. Seeing me, it leapt with remarkable agility.

I ducked down instinctively, but the thing never reached me. It hit an invisible barrier as if I was contained within a glass jar. There was a soft explosion. The *homunculus* hit this barrier like mud striking a wall and it splattered apart in a rain of flesh and blood. It spread around the edge of the carpet, not touching it, smouldering and rendered lifeless.

Villefranche had staggered back as the *homunculus* had been smashed, his face a mask of horror. He glared at me, unable to comprehend what had happened. Slowly another shape formed, a blood-red parody of a thing, its veins and arteries pulsing within it. I thought at first the head was a copy of the Androgyne one I'd impaled on the back of the door, but it was the original, somehow merged with the arterial construct. It was this grotesque parody of humanity that had obliterated the *homunculus*.

By the time it had dawned on Villefranche what had happened, it was too late to stop the second *homunculus* from throwing itself at me. However, it suffered the same fate as its predecessor, striking another barrier, another bloody shape, equally as hard. The *homunculus* disintegrated in a deluge of torn flesh. All energy was drained from it by the explosion. Villefranche gasped as if he had been punched in the gut and fell to his knees, his face momentarily screwing into an agonised expression. He crawled backwards, away from me.

I was watching the last of the hunched creatures. This one wasn't going to blow itself apart on the Androgyne-things, which were confined within the carpet's circumference. The *homunculus* seemed to be waiting for Villefranche to recover. Its power was linked to him. Destroying either of them, I realised, would seriously impair if not actually kill the other. I knew, though, that if I remained inside the protective barrier, neither the *homunculus* nor Villefranche would attempt to attack me. I was too well protected by the Androgyne-things. We would have hit an impasse.

Villefranche remained on his hands and knees. I could rush over to him and finish him, but I knew the *homunculus* would be on me in a flash, its speed incredible. So instead I chose to attack it before he could interfere. I stepped out off the carpet and outside the protective barrier.

The last *homunculus* was driven by Villefranche's violent emotions; for the moment rage governed them. I was banking on it clouding his judgement. The creature snatched at me and its claws tore at nothing, inches from my chest. If they had caught me, they would have opened me up. I ducked and drove the silver dagger at its gut, but it was quick to elude me, the point of my weapon touching no more than air.

I called on the additional strength and speed that imbues Redeemers as I looked for an advantage. I couldn't delay this – Villefranche was recovering with every passing moment and so giving more energy to the *homunculus*. I extended myself and almost dug home my blade, but the creature somehow twisted clear. I fought for balance and my left leg bent to take my weight as I swung forward into the attack.

The bloody debris around the carpet was like a thick oil slick. As my foot came down, it skidded, losing purchase. I hit the floor hard. My back and neck jarred and I rolled aside to avoid the driving punch of the *homunculus*. It passed within a hair's breadth of my flesh and, unleashed with such power, like a steam-driven piston, smacked up against the invisible barrier maintained by the Androgyne-things. I watched as the fist, forearm and upper arm of the *homunculus* all squeezed up like wet mud.

The *homunculus* couldn't prevent itself falling forward into the barrier. It struck it, though not with any real force. For a moment it was held there, like iron caught on a magnet, but I could see that it was going to tear itself free and come at me again. I swung round and drove my silver knife into its neck.

Its head flew back and it opened whatever passed for a mouth in a scream like steam issuing from a geyser, a long, drawn-out sound somewhere between agony and despair. I pulled out the knife and rolled well aside. The *homunculus* was shrivelling like a huge plastic sack. It was not long before its spasms ceased. All that remained of the three creatures was a liquefied mass, choking fumes rose from them. I watched their grey smoke curl upwards, strands of vapour that twisted towards Fellini's corpse. Gradually they were subsumed into it.

Villefranche had curled up into a foetal ball, almost underneath the writing desk, one hand gripping a leg for support. Maybe he thought it was his last contact with this world. The destruction of the *homunculi* hadn't killed him but it had wounded him deeply, perhaps fatally. At any rate, he wasn't able to crawl out of there and wouldn't be fit to walk for a while. He looked up at me through pain-filled eyes, trying to speak, but he was that badly crippled, the words wouldn't come.

I didn't much want to hear them anyway. I went over to Fellini's desk, where I'd seen a cigarette lighter earlier. I picked it up and found a clutch of papers, making a large spill. I ignited it and watched the paper catch. I dropped it into Fellini's blood-soaked lap. It didn't take long to start burning. The whole place would be an inferno in no time.

I was backing off from the already searing heat – and the stench of burning flesh – when I heard a sharp crack behind me. Simultaneously I felt something hit me hard in the lower back. Twice more. I almost staggered forward into the furnace, but somehow managed to turn around.

Villefranche had dragged himself to his feet. His mouth leaked blood like vomit, his eyes reflected the blaze, but he'd got hold of a gun. I hadn't checked the drawer under the drinks cabinet. It was open, so he must have found it there. And he'd discharged three bullets into me. He would have emptied the rest of the magazine into me, but his strength was collapsing like sand. He fell to his knees, the gun dropping on to the floor.

I was still able to go to him, although the pain from the bullets, the onset of death, was coming on me fast. I gripped his head in my left hand.

"Go back to your masters," he spat. He could not have broken my grip on him, but his hands clawed out and gripped my thighs. "Take all your memories with you. Let the last of my powers *curse* you with them. On the other side, you will retain them and live in misery with them forever. Your masters will have no use for damaged goods."

"I was right," I said, looking at the last remains of the things he had dredged up. "You were full of crap. But come and join us anyway."

I slid the silver dagger up under his heart, a clean kill. There wasn't much left in him to put up a struggle. I finished the business quickly and opened his throat with my razor, his flesh as unresisting as butter.

We died together.

*

The room was the same as it always was. So was the old armchair. I came to sitting in it. My suit was a little crumpled, but there were no bloodstains and my hands were clean. Villefranche must have been elsewhere.

I got up and walked around for a while, stretching and doing a few basic exercises. There was nothing to suggest I'd had three bullets pumped into my back. Villefranche had been right about one thing – this time I remembered it all. Whatever curse he had laid on me had enabled me to retain everything. I preferred it that way.

After a while the door opened and a familiar figure arrived, the junior of my two mentors. He waved me to the chair and I sat down while he slowly pulled a pen from his top pocket and scribbled something on his pad.

"Razorjack," he said in his usual unemotional way. "Any ill effects?"

192

"I seem to be intact. How about Villefranche? Have you secured him?"

His eyes betrayed his surprise. "You – remember him?"

I nodded. "Everything that happened. From the moment I left here until my return. The mission and what it entailed." I tapped my head. "It's all in here."

He continued to stare at me for a while. Then he scribbled something else down.

"You do have him?" I said. "Don't tell me I went through all that shit for nothing."

"Yes, yes, we have him. You did well."

"I'm glad someone's happy."

"You must excuse me for a moment," he said and quit the room. My words had obviously stirred him up.

After a while the other mentor arrived, the one I took to be the senior. This time he didn't have a chair, or a notepad. "Do you know your name?"

"Jack Krane, as ever."

"You say you remember everything about the mission?"

"Everything. I remember my life before Fellini and his goons murdered me, my subsequent work for you and the Villefranche mission. I know I saw to it that Villefranche was delivered to you. I killed Fellini and one of his henchmen, Mahlmann. And I Redeemed Rebecca Fellini. She's back in the live world."

"Ah," he breathed, straightening up. Clearly I was a disappointment to him.

I said, "I guess you have ways to wipe a man's memories. Part of the transition. But I ought to tell you that Villefranche reckoned he'd put some kind of curse on me. My memories are going to stick."

"Yes, he had the power to do such a thing. That's a great pity. You've shown remarkable promise. We had real plans for you." He seemed to be weighing things up in his mind.

"So – where to now?" I said glibly. "I suppose I could always convert to the other side."

He looked affronted. "I'll disregard that."

"I always was a bad penny. Listen – Villefranche offered me choices when I first met him. He wanted me to convert. One of the things he offered me was a return to the live world, for as long as I wanted. Assuming I didn't get run over by a bus or picked up a nasty disease, I could have lived a long life."

"You turned him down. Why?"

"Let's just say, I didn't like his outfit. They're the Bad Guys, right?"

"You've seen something of what they can do."

"I don't like their callousness, their cruelty, their complete disregard for human life and emotions. Power is all. Whereas you guys, well, you know about compassion, justice and all that stuff. And love. You know about love. I'd go as far as to say, it's important to you."

He almost smiled at that. "Go on."

"Maybe *you* should send me back to the live world. Perhaps not as a Redeemer, but in some capacity. No doubt the Adversaries are still active there."

"Always. The war never ends."

"Shame to waste my talents, wouldn't you say?"

I couldn't read his mind, but I knew he was thinking hard. I'd thrown him a curved ball. "Leave it with me," he said, going to the door.

"I'm not going anywhere."

I sat back in the armchair. I wondered where Rebecca was. If it was morning in the live world, the news would be breaking about the Fellini mansion. The fire I'd set would have taken a hold and done some real damage before anyone could get it under control. The Androgyne-things and the *homunculi* would have been completely destroyed. It would take the law a while to identify the three corpses, but Rebecca would know who they were. I just hoped she wouldn't do anything stupid.

Not till I got there.

ABOUT THE AUTHOR

Adrian Cole began writing at the tender age of 10, although he wasn't ready to submit professionally until he was much older – at 19. His first published work was a ghost story for IPC magazines in 1972, followed soon after by a trilogy of sword & planet novels, THE DREAM LORDS (Zebra, US) in the 1970s. Since then he has gone on to have more than 2 dozen novels and many short stories published and his work has been translated into a number of foreign editions.

He writes science fiction, heroic fantasy, sword & sorcery, horror, pulp fiction, Mythos (amongst other things) and has had two young adult novels published, MOORSTONES and THE SLEEP OF GIANTS (Spindlewood, UK)

His best known works are the OMARAN SAGA and STAR REQUIEM fantasy quartets and these have also been published recently as eBooks under the Gollancz SF Gateway imprint and have also been released as audio books (Audible).

His most recent novel is THE SHADOW ACADEMY, SF from Edge (Canada) and the anthology NICK NIGHTMARE INVESTIGATES (Alchemy UK) which collects the first arc of stories about his hard-boiled occult private eye, who confronts the various minions of Lovecraft's Mythos, as well as other monsters and horrors in different, bizarre locales.

He has been nominated for various awards, and was the recipient of the 2015 British Fantasy Award for best collection for NICK NIGHTMARE INVESTIGATES and has appeared in Year's Best collections. Short stories published recently include appearances in *Weirdbook*, *Spectral Press Book of Horror 2* and *Creeping Crawlers*.

A native of Devon, UK, he lives in Bideford with his wife, Judy, and enjoys frequent dips in the sea and an occasional bike ride up into the forests of the local area, about which the less said, the better.

For more information, visit *www.adriancscole.com*

Parallel Universe Publications

CLASSIC WEIRD 2 selected by David A. Riley
ISBN: 978-0-9932888-4-5

OTHER VISIONS OF HEAVEN AND HELL by Jessica Palmer
ISBN: 978-0-9935742-1-4

A SAUCERFUL OF SECRETS by Andrew Darlington
ISBN: 978-0-9935742-0-7

THE WINTER HUNT AND OTHER STORIES
by Steve Lockley & Paul Lewis
ISBN: 978-0-9932888-9-0

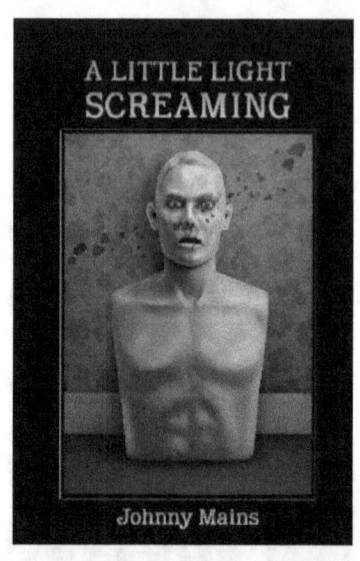

A LITTLE LIGHT SCREAMING by Johnny Mains
ISBN: 978-0-9932888-5-2

ENGLAND 'B': 90 MINUTES OF HELL by Richard Staines
ISBN: 978-0-9932888-7-6

AND NOBODY LIVED HAPPILY EVER AFTER by Kate Farrell
ISBN: 978-0-9932888-8-3

FISHHEAD; THE DARKER TALES OF IRVIN S. COBB
ISBN: 978-0-9935742-4-5

KITCHEN SINK GOTHIC: Selected by David and Linden Riley
ISBN: 978-0-9932888-3-8

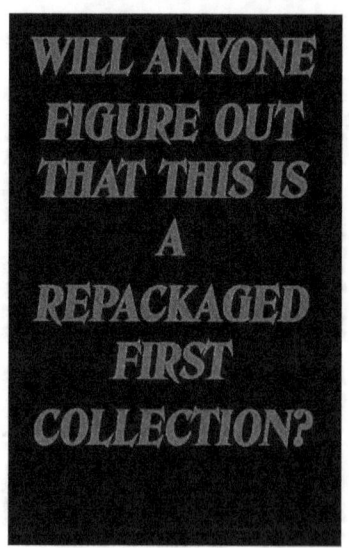

WILL ANYONE FIGURE OUT THAT THIS IS A REPACKAGED FIRST
COLLECTION? by Johnny Mains
ISBN: 978-0-9574535-7-9

BLACK CEREMONIES by Charles Black
ISBN: 978-0-9574535-5-5

**HIS OWN MAD DEMONS:
DARK TALES FROM DAVID A. RILEY**
ISBN: 978-0-9574535-8-6

THEIR CRAMPED DARK WORLD by David A. Riley
ISBN: 978-0-9574535-9-3

THE HEAVEN MAKER AND OTHER GRUESOME TALES
by Craig Herbertson
ISBN: 978-0-9932888-2-1

GOBLIN MIRE by David A. Riley
ISBN: 978-0-9574535-4-8

THINGS THAT GO BUMP IN THE NIGHT
selected by Douglas Draa and David A. Riley
ISBN: 978-0-9574535-6-2

CLASSIC WEIRD selected David A. Riley
ISBN: 978-0-9574535-3-1

MOLOCH'S CHILDREN by David A. Riley
ISBN: 978-0-9932888-1-4

Check our website:

http://paralleluniversepublications.blogspot.co.uk/